Vendetta

Vendetta

CATHERINE DOYLE

SCHOLASTIC INC. NEW YORK

First published in the United Kingdom by Chicken House, 2 Palmer Street, Frome, Somerset BA11 1DS. *www.doublecluck.com*

Library of Congress Cataloging-in-Publication Available

Doyle, Catherine, 1990–
Vendetta / by Catherine Doyle. — First American edition.
pages cm
Summary: "When five brothers move into the abandoned mansion next door, Sophie Gracewell's life changes forever. Irresistibly drawn to bad boy Nic Falcone, Sophie finds herself falling into an underworld governed by powerful families. When Sophie's own family skeletons come to life, she must choose between two warring dynasties—the one she was born into, and the one she is falling in love with"—Provided by publisher.

ISBN 978-0-545-69982-2 (alk. paper)
[1. Families—Fiction. 2. Love—Fiction. 3. Vendetta—Fiction. 4. Mafia—Fiction. 5. Youths' writings.] I. Title.

PZ7.1.D69Ve 2015
[Fic]—dc23

2014020255

10 9 8 7 6 5 4 3 2 1   15 16 17 18 19

Printed in the U.S.A.   23
First American edition, March 2015

Book design by Kristina Iulo

Bertrand Russell, *The Conquest of Happiness* (Liveright, 1996), copyright © 1930 by Horace Liveright, Inc.; copyright renewed 1958 by Bertrand Russell
Friedrich Dürrenmatt, *Incident at Twilight* (1952)
The publisher has made reasonable effort to contact the copyright-holders for permission, and apologizes for any errors or omissions, which will be rectified at the earliest opportunity.

FOR MY DAD

PART I

♥

"Of all forms of caution,
caution in love is perhaps
the most fatal to true happiness."

BERTRAND RUSSELL, *The Conquest of Happiness*

CHAPTER ONE

The Honeypot

I didn't see it at first, sitting between the cash register and a stack of order pads. It might have been there for hours — or longer — just waiting, while I spent another day of my summer dying of boredom inside Gracewell's Diner.

There were just two of us left to lock up tonight. I was hovering beside the register, drumming my fingernails on the countertop, while Millie, my best friend and partner-in-waitressing, glided around the diner and sang into the push broom like it was a microphone. Everyone else had left, and my uncle Jack — manager not-so-extraordinaire — had stayed home with a hangover.

The tables stood resolutely in rows, flanked by straight-backed, burgundy chairs and the occasional rubber plant. The door was locked, the lights were dimmed, and the window booths were clean.

I was trying not to listen to Millie destroy Adele when I noticed it: the jar of honey. I picked it up and studied it.

"I think I'm getting better," Millie called mid-song-murder from across the diner. The only thing she got right was the faint

British accent, but that's only because she *was* British. "I can hit that high note now!"

"*Big* improvement, Mil," I lied without looking up.

The jar was small and rounded. Inside, honey dotted with crystals of gold swayed lazily as I tilted it back and forth. A fraying square of cloth covered the lid and, instead of a label, a thin velvet ribbon encircled the middle, finishing in an elaborate bow. It was black.

Homemade? Weird. I didn't know anybody in Cedar Hill who made their own honey, and I knew almost *everyone* in Cedar Hill. It was just that kind of place — a little pocket on the outskirts of Chicago, where everybody knows everybody else's business; where nobody forgives and nobody forgets. I knew all about that. After what happened with my dad, I became infamy's child, and infamy has a way of sticking to you like a big red warning on your forehead.

Millie hit the last note of her song with ear-splitting vigor, then skipped behind the counter and stashed the broom away. "You ready to go?"

"Where did this come from?" I balanced the jar of honey on the palm of my hand and held it out.

She shrugged. "Dunno. It was here when my shift started."

I looked at her through the golden prism, which made her face distorted. "It's weird, right?"

Millie rearranged her features into a classic I-don't-really-care-about-this-topic-of-conversation look. "The honey? Not really."

"It's homemade," I said.

"Yeah, I figured." She pulled her eyebrows together and reached out to touch the glass. "The ribbon is kind of odd. Maybe a customer left it as a tip?"

"What kind of customer tips with pots of honey?"

Millie gasped, her face lighting up. "Did you . . ." She breathed in dramatically. "By any chance . . ." She exhaled. "Serve . . ."

I leaned forward in anticipation.

". . . a little yellow bear . . ."

I can't believe I fell for it.

". . . called Winnie-the-Pooh today?"

Her laughter set me off, it always did. That sound — like a duck being strangled — was what drew me to her when she moved to Cedar Hill five years ago. At school we would always find ourselves laughing at the same things. It was the silly stuff — making stupid faces; giggling inappropriately when someone tripped and fell; enjoying long, nonsensical conversations and discussing ridiculous hypothetical situations — that brought us together. Back then I didn't know it would be the only friendship that would survive what happened to my family eighteen months ago, but it didn't matter anymore because Millie was the best friend I'd ever have, and the only one I really needed.

We laughed all the way through closing, until we were outside in the balmy night air.

Located on the corner of Foster and Oak, the diner was a modest, low-lying building made from faded brick. It was perfectly symmetrical, its squareness reflected in the boxy windows that dominated the exterior and the small parking lot that surrounded it on all sides. Along the overhanging roof, a scrawling

"Gracewell's" sign was half-illuminated by streetlamps that lined the periphery of the lot. Right across the street, the old library loomed against the night sky, half-hidden by a line of neatly clipped trees that continued west past the general post office and on down the sidewalk.

I was still holding the well-dressed pot of honey as we crossed the empty parking lot. It's not like anyone would care, I told myself — with my uncle Jack at home nursing his self-induced headache, there was no one official around to claim it. I'd only done what any jaded, underpaid employee would do in my situation — claimed a freebie that I had no immediate use for and walked away from the diner feeling triumphant because of it.

"So I've been thinking." Millie slowed her pace to match mine.

"Be careful," I teased her.

"Maybe *I* should take the honey."

"Finders keepers," I sang.

"Sophie, Sophie, Sophie." She put her arm around my shoulder and pulled me toward her. We were almost the same height, but while Millie was curvy in all the right places, I was boy-skinny and chipmunk-cheeked like my father, though I had inherited his dimples, too, which was somewhat of a silver lining. Millie squished her cheek up against mine, as if to remind me of that. I felt her smile. "My *best* friend in the *whole* world, *ever*. Oh, how dull would my life be without you in it? The stars wouldn't shine half as bright, the moon would be but a shadow of its former self. The flowers would wither and — "

"No way!" I slithered out of her grip. "You can't compliment your way into my honey stash. I'm immune to your charm."

Millie scrunched her eyes tight and released a soul-destroying whine. "You already get the whole freakin' diner. Can't I just have the honey?"

Even though she was right, inheriting the diner when I turned eighteen was hardly my life's greatest ambition. They were my father's instructions before he went away, which would no doubt be enforced by my gloriously grumpy uncle Jack, who happened to exude a particularly pungent aura of I-don't-take-no-for-an-answer. It didn't matter anyway. Millie and I both knew the diner wasn't something to be excited about. It was just one big, dead-end headache waiting to crash into my life. But the black-ribboned honeypot? That was pretty — a nice surprise to lift the monotony of the day.

Millie shuffled behind me. "Sophie, this is your conscience speaking," she whispered over my shoulder. "I know it's been a while since we've talked, but it's time for you to do the right thing. Millie is so nice and pretty. Don't you want to give her the honey? Think of how happy it would make her."

"I didn't know my conscience had a British accent."

"Yeah, well, don't read too much into it. Just give her the honey."

I stalled at the edge of the parking lot, where we would peel off separately into the night. Before my parents' income was halved, Millie and I used to walk in the same direction, to Shrewsbury Avenue, where there were housekeepers and gardeners, giant pools, and crystal chandeliers hanging inside actual foyers. Now my walks home were a whole lot longer than they used to be.

"Millie doesn't even like honey," I hissed. "*And* she has no respect for bees. I saw her stamp on one three times last week to make sure it was dead."

"It's not my fault this country is overrun with obnoxious insects."

"What do you expect? It's the middle of July!"

"It's a disgrace."

"*And* you were wearing Flowerbomb perfume."

"He was being inappropriate."

"So you murdered him."

Millie shot out her hand. "Just give me the freaking honey, Gracewell. I need it to bribe my way out of a grounding."

I raised my eyebrows. We had just completed an eight-hour shift together and she hadn't mentioned this. "Grounded?"

"Total injustice. *Complete* misunderstanding."

"I'm listening . . ."

"Alex called me a *braceface*." Millie paused for effect. "Can you believe that?"

Well, she did have braces. And they were technically on her face. But I didn't say that. Instead, I did what any best friend would do. I adopted an expression of pure outrage and pretended to linger over what a rude tyrant her not-so-mature-but-definitely-hot brother was.

"He's *such* an ass," I offered.

"He's literally the worst human being on the planet.

Anyway, one thing led to another, and his iPhone fell out the window . . . Well, it sort of fell out of my hands . . . which were coincidentally dangling outside of his bedroom window at the time . . . He *completely* freaked out on me."

"Oh, siblings . . ."

"Well, you're lucky you don't have to share your house with any douchelords," she ranted. "What kind of nineteen-year-old guy *squeals* on his younger sister? I mean, *where* is the honor in that? He's a total disgrace to the Parker name. And how was I even supposed to know his phone would break?"

"Weird." Honey still in hand, I leaned against a nearby streetlamp and watched my shadow curve inside its puddle of light. "I could have sworn the latest iPhones had tiny built-in parachutes."

Millie started to swat at the air, like the problem was floating around in front of her. "If I give my mum that thoughtful jar of honey to use in one of her baking recipes, then she'll see me as the kind, caring daughter that *I am*, and take back the unjust grounding, which was unfairly handed out because of my ignorant, pigman brother."

I straightened up. "That's never going to work. I'm keeping the honey."

"Whatever," she said, with an elaborate flick of her poker-straight brown hair. "It's probably poisoned anyway."

She stuck out her tongue and flounced off into the darkness, leaving me alone with my hard-won bounty. I slid the jar into my bag, watching the wisps of black ribbon fall away from me.

I crossed the road and paused, trying to decide which way to go. After six shifts in a row, the balls of my feet were throbbing, and because Millie and I had stalled for so long, it was already later than it should have been. The longer way home was usually my preferred option — it was well lit and well traveled — but the shortcut was significantly shorter, bypassing the center of town, winding up the hill instead, and looping around the haunted mansion at the end of Lockwood Avenue.

CHAPTER TWO

The Boy with Haunting Eyes

The moon was full and high but the evening seemed darker than usual. After fifteen minutes with only the sound of my footsteps as company, the turrets of the old Priestly house climbed into the sky ahead of me, peering over the neighboring houses like watchtowers.

Beautiful as it was, the mansion had always reminded me of a child's dollhouse that had crumpled in on itself. Its whitewashed wooden exterior caved in at strange angles while corners jutted out like knives, piercing the overgrown masses of ivy. A stone wall covered in leaves snaked around the exterior; it was the only house in Cedar Hill that could boast such privacy, but its gothic aura did more to repel intruders than its boundary.

People who knew the house spoke of it with equal amounts trepidation and wonder, and often, to pass the time, would imagine their own stories about it.

When I was seven years old, my mother told me of a beautiful princess who would spend her days high up in the turrets of the old house, hiding herself away from an arranged marriage with a miserable and boring prince. By the time I turned ten, kids in the neighborhood had decided it was the spellbound home of a wily old witch. She would fill the sprawling rooms with cats and frogs, cauldrons and brooms, and, deep in the night, she would fly out into the sky and scour the neighborhood for stray children who should have been fast asleep in bed. When I met Millie, she told me about the vampires, who stood just inside the cracked windowpanes, peering out with glistening crimson eyes.

Then, at fourteen, when I was completing a school history project about Cedar Hill, I stumbled across the chilling reality of the mansion. There were no witches, no princesses, and no vampires — just a story about a young woman named Violet Priestly, a frontline nurse during World War II who had come out the other side as a drastically different version of herself. Traumatic memories haunted her like ghosts until her hallucinations became too strong to ignore. Not long after poisoning her husband and their young son, she hanged herself in the foyer of the old mansion.

Of course, no one wanted to buy it after that.

Nothing could sweep away the darkness that huddled around the Priestly corner. Even during the hottest summer days, when the streets shone with mirages, there was an unmistakable iciness shrouding the mansion. And so it endured for decades, as a beacon from another time and place, resolutely empty, and utterly unconquerable.

That was, until tonight.

As I drew closer to the mansion, rubbing the warmth back into my suddenly chilly arms and second-guessing my decision to come this way in the first place, I realized with a start that the house had changed entirely since the last time I had seen it. Someone had finally done it — *really* done it. The abandoned Priestly mansion had been dragged into the twenty-first century, and now, it was alive again.

I stopped walking.

The rusted wrought iron gates were wrenched open and pushed against hedges that no longer languished across the garden wall. The weeping willows had been pruned to an almost unnatural neatness, revealing windows on the second story that I didn't know existed. The ivy had been cut away to reveal sturdy wooden boards and a newly painted red door lit up by a teardrop lantern on either side.

And in the light of the lanterns were two black SUVs parked side by side on freshly strewn gravel.

My phone buzzed against my hip — a text from Millie letting me know she had made it home safe, and an inadvertent reminder that I hadn't. Reluctantly, I moved to continue on my way, but something inside was stopping me. The Priestly mansion, the frozen heart of Cedar Hill, was beating again, and lateness be damned, I had to know more about it.

And that's when I sensed something. I shifted my gaze up past the trees and caught sight of a flickering figure in an upstairs window. It was a boy. I couldn't be sure of his age, but even from a distance his bright eyes were unmistakable. They were too big for his delicate face and as they watched me from what seemed like another world, they rounded into discs that grew unnaturally. He leaned forward and pressed his palms against the glass, like he was about to push the pane from the window frame. Was he waving? Or telling me to go?

I raised my hand to him but it stalled, clammy and unsteady, in midair. And then, as quickly as I had noticed him, the strange boy was gone, vanished into the darkness behind him until the house, with its brand-new face, was still again.

Frowning, I let my eyes slide down from the empty window-pane across the driveway as the darkness ahead of me came alive. The faint sound of rustling wafted through the air, and I squinted until I could make out another figure behind one of the SUVs. He was hunched over, searching for something inside.

I tried to fight the desire to investigate, but my palms grew shaky at my sides as curiosity overwhelmed me, pushing me toward the house. I shuffled forward from the sidewalk, creeping just inside the open gates, and the rustling stopped. A car door shut and the sound of loose gravel shifted in the darkness. The figure straightened, his head appearing from behind the vehicle, moving in tandem with the noisy gravel until he stood between the house and the gates, watching me watch him.

Even beneath the lanterns, he was just an outline: a tall shadow with broad shoulders and sure movements. He paused and lowered his arm, easing a duffel bag toward the ground with deliberate slowness until it was settled at his feet. He stepped to the side and pushed it with the force of his boot until it disappeared behind the closest SUV and away from my prying eyes. But I had already seen it, whatever *it* was, and we both knew it.

He tilted his head to one side and stepped closer, one purposeful stride and then another, as he closed the space between us. With each step, my heart thumped harder in my chest. My curiosity evaporated, leaving reality in its place: I had been caught trespassing, and now this shadowed figure was stalking toward me.

I turned and stumbled back out onto the deserted street. As the sound of heavy footsteps split the silence behind me apart, I broke into a run, completely unprepared for the cat that hurtled out in front of me with a shrill meow. As I skidded to a halt, my arms flailing at my sides, he crashed into my back, silencing me midscream by jolting the wind from my lungs, and sending me flying through the air. I dropped my bag and landed on the sidewalk with a thud, my hands and knees scraping the pavement. Dizziness flooded me, sloshing the contents of my dinner back and forth in my stomach.

Before I could piece together what had happened or just how exactly I was going to be murdered, I was lifted out of my bubble of pain, away from the asphalt and onto my feet again, to where I had been standing seconds before, like someone had pressed REWIND.

Only this time, something was different. There was the feeling of strong hands on my waist. They held me upright as I wobbled back and forth, trying to find my balance.

"*Stai tranquillo, sei al sicuro.*" The words were so strange and unexpected, I thought I had imagined them.

I dropped my gaze and found his hands around me and suddenly I saw myself, as if from above, relaxing into the arms of a complete stranger on a deserted street in the middle of the night, in front of the most notorious house in Cedar Hill.

A stranger who had just caught me trespassing and then knocked me to the ground.

I had seen enough romantic movies to appreciate a swoon-worthy moment — but I had also watched a lot of *CSI*. With a start, I pushed the unfamiliar hands away from my body and leapt forward. I crouched and grabbed my bag from the ground, catching a glimpse of the thick silver buckle on his leather boot before springing back up and hitching my bag onto my shoulder hastily. I looked up at him, wishing I had something weapon-worthy in my handbag, just in case. But he stood still, his face a collection of shadows in the darkness. He didn't make another attempt to attack me, and I didn't wait around to give him the chance.

"Don't follow me." My voice sounded stronger than I felt.

I turned and started to run.

I heard him call out, but I was already gone.

I didn't turn around, but I was sure I could feel the shadow's eyes — *his* eyes — on the back of my neck as I ran. The distant sound of laughter followed me through the darkness.

I got home in record time. After depositing the pot of honey on the kitchen windowsill and trudging upstairs, I rubbed some ointment on my stinging knees and crawled into bed. After what felt like hours of staring wide-eyed at my ceiling and listening to the urgent thrumming in my chest, I fell into an uneasy sleep during which dreams of boys in windows dissolved into nightmares about shadowed figures and black-ribboned pots of honey.

CHAPTER THREE

The Gossip Merchant

There wasn't a whole lot that irritated me. However, the source of such rare annoyance had managed to slither into my house and ruin the sunny morning barely before it began.

". . . It's not a good omen, Celine. I have a sixth sense about these things . . ."

Rita Bailey's voice, which was shriller than a police siren, had no trouble infiltrating my bedroom despite the fact she was an entire floor below me. I scowled at my ceiling. I didn't want to hear about Lana Green's affair, Jenny Orin's worsening psoriasis, or the Tyler kids' lice scandal. But the volume of the old lady's voice left me with no other option. I would have to suffer it either way, and, given the depressing messiness of my bedroom coupled with my desire to eat breakfast at some point, I decided to face her head-on and get the most unpleasant part of my day over with.

I rolled out of bed, crawling between crumpled jeans and inside-out T-shirts to fish out a partially obscured bra. Springing to my feet and swiveling around without touching anything — because sometimes I liked to make a game of it — I swooped a pair of denim shorts off the ground and pulled them on before settling on a white tank top and my favorite pair of Converse. After putting on some moisturizer and pulling my hair into a messy braid, I crept downstairs, steeling myself for what I was about to hurtle into, coffee-less and overtired.

Rita Bailey, an old, portly woman with cropped white hair and pinched, shrunken features, hunched over the kitchen table, sipping her coffee in an outrageous pink pantsuit. Beside her, my mother was politely enduring her company, offering a tight smile and a robotic head nod at appropriate times. She had even cleared part of the table, which was usually buried beneath stray sewing projects and piles of fabric samples. Now confined to just one square foot of space, they balanced precariously against the wall, threatening to topple over them.

When we lived in a spacious four-bedroom house on Shrewsbury Avenue, my mother had two whole rooms dedicated to containing the explosions of materials needed for her dressmaking, but here, her works-in-progress always seemed to spill from room to room, following us around our cramped home in every shade and pattern imaginable. Yards of Chantilly and ivory lace stretched along armchairs, jostling for space beneath mannequins in short summer dresses and rich evening gowns. On several scarring occasions since we'd moved here a year and a half ago, I had woken up screaming at the sight of a half-finished dummy bride perched in the corner of my room, or a denim dress that should never see the light of day.

It wasn't that my mother didn't have some sort of system in place, it's just that no one but her could ever figure it out. She was probably the most organized disorganized dressmaker in all of Chicago, and I think she liked it that way. Mrs. Bailey, who was staring narrowed-eyed at the teetering pile of fabrics across the table, evidently did not.

I swept into the kitchen, pulling her attention away before her frown became so intense it broke her face. "Good morning, Mrs. Bailey." *That wasn't so bad.*

She refixed her stare on me. "Good morning, Persephone."

I winced. It had been a while since I had heard my name in its hideous entirety and, unsurprisingly, nothing had changed — it still sucked. But the way the old lady said it always seemed to make it worse, drawling over the vowel sounds like she was talking to a five-year-old child — *Purr-seph-an-eeeee.*

"I prefer Sophie," I replied with a level of exasperation that usually accompanied the topic.

"But Persephone is so much nicer."

"Well no one calls me that." It wasn't my name and she knew it. It was just a symbol of my mother's fleeting obsession with Greek mythology, which had, rather unfortunately, coincided with the time I was born. Thankfully, my father had given up on the mouthful within the first year of my birth. It didn't take him long to think of "Sophie" as a passable alternative — the name I suspect he wanted all along and one that rendered me eternally grateful to him for two reasons: 1. that I didn't have to go through life with a barely spellable relic for a name, and 2. that he didn't nickname me "Persy" instead. When my mother conceded defeat, I became "Sophie" for good. Plain, simple, and pronounceable.

"How do you even know to call me that anyway?" I added as an afterthought. For all the times Mrs. Bailey had intentionally wrongly addressed me, I had never thought to ask her how she had discovered one of my best-kept secrets. Then again, she was the first person to discover the location of our new house when we moved, despite the fact we had actively tried to hide it from her, *and* it was nearly an hour's walk from Shrewsbury Avenue. Maybe she *was* clairvoyant after all.

"I saw it on a letter once."

"Where?"

"I can't remember." She sounded affronted by the question. "It may have fallen out of your mailbox."

"Mmhmm." *Snoop*, I noted mentally.

Beside me, my mother was circling the top of her mug with her finger. "Sophie," she chided gently, "why don't we talk about something else?"

"Why? Are you still trying to shirk the blame for naming me the most hideously embarrassing thing you could think of?" Even though my voice was light, I was only half-joking. Not that it seemed to matter to my mother; she found my name-based indignation inexplicably amusing. I guess it made sense. The whole joke was hers in the first place and now it was following me around through people like Mrs. Bailey or Uncle Jack, who used it like a weapon when he was angry at me for taking impromptu nap breaks at the diner.

"I think the name Sophie is just as lovely. It suits you," my mother pandered, smirking into her mug until all I could see were the tips of her delicate pointed brows. I felt a tiny pang of envy for their symmetry. Everything about her was dainty and refined, like a pixie. Through the magic of genetics, she had only passed her sunny blond hair and her heart-shaped face to me. But, by the wonder of mimicry, I had also acquired her tendency for extreme messiness and her inability to cook properly. I was reserving judgment on where my diminutive height came from, because I was still hoping to miraculously grow another three inches before my seventeenth birthday, which was rapidly approaching.

At the word "Sophie," Mrs. Bailey emitted a long noise of ragged disapproval. It sounded like she was choking, and, fleetingly, a small, morally devoid part of me hoped she was.

I crossed over to the countertop to fill my mug and caught sight of the honey jar on the windowsill. Streaks of sunlight winked at me through the glass, as if to say "Good morning!" *It would be a shame not to try it*, I resolved. I grabbed a spoon and pried the lid from the jar, setting aside the frayed square of cloth that covered it and taking care not to disturb the black velvet ribbon.

Behind me, Mrs. Bailey was practicing her favorite hobby — the art of lamenting, "Persephone is *so* much more elegant. It might not suit her now, but she could always try and *grow* into it."

"Thanks, but I think I'll just stick with Sophie and continue to live in the modern world." I dipped a spoon inside the jar and twirled it.

"You look *so* tired this morning, Sophie," Mrs. Bailey informed the back of my head, laboring over my name like it was difficult to pronounce.

Ignoring her taunt, as well as the civilized option to put the honey in oatmeal or on toast, I stuck the heaping spoonful of it straight into my mouth.

"She'll be bright and chirpy once she's had her caffeine fix," my mother explained over my shoulder. The edge in her usually calm voice informed me that her patience was finally wearing thin. Even after my father's screwup, my mother had managed to retain her inhuman level of kindness, which meant she was still too polite to turn a sixty-something, lonely, *annoying* Mrs. Bailey away, even when her conversations mainly consisted of disapprovals and backhanded compliments.

"Are you sure, Celine? She seems so exhausted. She's a shadow of what a sixteen-year-old girl should look like. She should be out in the sun, getting a tan. She used to be such a pretty little thing."

Seriously? I would have responded with bitchiness in kind, but the honey was sticking my teeth together.

My mother released a small sigh — a specialty of hers. It was ambiguous enough to mean anything to anyone — "I'm tired/ happy/disappointed" — but I had a feeling it was intended to politely draw the topic to a close.

Fighting the urge to take my coffee and run, I turned around and seated myself firmly at the kitchen table, dragging the chair legs against the floor as noisily as I could and reveling in the look of discomfort on Mrs. Bailey's face.

OK, lady. Let's go. "I hope I didn't interrupt anything important." The labored, honey-laden words masked the sarcasm in my voice. I took my first, glorious sip of coffee and felt the steam rise up and warm my nose.

"Well actually, you *did*."

Quelle surprise. I always seemed to be interrupting Mrs. Bailey's groundbreaking news bulletins.

"I was just telling your mother that a new family has moved into the Priestly house on Lockwood Avenue."

I was utterly shocked by my unexpected interest in anything Mrs. Bailey had to say. But suddenly there I was, glued to Cedar Hill's resident gossip merchant like she was about to announce the finale plot of my favorite TV show. An onslaught of questions formed inside my brain. *Where do they come from? How are they related to the Priestlys? Why are you wearing that crazy pink suit?*

"Well, I bet it will be good to have some new faces around the neighborhood," my mother interjected before I could begin.

The old lady shook her head like she was having a seizure. She leaned across the table and looked pointedly at each of us in turn as if calling for our undivided attention, which she knew she already had. She dropped her voice. "You know I have the gift of sight, Celine. I've been seeing things ever since I was a child . . ."

I had to blow into my coffee to hide my smirk.

"I was walking by the old Priestly place a couple of weeks ago and I got the most unsettling feeling. When I saw the renovations and the moving vans, it all started to make sense. The house is full again and I just *know* it's not good."

"Maybe we shouldn't jump to conclusions," my mother offered. I could tell by the airiness in her voice that her attention was beginning to wander. She started to pick at a stray thread in her capri pants, frowning.

I considered telling Mrs. Bailey to chill out, too, but she had already redirected her gaze toward our backyard as if she were looking into another secret dimension. But in reality, she was just staring at the potted plant on the windowsill. She squinted her eyes and sighed, probably noticing it was dead.

"Nothing good will come of having five young men making trouble in the neighborhood, because that's *exactly* what they'll do, Celine. You mark my words."

She shook her head again, but every cropped white strand of hair remained perfectly static, like they were frozen in place.

"Wait, did you say *five* guys?" I had already seen two of them. Well, one of them, sort of. The second one had knocked me over. I frowned at the memory. Even after a night of reflection, I still wasn't sure what to make of it.

Mrs. Bailey was, of course, scandalized by my interest. Her mouth was bobbing open and closed, like she was trying to find the exact words for how much of a disgrace I was. "Five young, *troublesome* men," she heaved at last, clutching at her chest for added effect. "I saw them move in and I can tell you, they do not seem like the respectable type."

Isn't that what you said about my father? I wanted to ask, but I stopped myself. The argument wouldn't be worth it. It never was. And besides, I had gotten all the info I needed: There was a new family of boys in the neighborhood. Millie was going to keel over with happiness when I told her.

Distracted, I got up to take my half-filled mug to the sink. "I think having new neighbors is pretty cool."

"What's *cool* about it?" Mrs. Bailey threw the question at my back like a dagger.

I turned around. "What's *not* cool about it? Nobody ever comes to Cedar Hill willingly. This place is so boring. It feels like any minute now we're all just going to fossilize." *Maybe some of us already have . . .* I stopped myself again.

"There's no need to be so dramatic," she returned.

I blinked hard to suppress an inadvertent eye roll.

"I'm sure those boys are perfectly fine," reasoned my mother, who was rifling through her sewing kit. I could tell she was more interested in finding a needle to fix the single thread on the pants that had betrayed her.

Mrs. Bailey was still wearing a frown that was beginning to twitch from the effort of keeping it in place. "No, Celine, there's something not right about it. That house has been empty for too long. And we all know the reason."

"Ghosts," I whispered dramatically. I wanted to add an "*Oooooo*," but I figured that might be going too far.

Mrs. Bailey rose abruptly from her chair, shrugging on her shawl in a show of clumsy indignation. When she spoke again, her voice was low. "You can make jokes all you like, Persephone, but you just better be careful."

I glanced at my mother and was surprised to find that she had returned her attention to our conversation.

"Notoriety attracts notoriety," Mrs. Bailey was muttering without looking at either of us. "And with what your father did, it's best to be aware of — "

"I think that's enough, Rita." My mother rose from her chair, fixing the old lady with a dark look. "Sophie can handle herself. She knows how to be careful."

"Yeah," I echoed, feeling a million miles away. I was thinking about how I had steered myself into trouble the night before. The stinging in my knees resurfaced at the memory.

CHAPTER FOUR

The Letter

Mrs. Bailey's words had kindled something I had become all too accustomed to during the last year and a half of my life: Dad-related guilt.

Back in the welcome privacy of my bedroom, I sat cross-legged on my perpetually unmade bed. Clutching the latest prison-issue envelope in one hand, I carefully removed the letter from inside it and dipped back into my father's life, which, for now at least, was confined to the pages he sent me every couple of weeks.

Dear Sophie,

Sorry I haven't written in a while. I like to wait until I have something to say, even if it's not as interesting as life back in Cedar Hill. I would hate for you to think I'm becoming more boring than I was before I left. In truth, I am trying to make the most of my time here. I want to give you something to be proud of again.

You'll be happy to know that I finished Catch-22 *in just two days, which means I am finally getting faster at reading. I will have the* knowledge of an English professor by the time I come back, and maybe I'll even write a book of my own.

I hope your summer is going well. Try not to worry too much about not getting out in the sun — you will have the last laugh when all your friends are aging prematurely and you still have the skin of a teenager.

How is everything at the diner? I hope Uncle Jack is looking after you. I know he is really trying his best, so go easy on him. If you ask him, I'm sure he will give you some time off so you can get away with Millie — go on an adventure.

On the subject of your uncle, I was thinking that you should suggest some reading material for him, too. It would be a good way for him to de-stress. Maybe something with colorful pictures and big block letters? Just kidding. Don't tell him I said that! I do worry about him, which might sound ironic given the circumstances, but I am relying on you to keep an eye on him and his blood pressure. We are not getting any younger, unfortunately.

How is your mom? Has she remembered to get the dishwasher repaired or have you had to go through with your sink-filling plan? I hope she has stopped overworking herself, but I know how unlikely that is. Please let her know I am thinking about her if she asks, which I hope she does. I haven't heard from her in a while, but I know she is still processing everything. It is difficult for her, as I expect it is for you.

It has been so long since I've seen you. I would really love for you to visit when you get some time off. What about after your birthday, when everything has settled down again? Jack will give you a ride if you ask him. I do miss your teenage sarcasm, despite what you may think.

That's all for now. I look forward to your next letter and, as always, I am thinking of you and counting the days.

Love,
Dad

I slipped the letter back inside the envelope and placed it on the nightstand. I tried to shake the melancholia out of my head. Even after all my father's letters, I still felt sad reading them, but I knew, too, that not to have them at all would be a thousand times more painful.

With a heavy heart, I propped my notepad against my knees and began my reply, censoring the negative parts of my life and highlighting the positives as I wrote. Even if the world was falling down around me, I would not tell my father, because he, above all the people in my life, needed good tidings in whatever form he could get them. And no matter how angry and frustrated I was, I would give him what he needed to survive.

Hi, Dad,

As I write this I am balancing my notepad on two skinned knees and writing with a sore hand. If you're wondering why, it's because on my way home from work last night I face-planted into the pavement.

A freaky shadow chased after me and knocked me to the ground. But it's OK because I didn't let him murder me (you're welcome), and now I'm pretty sure that wasn't his intention in the first place. He was probably just chasing after me like a maniac so he could ask why I was snooping around his driveway in the middle of the night on my own. Teenagers, right?

Luckily I have lived to tell the tale, though I can't say my pride has survived. Still, I think it makes for a fitting opening to this letter, and I bet it made you smile a little.

I hope something good came of the incident, because I bolted home in a state of pain and paranoia.

It's nice to know you are reading. I think writing a book is a great idea. They say it's very therapeutic.

I don't know who "they" are or whether that's even true. And I really hope when you say *book* you don't mean a biographical one, because I'm not crazy about having to relive the story of your murder trial in paperback format, no matter how soothing it is for your psyche. And I don't relish the thought of watching Mom go through another anxiety attack anytime soon, either.

I haven't gotten a chance to do very much other than work this summer, which I am getting used to.

I have resigned myself to the current monotony of my life.

Uncle Jack is great. He is still doing his best to step into your role, though he is a little grumpier than you. Maybe that comes with middle age? ;-) He goes back and forth to the city a lot. Millie and I have developed a theory that he has met a woman there, because what kind of "city business" would he be attending to so often? What do you think, our Jack, a Casanova? Hmmm . . . food for thought. If it is the case, then I don't think we need to be worrying about his health, as long as his heart is doing OK.

Though, knowing Uncle Jack, I bet it's more of a sordid affair than an epic romance. So far, nothing has coming close to filling the void you left in his life.

Thank you for saying I will have the last laugh when all my friends wrinkle up like prunes in later years for spending the time they have now in the sun.

I am flattered you implied I still have more than one real friend and I hope you really do think that. If you knew how many people turned on me, I think it would break your heart.

And, honestly, I am happy to be out of the sun, because I know my time indoors is all part of the end goal of buying a car. I don't know what I will do to celebrate my 17th birthday, but it will probably be something low-key.

Millie's parents are going away, so she and Alex are going to throw a *huge* house party, complete with all his college friends. If you were here, you would definitely disapprove. But you're not.

I think Mom wants to make me a dress for my birthday. Every time she sees me in sweatpants, I see the light in her eyes dim a little bit. If I don't wear something ladylike soon, she might die inside. Last Saturday morning I caught her measuring me in my sleep.

If I see one frill or even the hint of bedazzling on it, things will get ugly.

She's working more than ever, which she really seems to enjoy.

Most of her friends have deserted her, too, in the wake of everything that happened, and those that didn't don't come around much anymore. I think Mom has lost her social sparkle.

I know last year was really hard for all of us, but now she seems happier, and I'm sure she is missing you as much as I am.

Sometimes it feels like she hates you and everything your incarceration has put us through. Sometimes I feel that way, too.

Mrs. Bailey has started to come by on Sunday again. I decided earlier that she is probably the most annoying person to ever live on this planet. Do you think she might be descended from Lucifer? Just a thought.

Annoying is putting it mildly. You don't know any of the crap she's been saying about you. And Millie's probably only told me half of it.

She was here this morning, talking about a new family who have moved into the old Priestly mansion. I guess they must be distant relatives. Weird, huh? I thought that place would be empty forever.

It's full of boys boys boys!

I will come and see you in a couple of weeks, after my birthday, when I get time off from the diner. I really can't wait.

I am dreading seeing how gaunt and unhappy you look. It makes me want to collapse in tears every time.

That's everything for now. I miss you so much.

Sometimes it physically hurts.

Thinking about you always.

I wish I could turn it off, like a switch.

And counting the days.

Counting the years.

Lots of love and hugs,

Sophie X

CHAPTER FIVE

The Priestly Brothers

I stood facedown with my nose pressed against the countertop, willing time to speed up. Even during the busiest hours of the day, the diner was never overrun with customers, but tonight it was unusually quiet. There was just one more hour to go until I could go home, and the minutes were dragging by. To make matters worse, the air conditioner was broken, the stifling humidity was frizzing out the ends of my hair, and the deliveryman hadn't shown up for the third day in a row, which meant we were low on some of the menu's ingredients.

Millie hovered behind me, prodding my shoulder. She was, after all, part-female, part-question. "So if these random Priestly relatives *just* moved in, then the shadow guy probably *was* one of the five boys?"

"Yeah," I replied through a yawn. "Probably."

She laughed like it was the funniest thing she'd ever heard. "How embarrassing for you."

I lifted my head. "Better embarrassed than dead."

She grinned. "Oh come on, Soph, *where* is your sense of adventure?"

I pretended to contemplate her question. "I think it's buried deep beneath my natural instinct to survive."

"You could have made out with a shadow!" Her face was glowing.

"*Or* been brutally murdered by one," I countered.

"Ugh, you are *such* a killjoy."

"How about this," I said. "Next time I'm in a risky situation with a complete stranger, I promise I'll try and make out with him."

"Bah! Don't make promises you won't keep. I don't want to get my hopes up."

The bell above the door jingled and three girls sauntered into the diner. I recognized two of them from school. Erin Reyes and Jane Leder were all bitchiness and long legs, and could have made a full-time career out of judging people. I was surprised to find them at Gracewell's — it was far from the expensive hangs they seemed to enjoy. Then again, the diner did have their favorite main attraction — me. It might have been nearly a year and a half since my father's incarceration, but it was *still* Erin's favorite topic.

She caught my eye and smirked, and I tried not flinch as she stage-whispered to the third girl, who was already studying me with rapt attention. "That's her. She *actually* works here, in the place where it *happened*. Can you believe that?"

The other two giggled, and I felt my cheeks grow hot.

"Ugh," said Millie, who had as much patience for routine bitchiness as I did. "I'll get this one. And if they're not careful, I'll bring them their menus with a side of my shoe up their . . ."

She trailed off, rounding the counter to attend to them.

I smiled graciously at the back of her head. Gracewell's Diner mostly catered to people who worked in town or local families who had been coming here for years. But every so often, nosy vipers from school would stop in to gawk at the infamous Michael Gracewell's restaurant, and Millie would take the hit and serve them so that I wouldn't have to.

Absentmindedly, I started to fix the errant strings on my apron, looping them into an uneven bow.

"Are you going to do *any* work today, Sophie?"

Ursula, Gracewell Diner's assistant manager, had returned from the kitchen. She was nearly as old as Mrs. Bailey but was *infinitely* cooler because she could rock purple hair and was able to have conversations that didn't negatively affect my will to live. She gestured toward Millie, who was handing menus to the three girls.

"Oh, come on. There's no one else here, and I can't exactly wait on ghost tables," I protested.

Ursula's laugh was husky, betraying her enduring smoking habit. "I'm just saying you seem distracted tonight." She pushed her circular spectacles up the bridge of her nose until they settled and magnified her eyes twofold. "Or should I say more distracted than usual."

"That's because she *is* distracted, Ursula." Millie was back, and whipping off her apron. She was leaving an hour before me, and in that moment I slightly resented her for it. "We should tell Ursula."

"Yes, we should," Ursula echoed, shuffling sideways so she could prop herself against the wall beside me. We were exactly the same height, so she could bore her eyes right into mine very effectively with little effort.

"But I don't *have* anything to tell," I swore.

"Lies!" Millie slipped in front of the counter, hoodie in hand. She shrugged it on, smiling so broadly nearly all of her clear braces were visible at once. She zipped it up and her name tag, MILLIE THE MAGNIFICENT — I don't know how she had snuck that one past Uncle Jack — disappeared. Then she leaned forward until her hair brushed the countertop, and dropped her voice. Ursula responded like a magnet, coming closer, and training her attention on Millie.

"Well, you probably won't believe this," Millie began, gesturing subtly at me with her thumb. "But Sophie has developed a crush on a shadow. A real bona fide shadow-crush. Rare as a solar eclipse, but they do happen. Our Sophie is a shadow-creeper."

Ursula pulled her eyebrows together until they almost touched. "What?"

"She's just kidding," I explained, throwing Millie a death stare.

"Am I, Sophie? Am I?" She smirked suggestively, in the way only Millie could. "Ursula, I'll need you to take over that table of *wonderful specimens* now that I'm leaving," she said, gesturing toward Erin and her friends in the corner, before crossing the diner and shouting, "See you guys tomorrow!"

Once Millie had disappeared, Ursula turned her penetrating gaze back to me. "So what's this shadow thing all about?"

"It's nothing, really. There's this new family living in the

Priestly place and I think I bumped into one of them the other night, but then I ran away from him, and now Millie thinks it's the funniest and most tragic thing she's ever heard." I grabbed a cloth and started to wipe down the countertop, which was already gleaming.

Ursula narrowed her eyes as if trying to determine whether there was more to my story, but before she could chase up a line of questioning, the bell above the door jingled.

Against the backdrop of our abrupt silence, two figures swept through the door.

I tried not to gape. One tall, dark, handsome boy is difficult to ignore, but two is near impossible.

They paused inside the door, their broad shoulders brushing as they stood side by side. They began to militarily scan the diner, as though they were looking for something that could have been under any of the tables or swinging from the ceiling fans.

Without meaning to, Ursula and I both took a step forward.

There was something effortlessly fashionable about them — their dark, straight-leg jeans were tailored to break perfectly above expensive leather boots that probably cost more than my entire wardrobe, and they wore designer T-shirts accented by the simple silver chains around their necks.

I studied the boy on the right, feeling something stir inside me. I knew his shape, his height. I dropped my gaze and recognized the silver buckles on his boots.

Ursula and I weren't the only ones hopelessly distracted; fleetingly I noticed how the three girls in the corner had fallen out of their conversation and suddenly looked a lot hungrier than they had been a moment ago. I didn't blame them. The boys were like something out of a movie.

Without glancing toward us, they glided — yes, glided — over to a window booth and slid in, keeping their attention on their own whispered conversation.

"Can you take this one, hon?" Ursula sighed. "I don't think I can stand next to them. It's too depressing." She made her way across the diner to tend to the girls in the corner instead.

My midnight encounter had seemed like little more than a bad dream, but now that Shadow Boy was here, I realized I would have to confront the reality of the situation — he was Mount Olympus, I was Gracewell's Diner, and I still had no idea why he knocked me over. With any luck, there was every chance he wouldn't even recognize me.

Although their distinct appearances and obvious similarities had led me to assume they were brothers, the fact that they were speaking Italian when I approached their table confirmed it — it was that same lilting dialect that Shadow Boy had spoken to me.

"Hi, my name is Sophie and I'll be your server this evening," I rhymed off briskly, handing them each a menu.

Shadow Boy snapped out of his conversation. He turned and, up close, he was younger than I expected — still older than me, maybe, with chestnut brown hair that curled beneath his ears and dark, almond-shaped eyes flecked with gold. I was struck just then, not by his handsomeness, but by his familiarity. I couldn't shake the sense that I had seen his face before — long ago — and though it was undeniably handsome, I had the unpleasant compulsion to look away from him. I tried to blink myself out of it.

He had just thrown me off. If I had seen him before, I wouldn't have forgotten him.

"Sophie," he said quietly, meeting my gaze. "I think we met the other night."

My face fell. I folded my hands in front of my body as his eyes searched mine with an intensity I was completely unused to. His brother, who seemed completely disinterested in our exchange, was studying his menu in silence.

Shadow Boy smiled. "I was just trying to help you up, you know."

"Ah," I said, returning what I hoped was a nonchalant expression. "You mean from where you put me in the first place? How kind of you."

If he was affronted, he didn't show it. "You stopped running so quickly I didn't have time to slow down . . . And I *did* try to apologize, but, if I recall, you ran away."

I smiled awkwardly. "I may have overreacted . . ."

"No harm, no foul," he offered, holding his hands in the air. "But are you always so defensive?"

"That depends, are you always so . . . assaulty?"

"*Non lo so,*" he said quietly, and across from him, his brother, who had been concentrating on his menu, released a low chuckle. I was struck by how effortlessly he moved between both languages, and slightly curious about whatever amusement was passing between them.

"That's a loaded question," Shadow Boy continued after a beat, as if sensing my annoyance. He furrowed his brows and leaned across the table. "I am sorry about the whole thing, Sophie.

I just wanted to ask you something. But then you stopped running so abruptly and . . ." He trailed off, doing his best to look ashamed of himself.

"There was a cat, and I didn't want to trample it."

"Ah, I see."

"But then *you* went ahead and tried to trample me, so I'm not sure it was worth it."

"I told you," he said conspiratorially, "I wanted to ask you something."

"Do you always ask your questions so aggressively? I'm not sure you'd make an effective interrogator."

"Perhaps you're right," he conceded with a small smile. "But I'm too impatient for that line of work anyway."

I zeroed in on the golden flecks in his dark eyes, trying not to lose my train of thought. There was just something about them . . . "So what's the question?"

"Well," he said. "At first I wanted to know why you were spying on my house. And then I started to wonder why you suddenly decided not to stick around when I noticed you?"

He wasn't smiling anymore; he was studying me and I understood what he meant — he knew I had been running away and he knew I was scared of him. But now, looking at him, I couldn't remember why I had felt that way.

"Were you running away from me?"

I shook my head too hard, making my cheeks jiggle. "Nope, definitely not."

"Oh, really?" he pressed, smiling broadly this time. It

rearranged his face beautifully, raising his brows and softening his jaw.

"I prefer to think of it as casual hobbling."

He pulled back from me and, slowly, I became aware of the rest of the world again. "I'd call it frantic sprinting."

"Semantics."

"I'm sorry if I hurt you," he said. "I'm Nic, by the way, and this is my brother, Luca."

Even though I was standing between the brothers, I had barely registered Luca. He had stopped studying his menu and was resting his interlocking fingers on top of it. I offered him a smile. "Welcome to Gracewell's."

"That was boring for me," Luca replied. His voice was sharp with impatience, and scratchy, too, as though he had a sore throat. "But it's nice to know you're planning on being somewhat professional this evening, Sophie."

I blanched. *How rude was this guy?*

He gestured back and forth with his index finger, first at Nic, and then at me, like our conversation was *his* business, too. "Are you ready to focus now, Nicoli?"

Nicoli. His full name suited him. It was beautiful.

Nic shifted in his seat so that he was closer to me, and the two of us were side by side, facing his brother. "Chill out, Luca."

Luca's eyebrows climbed. "My brother, *l'ipocrita.*"

Nic swatted his hand in Luca's direction. *"Stai zitto!"*

"Have you worked here long, Sophie?" Luca cut to me again. He dragged a hand through his hair, settling the unruly black strands away from his face and behind his ears. I found myself entranced by his bright blue eyes, now that I could really see them. They were searing, and seemed to shine unnaturally from his tanned face. *Is he the boy from the window?* I wondered. No, he was too hard, too unyielding. It wasn't him. I was almost sure of it.

"Well?" he pressed.

"Luca," Nic rumbled. "Can you not do this — "

"Let her answer."

"No, I haven't worked here for long," I replied quickly, hoping it would ease whatever tension was mounting between them. Maybe they'd just had an argument before I turned up. Or maybe Luca didn't get out much and this was his idea of socializing. "It's just a stupid summer job."

I felt guilty lying about the diner's role in my life and my future, but suddenly I couldn't stand the thought of them thinking I was as ordinary as I was; that my life was bound to a place that hadn't been redecorated in nearly twenty years, a place owned by an incarcerated man, a place where nothing exciting ever happened to anyone.

Nic pulled his arms from the table and folded them. He kept his narrowed gaze on Luca, like he was almost daring him to do something.

"Do you like it?" Luca appeared unaffected by the death stare.

I shrugged. "As much as anyone can, I guess."

"And what about your coworkers? Do you like them?"

"*Smettila!*" Nic hissed, his accent flipping effortlessly again.

"Does it matter if I like them?"

"You tell me," said Luca.

"Yes, they're nice, mostly," I returned evenly. "Why? Are you doing a police survey or something?"

For the first time since our rocky introduction, Luca smiled at me, revealing sharp teeth and pronounced cheekbones.

"Sophie," Nic murmured. "Don't worry about my brother. As you can see, he's *completely* socially inept."

The softness in his voice settled me, and I let myself be charmed by him, if only for a second, before leaving them with their menus.

"Look at those fine specimens!" whooped Ursula when I returned to the counter. "So *these* boys are the new Priestlys?"

I nodded subtly. Across the way, Nic and Luca were enthralled in another conversation. They were in their own beautiful little world again. And Ursula and I were on a planet beside that world, stalking them unashamedly.

"Is your shadow crush the black-haired one?" she teased.

"No, the other one."

Suddenly he turned his head a fraction, like he could hear us. I held my breath — without knowing why — and squeezed Ursula's arm, but she didn't notice because she was too busy trying not to drool. And then he was engrossed again. It was as though he'd needed a breather from the intensity of his discussion; now that he had taken it, he was back in. And so was Luca. Their mouths sped up and their gestures became more expressive.

"It's hard to look away," Ursula teased, undeterred by the mounting anger in their conversation. "And just *look* at those eyes. Where are they from?"

"Heaven?" I guessed, and we both laughed. They were so exotic, so different from anyone I had ever seen around Cedar Hill.

"Do angels eat?"

That's when I remembered I had completely forgotten to take their order. I slid around the counter and scurried back over. "What can I get you?" I grabbed the pad from my apron and flicked it open, ripping the bottom of the sheet.

Luca looked alarmed by my interruption, like he had forgotten where they were. He opened his menu again, scanned it for five seconds, and pulled back with a frown. "A coffee. Black. Strong."

He gestured at Nic.

"I'll have the steak sandwich, rare, with fries. And a glass of milk," Nic said finally, before shutting his menu and shifting his gaze back to me, "please."

"Is that everything?" I held eye contact with him, feeling my lips twitch into a shy smile.

"*Cazzo*, that *is* all!" Luca hissed into the space between us.

By now, I was used to dealing with difficult customers, but Luca's attitude was unparalleled, and I found myself losing my temper quicker than I normally would have. "I'm sorry, but is my presence in the *place where I work* offending you? Because you don't have to stay here."

He threw me a contemptuous stare, and I held it.

"Just don't spit in my coffee."

I bit my tongue and left them again.

After I passed the order through to Kenny in the kitchen, I joined Ursula, who was cleaning up after Erin and Co. We busied ourselves wiping down the remaining tables and sweeping the floor as the minutes dragged by. When I served Nic his steak, I caught sight of the beginning of a tattoo above the neckline at the back of his T-shirt, then spent the following ten minutes behind the counter figuring it was probably the top of a large, ornate cross.

Five minutes before closing time, when I was balancing the books for the night, Luca's phone rang, and he got up and left abruptly.

Nic approached the counter timidly, like he was walking into open gunfire. That same uncomfortable flicker of recognition stirred inside me but I pushed it away. *Get a grip.*

"Sorry about my brother." He swatted his arm at something behind him. "We think he was dropped on his head as a baby . . . several hundred times."

"I don't think I've ever met someone so inquisitive," I noted. It was the only non-negative thing I could think to say about Luca.

Nic jerked his head, like there was a bee buzzing in his ear. Maybe that's how he thought of his brother. "I guess I'm just used to it by now. Don't let him unnerve you."

"He didn't."

"You don't find Luca intimidating?"

I shook my head.

Nic's gaze adopted a sudden fierce intensity, and I was instantly hyperaware of how loud my heartbeat was.

"Good," he murmured.

"He's definitely weird, though," I added as an afterthought. "And unbelievably rude."

"We should bring him here more often so you can keep him in line." Nic produced a black credit card that gleamed with a level of affluence I could only dream about, and handed it to me. Suddenly every part of me was standing at attention, and I wondered if he knew it. He was probably used to having this effect on girls.

"So when did you move in?" I asked, trying to keep focused.

"Last week." Then I couldn't possibly have known him. My mind was playing tricks on me. Nic gestured behind him in the direction of the old house with a casualness that implied it was one of many sprawling mansions frequented by his family. Not that that surprised me; he had a certain look about him, the look of a wealthy kid who could afford European vacations and Aspen ski retreats. He had the kind of bloodline that stretched beyond somewhere as ordinary as Cedar Hill. "But you probably already know that, since you were spying on our house."

I felt my cheeks reignite. "I was *not* spying on your house!"

His smile grew. "Sure seemed that way."

I slid the credit card machine toward him and waited as he entered his PIN code. My gaze fell on the knuckles of his right hand, which were covered in pooling purple bruises and deep red gashes.

"What happened to your hand?" I asked, startled by the horror in my own voice. It was unpleasant to look at, and I couldn't understand why he wasn't flinching in pain.

Nic pulled his hand away from the machine and stared at it in surprise. "Oh," he said slowly, rotating his wrist and studying the injury.

The mechanical printing of the receipt filled the silence.

"Are you OK?"

"I'm fine."

I got the sense I had upset him. I ripped off the receipt and gave it to him, and this time he took it with his other hand.

"I didn't mean to pry . . ."

"No, of course not." Nic cleared his throat. "I had just forgotten about it, that's all. I got locked out the other day and I had to punch in a boarded-up window at the back of our house to get in. The perks of moving and all that . . ."

"It looks painful," I said, doing my best impression of Captain Obvious.

Nic shook his head a little. "I've had worse."

I couldn't tell if he was joking or not, and before I could think of a reply, he was turning from me.

"I should probably go, Sophie."

"Good-bye," I offered.

"Maybe I'll see you soon?" he called over his shoulder.

"As long as you don't try and kill me again."

"I'll try not to, but you're certainly more than welcome to come back and stalk my house." He winked, the lightness in his voice back again.

"I wasn't stalking it!"

"*Buona notte*, Sophie."

CHAPTER SIX

The Drowned Man

I arrived home to find a silver Mercedes parked on the street outside my house. I rounded the car, which exaggerated the pitiful state of my mother's battered Ford just by being near it. The Mercedes may have been sleek, but it was empty and unfamiliar. What's more, my mother was usually in bed at this time of night, *not* welcoming rich visitors. I might have been infamy's child, but she was infamy's wife, and that meant her social calendar was a lot more open than it used to be. Now, instead of friends, she had projects.

I began to panic that she *was* welcoming a visitor — the kind of visitor who was going to try and replace my father. Maybe my mother was already tired of waiting. Maybe she didn't want to face the next four years alone, fielding questions from nosy neighbors and fair-weather friends, and spending every Valentine's Day crying over the night my father was taken away from her. Maybe this was the car of the man who was going to try and fix it all.

I centered myself. There was really only one thing to do. And that one thing was not to stand outside panicking. No. I was going to march inside, muster up every strand of teenage sarcasm and moodiness I had in me, and use it to scare away whoever this mystery suitor was.

I let myself in through the front door and shut it quietly behind me. Deep vibrations were wafting from the kitchen — a man's voice! I padded down the hallway, stopping just behind the door that led to the kitchen. It was ajar.

"I don't know why you're acting so jumpy. You're going to terrify her," my mother was saying.

"Will there ever be a time when you take my advice, Celine?"

The strained voice of my uncle Jack surprised me more than if it had been a different man entirely. Historically, my mother and my father's brother had never gotten along. In my mother's mind, Jack was always getting in the way. And even when he was getting in the way with concert tickets or take-out pizza, he was still a nuisance. He was about the only person in the world who she refused to tolerate. He ranked below Mrs. Bailey on the I-don't-want-you-in-my-house scale, and *that* was saying something.

Growing up, my father and my uncle only ever had each other — a result of two absent, alcoholic parents — and with Jack being younger, and always refusing to settle down, he had relied a lot on my father, pulling him away for nights at the local bar, or sweeping into his life during private moments that my mother had wanted to keep for just us three. In short, Jack was always there, and was, in my mother's esteem, a bad influence.

But I knew the other parts of him — the man who took me into the city to see *Wicked* at the Oriental Theatre just because I once said in passing that I liked musicals; the man who purposefully lingered around my conversations with Millie at work so he could chime in with his idea of sage advice about our boy problems; the man who ruffled my hair when I was trying to complain about something completely serious, who would buy me the new iPhone on a whim, "just because," and who would insist on driving me to school when it was snowing out so I wouldn't have to walk through the slush to reach the bus. I saw the man who did his best to step in and protect me when my father went to prison, and even though he didn't always succeed in shielding me from the cruel jibes and the rescinded party invitations, at least he tried.

I pressed closer to the door.

"I don't want you getting Sophie involved in your conspiracy stuff," my mother snapped. "Haven't you learned anything?"

"It's my prerogative to look out for her, Celine. I made a promise to Mickey."

"I think you've already done enough," my mother replied in a dangerously quiet voice reserved only for her most terrifying moods. I flinched in sympathy for my uncle.

"When are you going to let all this shit go?" Jack spat.

"When you accept your part in it!"

I peeked around the door. My mother stood at one end of the kitchen, wearing her bathrobe and slippers. Her short golden hair lay messy around her face, and her features were pinched in disgust. She had folded her arms and was leaning to one side, her hip hitched up at a defiant angle. Small as she was, nobody wanted to be on the wrong side of Celine Gracewell. I, of all people, could certainly attest to that.

"I'm just trying to keep Sophie safe," Jack said, his shoulders dropping in resignation. "Why won't you let me?"

"Because I don't trust you. Not after everything."

With a frustrated sigh, my uncle stepped back and shook his head. "You've never trusted me."

"Oh shut up, Jack."

Feeling like I had heard enough to make me feel sufficiently uncomfortable for the rest of the year, I kicked the door wide open.

"What the hell is going on?"

Jack's face flooded with relief, settling the high color in his cheeks. "There you are!"

"Yeah." I pointed at myself for added effect. "Here I am. What's all the yelling about?"

"Nothing, nothing." He ran his hand along his graying buzz cut, stopping to scratch the back of his head. "I'm just stressed."

Jack was always stressed about something.

"What are you doing here?"

"Being dramatic," my mother hissed before he could reply.

Yikes.

"Is that your new car in the driveway?" I asked, coming to stand between my uncle and my mother and trying to alter the mood. "If you're making that kind of money from the diner, you should probably give me a raise."

He wasn't amused by my joke. "I borrowed it from a friend. I'm not driving my car right now."

"Feeling too conspicuous these days?" I tried to lighten the mood again.

There really was nothing more uncomfortable than awkwardness. And besides, Uncle Jack drove a red vintage convertible — an homage to his midlife crisis. It was only fair I got to make fun of him for it.

He sighed. "Something like that."

My mother moved around me to fill a glass of water. "Just say what you want to say to her so we can get back to our lives."

"What are you doing here so late?" I asked again. "And why haven't you been at work? The deliveryman still hasn't shown up."

My uncle shuffled his feet like a lost child, unsure of where to put himself. "I know," he said, his voice thick with weariness. "Luis died on Friday night."

"Oh," I said, feeling a sudden pang of guilt. The deliveryman had a name — Luis, yes, I remembered. And now Luis, who was barely forty, was dead. "What happened to him?"

"He drowned."

"Drowned," I echoed. "At night. Where?"

"In his bathtub," said Jack, simply, like there wasn't anything bizarre about that statement.

"Oh dear," said my mother, covering her mouth.

I, on the other hand, was gaping. It just seemed so illogical. "Was it suicide?" The last time I signed for a delivery, Luis was chattering on about how great the weather was.

"Luis had too much to live for," Jack replied matter-of-factly. "He didn't do it to himself." What did *that* mean? A sudden coldness rippled up my arms. My uncle continued, undeterred by the implication, leaving me to ponder it in silence. "Eric Cain and I are going to see Luis's family tomorrow. I want to see that they're taken care of while they deal with . . . all of this. His wife is inconsolable."

I was starting to feel like a royal ass. I had met Luis maybe twenty times and I barely knew his name; my uncle knew his story, his family, and now he was going to go out of his way to make sure they were OK.

"That's really good of you," I said, looking to my mother for her agreement — surely she would give Uncle Jack credit for this — but she wasn't paying attention to me.

"That poor woman," she said quietly instead.

"It's the right thing to do," said Jack, to me.

"Are you OK?" My uncle wasn't one for big displays of emotion, but I could see by his face that he was upset.

"Yeah," he said, brushing off my concern. "I just wanted to come by and talk to you before I left."

"You could have called me," I ventured, not unkindly, but there's just something so unnerving about people visiting you without calling first. "I'm permanently contactable."

"I lost my phone. I have to get a new one."

My mother circled the table and sat as far away from Jack as she could. She started drumming her fingernails along the table — a not-so-subtle hint — while still keeping a watchful eye on our conversation. If I thought Luis's death had softened her obvious disdain for my uncle, I was wrong.

Jack ignored her exasperation, and I felt like I was the only one left experiencing the full awkwardness of the situation.

"So . . . what's up?" I asked.

He pulled a chair out and sat down, propping his elbows on his knees. His shoulders sagged. "After I visit Luis's family tomorrow, I'm going to go stay in the city. I won't be back in Cedar Hill for a while. But I want to talk to you about something before I go away."

He looked at me with solemn gray-blue eyes — they were my eyes, my father's eyes, and with a sudden pang I was reminded of just how similar they were. Before, they could have been mistaken for twins, but not anymore. Prison life had been unkind to my father's appearance, while my uncle's face remained mostly unlined, his hair neat and his skin lightly tanned from being out in the sun.

"What do you want to talk about?" I backed up against the counter and gripped it a lot harder than I meant to, sensing something was wrong. This was what they were arguing about. My mother continued to drum her fingernails on the table.

"A new family have moved into the neighborhood, and I need you to be careful of them."

I felt alarm spread across my face. "What?"

He surveyed me warily. "Do you know what I'm talking about?"

I nodded slowly, trying to figure out where this was coming from and why it was making me feel panicky all over again. "What's wrong with the Priestlys?"

I watched my mother's reaction for more clues.

"Theatrics," she murmured, with a dismissive flick of the wrist. Still, she stayed where she was, monitoring our exchange.

"Persephone" — I grimaced on instinct. I hated when Jack

full-named me. "I'm not going to get into it," he said. My uncle's stern voice was so like my father's, it sent a shudder down my spine. For a second I wanted to close my eyes and pretend he was there, that everything was back to the way it should be — that we hadn't just discussed somebody drowning in their own tub, and that we weren't about to slap a big fat warning sign over the hottest boys in the neighborhood. "Just do as I ask."

I couldn't help but feel skeptical. Even with his bruised hand, there had been something so soothing about Nic's presence.

"When will you be back?"

"I don't know yet."

Cagey as ever. I wished Millie the High Inquisitor were here. She could get answers from a mute. And she'd enjoy it, too.

"So that's all you're going to tell me?"

"That's all there is." Jack looked away from me, out the window and into the darkness behind our house. "Do you understand?"

I was about to answer that I didn't really understand *anything* about it, but then the most peculiar thing happened. He sprang to his feet like something had bitten him. The chair tumbled backward and he darted across the kitchen.

"What on earth?" My mother's chair screeched against the floor.

Jack lunged at the kitchen sink and shot out his hand. I thought he was going to punch through the window, but instead he grabbed the jar of honey from the sill. When he looked at me again, his eyes were red and bulging.

"Where did this come from?"

"The h-honey?" I stuttered. I had never seen someone so freaked out by something so benign. "I found it."

He pinched the black ribbon between his fingers, rubbing it. "Where?"

I shrugged. "Someone left it at the diner. I found it when I was closing up."

The color drained from his face, turning his usually red-tinged cheeks an eerie paper white. "If you find one of these again, I want you to leave it where it is and call me immediately."

"Jack, it's just honey," I pointed out.

Why was everyone acting so strangely lately? I had already tasted it and lived to tell the tale, so it's not like it was poisoned.

"Just do it," he said quietly. "OK?"

"I thought you said you didn't have a phone," I reminded him.

"I'll call you when I get a new one."

"Jack?" In all the strangeness, I had forgotten my mother was still there. "I think you should go now. You're acting erratically and it's making me very uncomfortable. Sophie probably wants to go to bed."

I opened my mouth to protest — I wasn't tired — but then I stopped myself. My mother was right.

"OK." Jack looked at the ground, shaking his head. "Sorry, Sophie. I've had a very long day."

"It's fine." I offered him an encouraging smile. Between managing the diner and taking care of his investments in the city, Jack always worked himself into the ground, but lately he had been more unlike himself than ever; he was exhausted and jittery, and now that Luis had died, his behavior was stranger than ever.

"Good night, Sophie."

"Night," I returned.

Honey still in hand, Jack trudged toward the back door.

A half second later, the motion sensor in our backyard flickered to life, illuminating my uncle's shadow as it faced away from us, staring at the broken patio squares and the overgrown grass.

"What on earth is he — "

The rest of my mother's question was drowned out by an ear-splitting crash. I pressed my nose up to the window, but Jack was already disappearing from view. I looked down, where the light was winking off a hundred shards of shattered glass.

"That man!" my mother shrieked, coming to stand beside me at the window. "This is exactly why I don't want him around. Your uncle's behavior is completely irrational. He's been drinking again, and if he doesn't stop, he's going to wind up doing something he'll really regret . . ." She trailed off and started to rub my arm. "Are you OK?"

"I'm fine," I lied, pinning my hand against the window to stop it from shaking.

"I wish your father were here to keep him in line."

"I think if Dad were here Uncle Jack wouldn't be out of line," I said quietly.

My mother sighed. "I'll have to wait until morning to clean up that mess."

"I'll help you."

We lingered at the window together, and watched as honey oozed into the pavement cracks like dark gold blood.

CHAPTER SEVEN

The Crimson Falcons

Millie had an outfit for everything, so when she showed up at the riverside courts on Saturday, I was unsurprised to find her wearing a tiny pair of shorts and the tightest basketball jersey I had ever seen. She pushed her way through pockets of other teenagers, waltzing toward me in an explosion of black and red.

"I didn't know you were a Bulls fan."

"Oh, didn't you?" She smirked and plonked herself down beside me on the bottom bench of the courtside bleachers.

"Let me rephrase that," I said as she began to wind her hair into a ponytail. "I didn't even know you were a basketball fan."

"I guess you could say I'm more of a *boys* fan." She snapped the hair elastic into place. "The top belongs to Alex. It shrunk in the wash." She grinned unashamedly.

I looked down at myself: my mother's three-quarter-length jogging pants, a plain gray tank top, and an old pair of Asics with bright green stripes. My hair was tied high on my head, falling down between my shoulder blades in a straight ponytail. Already

I could tell the sun was bleaching the stray baby hairs that were too wispy to be tied back with the rest.

Millie ran her gaze along my outfit, scrunching her nose.

"You look . . ." she began uncertainly.

" . . . normcore?" I finished.

Exercise wasn't exactly my calling in life, but I was grateful to have something to distract me from my uncle's recent behavior. He had been gone for several days since his whole honeypot-patio freak-out and still hadn't tried to contact me. Ursula was in charge of the diner in his absence. She had reacted the worst to the death of Luis, and had resolved never to take a bath again, just in case she drowned herself. Millie and I were slightly less dramatic about it, but we were still glad to be free of her morbid rants, at least just for the day.

We never usually played in the Cedar Hill Summer Basketball Tournament. Not that the word "tournament" really summed it up. It was more of a basketball-related gathering hosted by the Cedar Hill Residents Association every July. As part of an ever-growing agenda that included park maintenance, a neighborhood watch, and outdoor movie nights, the CHRA were always coming up with ideas that would keep us teenagers off the street and out of trouble in a "socially desirable and positive way" during the summer. The basketball tournament was one of the few that had actually stuck, and over the years it had become a tradition that everyone made fun of but no one wanted to miss. It was really about the only thing the neighborhood kids actually did together; the rest of the summer we were like lazy suburban tumbleweeds, floating around the town in twos and threes.

For Millie and me, the whole thing had always been more of a spectacle enjoyed from the sidelines while eating ice cream and pointing out hot boys, but in the interest of "getting back up on the social horse," as Millie called it, we had decided to take part this summer. I was hesitant at best; if nobody wanted to hang out with the daughter of a murderer, who would want to play basketball with one? Thankfully, Millie's brother, Alex, had invited us to be part of his team. I suspected it was a way to make it more of a challenge for him — the trophies from the past three years were probably gathering dust on his bedroom shelf by now.

"We might actually win this thing, you know." Millie was reclining on the bench, arms splayed out behind her as she scoped out our surroundings.

As always, there were twice as many spectators squishing themselves into the bleachers and spilling out onto the grass that surrounded the courts. Erin Reyes and the rest of her gang had already secured a prime vantage spot at the top of the bleachers. Instead of playing in the tournament, they would most likely be practicing how to eat their Popsicles as seductively as possible. They were already doing an uncomfortably good job. Just beyond the courts the river flowed lazily, reflecting the clear sky, and along the bank, rows of young trees leaned over the water like they were peering inside for something.

"I remember the last time I played basketball," said Millie wistfully. She stared up at the sky and I could see the sun was already dusting freckles across her pale cheeks. "I was trying to pass the ball to Alex, but he missed it and it smashed the kitchen window."

"Good times," I remembered fondly.

"What about you?" She snapped her head down.

"Maybe never?"

Little creases rippled along Millie's forehead. "I'm sure you'll be good at it."

"You better be," someone interrupted.

Millie's brother, Alex, was stalking toward us, his grin revealing nearly all of his perfectly square teeth. He was accompanied by two of his friends — the first I recognized as Robbie Stenson, a stockier, *way* less attractive version of a Ken doll, who came complete with floppy brown hair and overly groomed eyebrows. He didn't walk so much as lope around, kind of like a stylish troll. The other boy I had seen once or twice at Millie's house playing video games, but he never seemed to say much. He had bright red hair, gangly limbs, and a forehead that was shinier than the rest of him.

Millie bounced to her feet. "It's about time you showed up. We have a tournament to win."

"Soph, you know Stenny and Foxy, right?" Alex indicated behind him.

Ah, boys and their stupid nicknames. "Yeah, hi." I waved.

Robbie Stenson gave me a too-cool-for-this-introduction head nod so subtle I barely registered it, while "Foxy" threw a fluorescent yellow vest at me. I fumbled it and had to bend down to pick it up. They were obviously less than thrilled about having me on their team.

Millie caught her vest on reflex and then dropped it like it was on fire. "No way. I'm not wearing this. It reeks of sweat."

"Are you serious?" Alex's voice was already weary with sibling-related fatigue.

Millie curled her lip in disgust. "I'd literally rather die." I suppressed my smile. Their British accents made even the most banal exchanges sound way more *Masterpiece Theatre* than they had any right to be.

Robbie, Foxy, and I put our vests on without protest; mine fell to my knees and halfway down my arms, engulfing everything but my luminous kicks. Eventually, and after some not-so-subtle peer pressure on my part, Millie wriggled into hers.

"You're such a tyrant," she muttered under her breath.

"At least your legs still look good," I tried to reassure her. But we couldn't hide from the ugly truth. We were both swimming in oversized fluorescence.

"We're up on court one first," Alex started, clapping his hands and rubbing them together. "Our team name is the Sharpshooters."

Millie and I grimaced. "That's the worst name ever," we chorused.

"Why don't you come up with something better, then?" Alex challenged.

"Oh, oh, oh!" Millie started hopping up and down. "What about Victorious Secret?"

Alex's face fell, and Foxy let out a groan.

"That doesn't even make sense," Robbie cut in.

"How about the Human Highlighters?" I suggested, gesturing at our hideously luminous vests.

"Fine." Alex threw his hands up in surrender, and Robbie and Foxy nodded their reluctant consent. "We'll change it."

Millie cupped her hands around her mouth and made her voice sound crackly. "That's one small step for Sophie, one giant leap for Alex's sense of humor."

Robbie sprinted off to reregister our name, leaving us with Foxy and Alex, who was already taking the whole situation a million times more seriously than we were.

"I've done a little recon," he said, conveying his info like a Navy SEAL. "A lot of the other players are younger than us this year, which gives us the advantage . . ."

Millie punched me in the arm and my attention fell away from her brother. "What?"

"Now *you're* literally going to die." Her eyes had grown to the size of saucers, and I swiveled to follow her gaze. "That's them, right? The Priestly brothers?"

She wasn't fully wrong about the dying thing. My heart definitely slowed down for at least a couple of beats. Across the far court, the Priestly brothers were coming toward us; there were four of them this time, their connection to each other made plain by their olive skin and dark hair.

"I never thought I'd actually find basketball shorts attractive on a guy" was all I could manage.

"I was just thinking that," said Millie.

What the hell are they even doing here? I wondered. Most of us had come for tradition's sake — it was a pleasant enough way to kill time, a last resort on a sunny day for a bunch of kids who had nothing better to do. But these boys weren't like the rest of Cedar Hill. I would have thought them above the idea of attending some Podunk neighborhood basketball tournament.

Luca was walking next to Nic, his face stern, and a new brother flanked them on either side. They probably could have nailed a five-legged race if they'd wanted to.

By the way the brothers seemed to zero in on Luca as he spoke, I assumed he was the eldest, though the others, the two I had yet to meet and who were remarkably similar to each other in appearance, could not have been that far behind — maybe eighteen or nineteen years old. They were shorter and more filled out, though they shared the same square jaws and strong cheekbones. I guessed Nic was the youngest of the four, though not by much.

"Holy handsomeness!" Millie was practically salivating. "Four Italian stallions carved from my dreams. Which one is Nic?"

My eyes hadn't left him. "The one with the dark hair."

"Ha-ha, very funny."

"Second from the right."

"Wow. And Luca?"

"Second from the left."

Millie whistled to herself. "*Hello*, blue eyes."

Alex prodded her in the shoulder. "Are you done? We're trying to talk tactics."

"Shut up," she hissed, shaking him off. "I'm in the middle of something." She narrowed her eyes, honing in. "OK, who's on the far right? The one with the slicked-back hair? And is that a *scar*?"

"I don't know. Maybe we should call him Hair Gel."

The closer they got, the more obvious it became that they were capturing the attention of every girl in the vicinity, and they looked like they knew it, too. I wondered where the fifth brother was — the bright-eyed boy from the window who'd raised his hand without a smile — but the thought vanished when Nic's eyes found mine and I nearly exploded with butterflies.

"Hi," he mouthed.

I smiled back, resisting the urge to clutch my stupid, backflipping stomach.

"Holy crap, that was seductive." Millie was hopping from foot to foot. "They're coming over. Be cool."

Like helpless magnets, we drifted toward the brothers, leaving Alex and his sidekicks to talk boring strategy behind us, determined, like every boy at the basketball courts, to ignore the new arrivals. My uncle's warning, which had seemed so urgent and important at the time, flittered away on the wind. If these boys were really bad news, as Jack seemed to think, then suddenly I was happy to be Icarus, ready to get all melty from flying too close to the suns.

"Hey," I called out. "I didn't know you'd be playing today."

Nic stopped a couple of feet away and the rest of his brothers closed in around us. "It was a last-minute decision. Now I'm glad we made it."

Millie pinched me. It was her silent version of an excited squeal.

"Nice vest, Sophie," said Luca, straight off the bat. "I can barely see you."

"Luca." I tore my attention away from Nic for the amount of time needed to throw his brother a contemptuous glare. "A pleasure, as always."

The brother beside him laughed. He had the stupidest

hairstyle: The top section of his hair was scraped into a short black ponytail, while the sides of his head were shaved, revealing a small golden hoop in his left ear. Despite the ridiculous plant hairstyle, he was attractive, but when he laughed, his eyes widened unnaturally and his opened mouth revealed two chipped front teeth that made him seem slightly maniacal. He reminded me of that one crazy hyena in *The Lion King*.

"Ignore Luca. That's just his bad attempt at trash-talking you," Nic cut in, sending his brother a glare on my behalf.

"And my way of pointing out that she's small," Luca added.

"Thanks, Sherlock. I know I'm small."

"Just making sure."

"Do you even have a brain-to-mouth filter?" I asked.

"I try not to overuse it," he returned blithely.

"Clearly."

"Don't cry about it, Day-Glo."

"Shut up, Luca." Nic threw his red vest over his head and pulled it down. "I think you make it look good, Sophie."

"*Cazzo*, here we go again," muttered Luca. He rolled his eyes and then leaned into Ponytail, adding in a calculated whisper, "*This* is what he was like at the diner. It was so annoying."

"You know, Luca, you're really good at strategically muttering things just loud enough to be offensive."

"Thank you, Sophie." His tone lifted, rendering his false sincerity almost believable. "I appreciate that."

"I should get you a medal."

"Don't bother," he said, a lazy smirk forming. "After today, I'll have a trophy."

I curled my lip. "I know what you can do with that trophy . . ."

Millie's laugh drowned out the rest of my reply. She hugged her arm around my side, pinching me through the vest. *Squeal, squeal, squeal.*

"So what's your team's name?" Nic cut in, strategically guiding the conversation out of the gutter.

I puffed up my chest and brushed the stray strands of now-white hair away from my face. "The Human Highlighters."

Luca snorted.

"What's yours?" asked Millie, but she wasn't directing her question at Nic; she was looking at Hair Gel, her teeth gently pulling at her bottom lip.

I zeroed in on his face — Millie was right, there *was* a scar. It was obviously an old injury, slicing through his left eyebrow and glowing silvery against his tanned skin. On instinct, I glanced at Nic's bruised hand, and felt an uneasiness bubbling in my stomach. I pushed it away.

"The Crimson Falcons," Hair Gel replied to Millie, falling right into her trap and watching her lips hungrily.

"Intense," said Millie, her expression entirely coquettish.

"It was either that or the Angel-makers," Luca added. His humor was so deadpan, sometimes I didn't know if he was funny or just insane.

"Stop it." Nic punched Luca in the arm with an audible thump, but his brother didn't flinch. If I had received that hit I would have been on the ground screaming for my mother.

"*Calmati!* I think I'd better defuse this," Hair Gel cut in, moving easily from one language to the next, just like Nic and

Luca did. It was hard to tell which was their real accent — American or Italian. Hair Gel leaned over to shake our hands, holding Millie's a little longer than mine and, I noticed, stroking his thumb over hers. Maybe Millie had finally met her flirting match. "I'm Dominico. You can call me Dom, though."

Millie broke into the creepiest giggle I've ever heard. "I'm Millie. This is Sophie. Welcome to the neighborhood."

Welcome to the neighborhood? I'd have to tease her about that later. Maybe she could stop by his house with a basket of muffins.

"Thank you. Do you work at the diner as well, Millie?" Dom lingered over her name like it was a beautiful flower. His charm offensive was almost as powerful as Nic's, but his eyes were darker, his expression intense. I studied his scar as he moved away from me, beginning his own hushed conversation with Millie.

I felt Nic's attention on me again. "Good luck today," he offered earnestly.

"Thanks, you too." There were other things I wanted to say to him, but with Luca and Ponytail watching us I could barely utter a word without feeling self-conscious.

"We don't need luck," Luca interrupted, prompting another exasperated thump from Nic.

"Luca," Ponytail whined. His voice was abnormally high and not unlike Marge Simpson's, and for a terrifying moment I thought I was going to laugh in his face. He frowned, and his eyebrows bled into one fuzzy caterpillar above coffee-colored eyes. "Can we just go register?"

"Yeah, let's go, Gino. We shouldn't be fraternizing with our competition anyway." Luca elbowed Nic as he retreated. *"Andiamo,* Loverboy."

"I should probably go get ready," Nic offered apologetically. "Wouldn't want to get on the bad side of our wonderful dictator."

"Same here," I said, but both of us still lingered. "Where's the rest of your team anyway? Don't you have a fifth player?"

He shook his head with more casualness than I was expecting. I was hoping he'd mention the fifth brother, at least give me a clue as to why he hadn't come or even that he did, in fact, exist, and I hadn't imagined a creepy ghost boy at the window that first night. "We're a foursome."

"So you're at a disadvantage," I noted. "That's a risky move."

Nic did something with his eyes that made the flecks of gold inside them glisten. I wasn't sure if it was a secret superpower or the effect of the sun, but it was damn effective. And a little jarring, though I still couldn't figure out why.

"You're welcome to be our number five," he whispered conspiratorially. "I promise I'll keep Luca away from you."

I bit my lip to keep my smile from bordering on disturbing. "I'm not sure Millie would ever forgive me if I jumped ship."

"Ah, I see." He feigned the look of a puppy that had just been kicked. "You're too noble for that."

"And surely you're too honorable to steal me from her."

"No, I'm not."

I felt a blush rise in my cheeks. "Well, I'll have to be honorable enough for both of us, then. Besides," I added, trying to justify my refusal to myself, "we're up in a minute, and we've already missed our strategy session. I don't want to annoy the rest of my team any more than I already have."

"Where are they?"

I gestured behind me at Alex and the rest of the yellow vests, who were in the middle of an intense set of jumping jacks.

Nic's smile faded. "That blond guy?"

"That's Millie's brother and two of his friends. I think she bribed them into letting us on their team."

Nic studied Alex and the others as they started to bend themselves into elaborate stretches. "I'm sure the bribe wasn't necessary."

"Soph." Millie was back and tugging on my arm. "We gotta go. Our game is about to start."

Dom had stepped away from her and I caught a glimpse of his scar again. Though he couldn't have been much older than us, something about it aged him, made him other than what he appeared. I couldn't put my finger on what it was. He caught me watching him and smirked, his expression suddenly wolfish.

I looked away, embarrassed.

"See you guys on the court!" Millie pulled me with her, wiggling her butt a lot more than she usually did as she walked.

When I waved at Nic he was still staring at Alex. He didn't wave back.

We won our first game in time to watch the Crimson Falcons play Saved by the Balls on the opposite court. The Priestly brothers were fascinating to watch; even Alex, who had expressed a deliberate disinterest in them since their arrival, was glued to the game. Nic and Dom were the most obviously athletic, whipping up the court in flashes of red. They scored most of their baskets, only occasionally deferring to Gino, who seemed to be more adept at intimidating the other players than actually playing against them. Maybe it was the ponytail.

Luca glided around the sidelines, and when the opportune moment arose, he'd strike from the shadows like a viper, snatching the ball out of the opposition's hands before the other player even had time to notice Luca was there. But that's all he did: intercept. I didn't see him make one single basket. He didn't even break a sweat.

Our game against Don't Hassle the Hoff started before the Priestly game finished, though it was clear that, like us, they would be advancing to the next round. We won by a comfortable margin of 62–39. Alex did most of the work, followed by Foxy and then Robbie. Millie was a very distant last, but she made it clear she didn't care. She was there to make an appearance, and if her fingers happened to brush against a basketball by accident, then fine.

We watched the Priestly brothers win their second game with more ease than we did. In our third game we were up against the Thunder Squirrels. I became acutely aware of Nic's presence on the sidelines and decided to make more of a conscious effort this time. Millie seemed to have concocted a similar plan, because for once she wasn't squealing and running away from the ball. She was actually chasing it.

By the end of our third quarter, the brothers were on the other court, winning their game as well, which meant both of our teams were going to the finals.

CHAPTER EIGHT

The Switchblade

"Crap," Millie said. The short parts of her bangs had frizzed out and she was frantically fixing her hair as we lingered on the court. "I don't want to play against Dom. He'll see how terrible I am and then he won't come to my house party next week."

"You invited him to the party already?"

Millie slow-blinked at me. "Didn't you invite Nic?"

"Um . . ."

"God, Sophie." She scrunched her eyes and started to rub her temples. "Sometimes I wonder what goes on in that head of yours."

"I hadn't even thought about it," I admitted.

"*I hadn't even thought about it*," she mimicked in the world's worst attempt at my accent.

"I'm not from the South," I pointed out.

"It's on your birthday," she countered, ignoring my jibe. "You should definitely invite him."

"I will." I tried not to feel nervous about the prospect of inviting Nic to a house party taking place on my birthday where a grand total of five people would actually acknowledge me.

"In the meantime, let's hope Dom doesn't lose all respect for me during this game."

"It's OK," I soothed, retying my ponytail. "He's already seen how bad you are."

She shot me a withering look. "It's bad enough he's already seen me sweat. It must be over a hundred degrees today."

Alex, Robbie, and Foxy joined us and started stretching again. They were so pumped it was almost laughable. "Just one more game, guys. We've nearly got this," Alex said.

"We *so* don't got this," whispered Millie.

I nodded my head solemnly. "We are screwed."

Alex turned his attention to us, his face awash with concern. We were loose cannons, and his awareness of that fact couldn't have been more obvious. "OK, the Crimson Falcons are a man short, which means Foxy, Stenny, and I can take the strongest three. Millie and Sophie, you stay on the tallest guy."

"I don't want to mark Luca!" I wailed.

"Can I mark Dom?" Millie asked hopefully.

Alex raked his hands through his hair, sweaty strands flopping back around his eyes. "No. If Luca's free to move around, he'll throw our game off."

Over Alex's shoulder I could see the Priestly brothers taking up their positions on the court. Nic was passing the ball back and forth between his hands, his expression focused. Beside him, Luca was smirking like it was going out of fashion. I wondered if he even had a facial expression that didn't read as "smug ass."

"Earth to Sophie."

"Huh?"

Alex was staring at me, his big blue eyes as wide as Millie's. Sometimes it was eerie how similar their expressions made them. "Did you hear what I said?"

I shook my head dumbly. "Were you speaking?"

He released a sharp sigh and placed his hands on my shoulders, locking gazes with me. Ordinarily I would have been giddy if Millie's hot older brother got this close to me, but my hyperawareness of Nic was distracting me. "I need you to keep Millie focused. I'll take care of the rest. The Crimson Falcons are going down."

"You have to stop calling them that. I can't take you seriously."

He pressed harder on my shoulders, as if to steady my resolve. I watched a stray bead of sweat slide down the side of his face and onto his neck. "Sophie, can *you* please focus?"

"Hey, man, I think she gets it."

Alex withdrew his hands and I pulled back to find Nic standing right beside him. He was giving him that look again — that I-don't-trust-you-and-maybe-I-want-to-kill-you look, but it was up close this time, and full of hostility.

"You're so worried about losing that you have to eavesdrop on our huddle?" Alex returned.

Nic arched an eyebrow. "You're so hyped up about this game that you're going to freak her out about it? Give her a break."

Alex squared up to Nic; they were almost the same height, but Nic had the advantage. "I like to win and so does she."

"I bet Sophie likes to have fun, too. Have you heard of that concept?" Nic clenched his jaw. "Leave her alone."

"Who the hell are *you*, anyway?" snapped Alex. "You don't know either of us, so why don't you get out of our business and worry about yourself?"

Nic didn't move. They stood almost chest to chest, and I could see by the way Alex was flicking his gaze toward Robbie and Foxy that he was angling for backup. Not for the first time I registered Nic's defensive stance, and understood his distrust of Alex was about me. By the way he was staring at him, it looked like Nic was trying to bore a hole through Alex's forehead.

"Boys, chill out!" I squeezed myself into the space between them, pushing them apart with my hands. Alex fell away, but Nic didn't budge as easily. I could practically feel the testosterone seeping through his pores. "Let's just start this thing, OK?"

"Fine." Alex's teeth were gritted.

"Fine." Nic turned on his heel and gestured to his brothers. They huddled up on the other side of the court.

Millie sidled over to me and dropped her voice. "I think Dom's going to ask me out."

Alex and Nic were getting into position for the jump ball.

"How do you know?"

A shout went up from somewhere behind us; the ball was in play and Nic had possession.

"He was flirting with me like crazy. And I thought *I* was shameless! I can tell he doesn't want to wait until the party to hang out."

Nic scored the first basket before I had time to reply.

The game moved so quickly I could hardly keep track. I barely touched the ball, and Millie only managed to bounce it once before Luca zoomed by and dribbled it out from under her. Every time Nic passed me, it felt like he was deliberately slowing down so I could feel him brush against me, and I kept blissfully forgetting I was supposed to be marking Luca. By halftime, we were behind by six points.

At the start of the third quarter, Robbie passed the ball to me — I was standing near the basket, wide open. I sprang up, but the ball was knocked from my hands before I could shoot. It bounced away as Gino barreled straight into me. I would have flown off the court if Nic hadn't jumped out of nowhere, catching me from behind. I stumbled against him with a thump.

"Careful," he panted, his breath unsteady on my neck.

"Nic!" Luca yelled. "Heads up!"

I looked up just in time to see a big orange blur whizzing directly at my face. My head slammed backward into Nic's chest, and he grabbed me as I slumped against him.

"Tu sei pazzo!" Nic screeched over my head.

Tears started to stream down my cheeks, mingling with the blood that was pouring from my nose.

A little crowd formed around me.

"Sorry." It was Luca's voice, but I couldn't focus on him. "I did say 'Heads up,' though."

"Why would you pass the ball to me when her face was in the way?" Nic seethed over me.

"Why would you be feeling her up in the middle of a basketball game?"

"Vaffanculo!"

I didn't need to understand Italian to guess what that meant.

Millie whipped off her vest and handed it to me. I started to dab my nose, pinching the bridge with my free hand to stop the bleeding and trying not to smell the years of stale boy-sweat that had been encased in the mesh.

"Can *everyone* just give her some space?" Millie demanded.

Nic pulled his hands from my waist and joined the others, who were all staring at me with various levels of concern. Except Gino, who was tracking the movements of a nearby butterfly and snickering to himself.

"Do you think you can keep playing, Sophie?" Alex asked.

Nic bristled, turning on him. "Are you serious, dude? That's all you can think to say?"

"What the *hell* is your problem?" Alex shot back.

Before Nic could retort, Millie was stomping her feet on the concrete like the angriest two-year-old imaginable. "What the hell is wrong with *both* of you? Stupid boys and your *stupid* competitiveness. Just shut up, all of you! Sophie and I are absolutely *not* continuing this *childish* game with you hotheaded *Neanderthals* so you can win some *stupid*, cheap-ass trophy. We want no further part in this pathetic charade."

"I — " Luca began.

"No!" Millie raised her index finger and pointed it directly into his eye like she was about to poke it. "Not another word from *you*. If you have something to say, you can write it in a card and send it to Sophie's house with the *nicest flowers* money can buy. And you can say how *sorry* you are for being a *giant* ass and nearly *killing* her. She could have *died*. Do you understand that? *Died!* And all you have to show for it is that smirk. I don't think it's one bit funny, and I'll have you know I am a great judge of humor. So why don't you wipe that smile off your god-awfully perfect face and grow a sense of humanity, you smug douchelord."

I couldn't quite fathom how everyone was managing not to laugh at Millie's ridiculous dramatics. If I had been in slightly less pain, I would have been doubled over on the ground myself.

"Mil — " Alex tried.

"No, Alex!" she shouted. "I don't want to hear your excuses, either. Where did you even *come* from anyway? I find it hard to believe we crawled out of the same womb. If you're not man enough to go through life without a fake trophy telling you something about yourself, then you're not man enough to speak to Sophie or me. And that goes for *all* of you morons." She grabbed me by the arm and started pulling me away from everyone. "We are going to the sidelines, where there is ice cream. And that is *final*!"

I could see the lingering shock in their eyes; they had obviously underestimated Millie. Nic was boring holes in his brother's forehead. If looks could kill, Luca would have been long gone from this world.

"Resume play?" I heard Alex say as we left the court.

"I can sit the game out to make it even." My heart leapt at Nic's suggestion.

"No way. We finish it like this. We'll still beat you."

Stupid Alex.

After the game, Nic found me on the sidelines nursing my nose with an unopened Popsicle. Millie had gone in search of Dom to try and salvage their burgeoning love after her crazy outburst on the court. Alex had stormed off in a huff, and Luca was probably strolling around somewhere with a giant trophy tucked under his arm.

"Congratulations on your win."

"Thanks." Nic sank onto the grass beside me and pulled his knees up, wrapping his arms around them. "But I don't think a two-foot plastic trophy is going to improve my life much."

"You probably would have lost if I had continued playing," I teased. I took the Popsicle away from my nose and wiggled it around to restore some feeling, relieved that it didn't seem broken.

"Good as new," Nic said. He leaned closer to get a better look and I noticed a small sprinkling of freckles across the bridge of his nose. "It's perfect."

"What is it about you boys and your incessant need to assault me anyway?" I asked. "Have you got it in for me or something? You could at least be more subtle about it."

"Must be something about you." Nic flashed me a roguish grin. "We're usually very discreet."

"Four boys and discretion. Those terms don't exactly go together in my mind."

"Well, actually there aren't just f — " Nic fell away from his sentence when something behind me caught his attention.

I looked over my shoulder.

At the edge of the riverbank, past the last court, I could just make out a ponytailed figure shoving someone with short blond hair behind the trees. Alex and Gino. It was hard to see, but they looked like they were fighting.

Nic sprang to his feet. I tried to keep up, but he was much faster than me.

Within seconds he was at the riverbank, pushing through the trees and pulling Alex off his brother. When I caught up with them, I found Gino doubled over, unmoving, with his head clutched loosely in his hands. Nearby, Nic was pinning Alex on the ground, and the two were trading insults.

Alex jerked his body to the side and kicked out at Nic, making him fall back onto his haunches.

"This has nothing to do with you!" Alex shouted as they both clambered to their feet.

"You just knocked my brother out!" Nic yelled, thundering into Alex and tackling him at the knees. He slammed him into a small tree that bent under their combined weight.

"Stop!" I tried to pull Nic away from Alex, but he wouldn't budge. I stumbled backward just in time to avoid Alex as he surged forward, head-butting Nic and knocking him clean over into the dirt.

"Alex!" I screeched. "Have you gone insane?"

"His brother started it!" He came to stand over Nic. "You're a family of dirty cheats! Go back to wherever you came from!"

Nic spat a puddle of blood on the ground. "Don't talk about my family," he threatened. He stood up with great effort, squaring himself against Alex's attempts to shove him back down. He righted himself and swung out. Alex ducked, leaving him grappling at the air. When Alex shoved him again, Nic didn't budge. Instead, he flung his arm out and pulled Alex into a head-lock, dragging him to the ground again.

As Alex cursed and pummeled his hands into his sides, Nic plunged his fist into his back pocket and pulled something out. With a flick of his wrist it doubled in length. He tightened his grip and hunched over Alex until the two were almost nose-to-the-ground. I couldn't see what he was doing, but I registered the glint in Nic's hand as he moved it between their struggling frames, and I screamed as the realization took hold.

"Nicoli, *smettila!*"

I jumped at the sound of Luca's voice. He appeared from behind me, running toward his brother. He grabbed Nic by the back of his neck and tore him away from Alex.

The color in Nic's cheeks faded as his brother whispered urgently in his ear. I scanned his open hands — the knife he had been holding was gone.

Beside us, Gino was slowly starting to rouse himself. He got to his feet, rubbing the back of his head. He regarded the scene groggily before nearly knocking me over as he stumbled up the bank toward his brothers.

Alex had gotten to his feet as well, and was shaking with anger. He started toward Gino.

"Don't even think about it," said Luca. "Just walk away."

"Two on one isn't fair," said Alex, starting to circle the brothers, two of whom were completely spaced-out. Nic hadn't said a word since Luca pulled him off Alex, and Gino was still having trouble standing upright. I could see Alex sizing them up, zeroing in on their injuries. "You should fight your own battles next time, Gino."

I came between them. "Alex, just go home," I said. "This doesn't need to get any worse."

He narrowed his eyes at Nic and then Luca, considering his options. Then, reluctantly, he relented. "Fine. Are you coming?" he asked me.

I glanced at Nic. *Not without an explanation.* "In a minute."

"They're bad news, Soph," he said, his voice laced with confusion. "Why are you taking their side?"

"I'll just be a minute," I repeated, trying to ignore the sense of betrayal in his expression.

"Suit yourself. I'm out of here." Alex started walking away, but not before adding a pointed "You're lucky!" over his shoulder. I wasn't sure which of the brothers he was talking to.

"No," said Luca. "You are."

Once Alex was out of sight, I turned my attention to the Priestly brothers. Nic was breathing hard, his expression unreadable as he scanned the grass around us. Beside him, Gino's hair was falling unevenly around his ears, like a lopsided mushroom. He held that same crazy look I had seen out on the court: darting and unfocused. Luca was regarding me calmly.

"We're going to go now," he said, as if he were leaving a party, not a brawl.

"What the hell was that about?" I asked, ignoring his flippancy.

"He called me a cheat," said Gino slowly, like the memory

was just dawning on him. He was obviously concussed, but I couldn't tell what was wrong with Nic, who was still uncharacteristically quiet, his eyes downcast. "He said I played dirty on the court."

"So what?" I asked.

"So I had to shut his stupid mouth up!" He raised his voice and I registered his pronounced lisp for the first time. It must have been the effect of his chipped teeth.

Luca rolled his eyes. "Relax, Gino."

"Fighting's not the right way to shut someone up," I said, stopping the phrase *you moron!* before it slipped out. I grabbed Nic's arm and tugged him away from Luca's grip. He pulled his attention from the grass and looked up, the embers in his eyes igniting; at last he seemed to register me.

"I'm sorry you had to see that, Sophie," he said quietly. "I was just trying to defend my brother and it got out of control."

"You think?"

"We're leaving," said Luca, gesturing for Nic to follow him. "Come on."

His dark eyes studied the space around me as he pulled himself away.

"Wait!" I said, following him.

He turned.

"I just saw you pull a knife on Alex. You can't just walk away from that!" As I said it, I couldn't quite believe it was true. It was such a dark thing to do.

Nic shook his head. "No, I didn't."

"I saw you," I countered. "You took it from your pocket."

"You don't know what you're talking about," said Luca without bothering to turn and look at me. "Come on, Nicoli."

Nic's forehead creased with concern. "I think you must have imagined that, Sophie."

"I didn't imagine it," I protested.

Nic wasn't listening to me. He was giving me that look — the one that adults use when they're patronizing you — the Mrs. Bailey look. "You had a traumatic incident earlier. I think you need to rest."

I recoiled from him. "I know what I saw."

I was angry now. One minute Nic was being lighthearted and attentive, and the next he was pulling a knife on my best friend's brother and then making me think I was crazy when I questioned him about it.

"We'll talk about this again, OK?" said Nic.

He gave me a brief nod before turning on his heel, leaving me glaring at the back of his head and wondering if I was going nuts or if he was the most convincing liar I had ever met.

I was about to go back across the courts and find Millie when something along the riverbank caught my attention. I followed the glint, and in a flash I was combing through the grass and picking up the switchblade I had seen Nic pull from his pocket — so *this* is what he had been looking for. And I had thought his downcast expression was a display of remorse. I felt a strange mixture of triumph and nausea as I turned the blade over in my hand. It was six inches long and razor-sharp. I flicked it closed. The handle was heavy and gold and, in the middle near the base, a crest had been etched into it. It was jet-black and inside it there was a perched eagle carved in ornate flourishes of deep red. Its half-spread wings brushed along the outline.

Below the crest, there was an inscription:

Nicoli, May 12, 1998

I almost dropped it. This wasn't just any switchblade; this was an expensive, *personalized* switchblade, inscribed with Nic's name and, I guessed, his date of birth. It was important; it had meaning. And I had no idea what that actually meant.

I turned the handle over again, zeroing in on the bird inside the crest. I knew what an eagle looked like, and at a second glance I realized this wasn't one. A hawk, maybe? Then it hit me. The bird inside the crest was a falcon. A crimson falcon. I didn't know what that meant, either, but I was sure now, right down in my gut, that it meant something to those brothers, and it sure as hell meant something to Nic.

The realization made me feel panicky, because I knew I wasn't in control of my reaction to it. Even if my uncle *was* right about the Priestly family, I still couldn't help the way my heart flipped every time I thought about Nic's dark eyes — there was something about him, something I couldn't ignore. I was developing feelings for someone who walked around with suspicious bruises on his hands and carried a weapon wherever he went, a weapon he was clearly prepared to *use*. A weapon he would come back for but wouldn't find. I knew I couldn't trust my illogical heart, and that meant I had to do everything in my power to stay away from him so I wouldn't have to.

CHAPTER NINE

The Break-In

My attempts at avoiding Nic Priestly and his brothers were short-lived.

By the time I arrived home from my dinner shift a couple of days later, the heavens had opened up, giving way to one of the worst summer storms I could remember.

I slumped against my front door as a roll of thunder groaned behind the clouds, raising the hairs on the back of my neck and heralding a fresh onslaught of rain. After rummaging through my handbag for the hundredth time, I conceded defeat. I had forgotten my keys, and since my mother was in the city at a client's dress fitting, I was locked out indefinitely. The battery in my phone had died, so I didn't know when she would be back, and I wasn't about to melt into my stoop waiting for her.

I picked myself up and, trying not to notice how the rain was welding me into my jeans, I hurtled back down the street, hopping over puddles as I ran. If I traveled at just below the speed of light, taking the fastest route, I would make it to the diner, which was nine blocks away, just as Ursula and the new waitress, Alison, were locking up for the night. Then I could slip inside, find my keys, and be out in time to swim back home again.

As I ran, the sky flashed and rumbled, rattling my nerves. It hadn't rained this badly since the night my father went to jail, and I was reminded, with an unpleasant twist in my stomach, of how frightening that storm had really been. Ever since that night, the sound of thunder terrified me — it had become a sign of something sinister, something unwelcome. And now, not long after our deliveryman was discovered drowned in his own bathtub, here I was, completely alone and trapped in one of the heaviest downfalls Cedar Hill had ever seen.

By the time I finally turned into the diner parking lot, my feet were swimming in shoefuls of water and my nose was completely numb. Inside the diner, all the lights were off. The whole restaurant was just a low, concrete square cowering against the night sky.

I was too late.

I sprinted across the lot, hoping to find shelter beneath the overhanging roof at the diner's entrance. I could wait out the worst of the storm, then make my way to Millie's house.

If I had been able to open my eyes as normal, and if the storm wasn't whipping my hair around my face in wet lashes, I would have seen the figure outside the entrance before I was charging into it.

"Hey! Watch it!"

I stumbled backward so that I was half in, half out of the shelter, but not before I'd seen that the stranger was pressed up against the door, his hands against the glass, like he was peering through. He turned and pulled his hood down.

"Nic?"

"Sophie?"

"What are you doing here?" we both asked at the same time.

"I left my keys inside, and I'm locked out of my house."

Nic nodded thoughtfully. I waited for his answer. After a long moment, he responded quietly, "I wanted to see you."

Another flash of lightning ignited the sky, and I saw his face fully. It was solemn, and oddly vulnerable. It was strange to think he had that side to him; I had thought of him as flawless, and confident to his core.

And dangerous, I reminded myself with a start. *Focus, Sophie.*

On instinct, I backed away from him and stood stock-still in the deluge.

"You shouldn't be here," I said, glad of the steadiness in my voice. "I don't think it's a good idea for us to hang out."

"What do you mean?" he asked, his voice suddenly guarded.

"I know you lied to me." The memory crashed into me, and I reached into my bag. I pulled the knife out. It was closed but I could feel my fingers shake as they clutched the cold metal handle. I didn't think he would snatch it from me, but a part of me wasn't convinced — how could I know for sure? I edged backward and tightened my grip on it, trying to ignore the rain soaking through my top.

Nic stepped closer. I could see his eyes drift to my hand but he didn't move to take the knife. Cautiously, I edged it higher so that it hovered between us. "Do you recognize this?"

He watched me with calculated stillness. There was nothing but the sound of his uneven breaths and the distant roll of thunder, as my hand shook.

"Well?" I asked.

The silence endured. His breathing evened out, but his expression remained unchanged, resolute. When he finally answered me, it seemed to take all of his energy. He pressed his lips together and pushed the words out, pronouncing them slowly, like his tongue was betraying him. "It's mine."

"I found it in the grass after you left." It was an unnecessary detail — he had probably come back for it after I left — but I felt compelled to remind him that I had been right and he had been wrong to try and convince me otherwise. He knew I knew it was his, and the less information he offered me, the more suspicious I became.

I lowered my hand and took a step toward him, pushing myself into his personal space beneath the awning, so that the wall between us would shatter.

His shoulders tensed.

"Why do you carry a knife with you?"

He stalled, pulling his fingers through his hair and grabbing at it in clumps so that it stuck out over his ears. When he dropped his hand, it was with a sigh of resignation.

"The switchblade was a gift from my uncle," he began slowly, as though he were reading from a script. "He can be a bit . . . eccentric."

I turned the knife over in my hand, tracing my thumb over the falcon crest and the inscription below it. "That's one word for it."

"In my family, when we turn sixteen, my uncle gives us a switchblade inscribed with our name and our birth date," he went on, sounding surer of himself. "It's something his father, my grandfather, used to do, and so he does it for us. It's just a family tradition."

"It strikes me as a little unsafe." I didn't try to keep the judgment out of my voice.

Nic shrugged, and in a quiet voice he conceded, "Yes, you could say that about Felice."

"Feh-*leech*-ay," I repeated, dwelling on the *leech* part. It suited a knife giver. "I got earrings for my sixteenth birthday. No weapons, though."

Nic dragged his thumb along his bottom lip, and I found myself fixating on the way he nipped at it with his teeth.

I shook the thought from my head, and stepped away from him again.

Focus.

"I saw you pull this out during your fight with Alex," I said. "Were you going to — " My voice wavered. "What were you going to do with it?"

"Nothing," he said with so much conviction I almost felt compelled to believe him. "I would never use it on anyone, especially not your friend's brother. But I thought if he saw it he would back off and leave my brother alone. He had already knocked Gino out, but he kept coming back for more. He was so competitive, so angry that we had won, and so convinced that we had cheated. I just wanted to get rid of him before the rest of my brothers got involved."

"So you were going to threaten him with *a knife*?" I asked, disbelief dripping from my voice.

"No," Nic faltered, shaking his head. "Not like that. I just, I don't know. I was trying to defuse it . . ." He trailed off.

I had to fight the urge to take his chin between my forefinger and thumb to hold his gaze still enough that he'd level with me. Was this the truth or a well-versed lie?

"Why do you even carry it around?"

"It's hard to explain," he replied, his expression suddenly sheepish. "I guess I carry it so I can feel protected, and so I can look out for my brothers if I have to. Ever since my father died, it's been hard for all of us. It changed us. It changed me. I don't know this place or the people in it, and I'm so used to having the blade with me for a sense of security that it's like second nature to keep it in my pocket. I don't really feel safe without it." He swallowed hard, burying the emotion that was causing his voice to falter. "I know it's a strange way to cope with something like that, but it helps me."

The knife suddenly heavy in my hand. "I didn't know that."

Nic shrugged. Another flash of lightning lit up his face, and I could see it was bleak with the memory. He slumped backward against the door, his stance defeated. Whatever game of truth we had been playing, I had won, and I felt queasy because of it. "It is what it is," he mumbled.

I had to look away from him. I had felt those feelings of grief and sadness, wallowed in them, even, and for what? A father who deserved to be where he was, and who would come back to me eventually. I knew there were things about Nic that might make him bad for me, but there were things about his life that he couldn't change, and that didn't make him a bad person, either. "I'm sorry for your loss."

"No, I'm sorry." He straightened up abruptly, as though someone above him was pulling him by strings, and the vulnerability drained from his posture. "I was an idiot to pull that knife out, but I wouldn't have hurt Alex with it, I promise. I would never do that. Please let Millie know that, too."

"I didn't mention the knife to Millie," I said, my stomach twisting with guilt. It was a telling revelation.

"Oh," he said quietly.

"Alex didn't see it, and I didn't want to make the whole thing worse. Besides, he texted me afterward saying he was sorry things got so heated, so I thought we could all just chalk it up to an isolated incident that got out of hand and maybe you could both just move past it." I spoke quickly, mashing the words together. Suddenly my cheeks felt like they were on fire. I didn't tell Millie everything. Did that make me a bad friend? Or just an idiot? Because despite knowing I shouldn't care about Nic, I did, and even though I was trying to avoid him, I had been hoping to see him — to give him the chance to explain.

"Thank you," he said earnestly. "I'm sorry if I scared you and I'm sorry I lied to you about it. I thought it would be easier, but I knew afterward it was the wrong thing to do. I wanted to come and talk to you about it."

"So that's why you're here?" I asked, wondering about the timing of his late-night visit.

Nic smiled, revealing a wedge of white teeth in the dark. "You got me."

I stashed the knife back in my bag and moved to peer through the diner door as he had done, not because I thought there was anyone inside, but because I was suddenly feeling shy and I didn't know what else to do.

"Can you get in?" he asked.

My wet hair swung around me like strings as I shook my head. "Everyone else has gone home."

"Maybe I could do something."

"Could you teleport me into my house?"

He took an uneven breath, and coyly he asked, "Do you want me to try?"

"To teleport me?"

"No." He cleared his throat. "I can try to open the door if you want."

"What? How?"

"Do I have your permission to try?"

I raised my hands in the air. "By all means."

"Do you mind standing back a little?"

"Are you really going to do this?"

He set his jaw. "Yes."

I might have agreed to anything he asked right then because, in the rain, he looked incredible. His wavy brown hair was wet and pushed away from his face, revealing the full effect of his chiseled cheekbones. I shuffled backward.

Nic turned his back to me and pulled something that resembled a fountain pen from his back pocket.

"What's that?"

"Another gift you'd disapprove of," he said simply, before moving closer to the door and obscuring it from my view.

For a minute or so all I could see were slight movements in his arms as he went to work on the door — first the upper lock, which yielded with a light click, and then the heavier one lower down, which took longer. Finally, he pulled the handle down and the door swung open in front of us, jingling the bell above it.

My mouth fell open. "You just broke into the diner."

"You gave me permission." He stashed whatever he had been using into his pocket and stepped back so I could enter first. "After you."

I stared at him as I shuffled inside to punch in the alarm code before it went off. "Do you make a habit of that?"

"No," he said, following me closely. "My brothers and I used to find tools that we could use to break into one another's rooms when we were younger. It was never anything more serious than bedroom warfare. It was just dumb luck that an old screwdriver could open that door tonight. The locks really aren't what they should be."

I flicked a switch so that a line of recessed lights sprang to life, illuminating a pathway to the other end of the diner.

"And you just happen to carry that with you because . . . ?"

"I was trying to get into the old barn at my uncle's house tonight so we could use it as a storage unit."

Nic trailed behind me, his attention wandering around the diner like it was the most fascinating place he had ever seen. "My mother ordered a truckload of antiques for the new house, but she doesn't want us moving them inside the place until she comes back from overseas in a few weeks. She wants to finish the painting first. So right now we're trying to find a place to stash them."

I slipped behind the counter and started looking for my keys. "So your mother's entrusting her sons to handle her expensive furniture in her absence?"

Nic slid in beside me, his arm brushing against mine as we searched side by side. "Pretty much."

"I'm not sure I'm completely convinced by that, but it does seem more likely than my other theories."

"What kind of theories?"

I tapped my chin. "How about that you're a notorious jewel thief?"

Nic angled his head to one side and smiled. The tension seeped from his shoulders. "That actually sounds kind of cool."

"Or what if you rob little old ladies when they're asleep in their beds?"

"Not cool."

I stopped searching for a moment and looked at him — his inky-brown eyes, the curve of his upper lip, the way his hair curled beneath his ears. There was something nebulous about him, something dark and uncertain. It ignited a kind of uneasiness in me that I hadn't felt in a long time. I thought of my uncle's warning to me, and not for the first time felt the weight of it in my mind. "The trouble is," I said, my voice catching in my throat, "I don't know *what* you are."

Nic held my gaze steady. "Maybe that's half the fun of it."

Too flustered to respond, I resumed the search for my keys, and Nic broke into a low laugh. I'm sure he didn't mean it to be seductive, but the sound of it coupled with our proximity was having that effect on me.

"So your mom went overseas and left all her sons alone in her new house?" I asked in a bid to distract myself. "She sounds very trusting."

"She's not," said Nic, laughing again. "It's just that her love for Venetian furniture outweighs the distrust she has in her five sons."

Five sons! So I hadn't imagined Priestly Boy Number Five and I definitely wasn't seeing ghosts that night.

"We *try* to be respectful of her wishes when she's away," Nic added as an afterthought. "Though sometimes we make a mess, and of course we end up fighting, too, as brothers do."

"I don't have any siblings, so I guess I wouldn't know a lot about the whole rivalry thing."

Nic nodded thoughtfully. "That's too bad. My brothers are my best friends."

"Even Luca?" I couldn't help myself.

Nic's smile was empathetic. *"Even Luca."*

"That's . . . surprising."

"He's not so bad."

I bit my tongue.

"There's nothing more important than the bonds of family," he went on. "When my grandfather was alive he would always say, *'La famiglia prima di tutto.'* It's written on his mausoleum."

Rich much? I bit my tongue again. "What does that mean?"

"'Family before everything.'"

"Cool," I said, somewhat ineptly. "When my mom's dad died, he had 'All dressed up with nowhere to go' written on his gravestone."

Nic's confused expression was unsurprisingly endearing.

"He was an atheist," I added by way of explanation.

"Oh." His bewilderment morphed into a wry smile. "A funny atheist."

"He died the way he lived — making jokes that pissed off my grandmother."

I bent down and started rifling through the cabinets behind the counter — there were folded aprons, grimy old sweaters, and somebody's pair of track pants. Probably mine.

Nic continued to rummage through the papers along the countertop. "Would your manager mind you being in here?"

"My keys aren't up there," I said, opening another cupboard and fishing around inside — nothing but dust bunnies and broken pens. "They're probably in one of these cubbyholes."

I looked up at Nic. He had picked up a menu and was studying it.

"Would he mind?" he asked again.

"No." I tried a different nook and felt the tips of my fingers brush against something jagged and metal. "I'll lock up after us. He won't even know we were here."

I could hear sheets of paper rustling around as Nic leafed through them, pausing at some before stashing them away again.

"Where is he anyway?"

I shifted my shoulder so I could reach farther inside the narrow nook. "Who?"

"Your manager."

"His friend died, so he went to visit the family. I don't know where he is now." I paused as my uncle's disapproving face meandered into my mind, all red and puffy. With a pang I realized I missed him. I hoped he would call me soon.

I closed my hands around the keys, feeling their familiar edges with a flicker of triumph.

Nic had stopped shuffling. "So he just didn't come back?"

I pulled them out — one brass diner key, another silver one for the smaller lock, my purple house key, and a glitzy Eiffel Tower key ring from Millie. I sprang to my feet and dangled the keys triumphantly in front of me.

"Got 'em!" I dropped them into my bag.

Nic's smile pulled more to one side, pushing against his right cheekbone. We stood a foot apart, no longer distracted by the search, and with nowhere else to look but at each other. Suddenly our surroundings felt a lot more intimate. Standing alone and sopping wet in the diner, my awareness of him spiked, and I was conscious of every exhale being louder than it should be.

"Do you want me to give you a ride home?" he asked. "It's still coming down pretty hard out there. I don't want you to melt into a puddle."

"Are you implying I'm a witch?"

Nic feigned a horrified expression. "Absolutely not. I am ever the gentleman."

"Except for when you're knocking over girls outside your house and breaking into diners in the middle of the night," I pointed out. I thought about adding a switchblade comment but stopped myself, thinking of his father and everything he had just confided in me.

He nodded solemnly. "Yes. Except for then."

I hesitated. "A ride home would be great."

I followed him back to the other end of the diner, focusing on the lighter streaks of chestnut in his dark hair.

As Nic glided toward the door, his hands stuffed deep into his pockets, he surveyed the diner again. "This place is so . . . retro."

"It's an acquired taste."

"Like my mother," he surmised with a soft chuckle. "In fact, sometimes I think I'm still acquiring."

"I feel that way about certain people, too." I smiled, thinking of Jack and deliberately *not* thinking of his warning. He could be difficult and unpredictable, but once he was in your life, he was there for good, like a mole that makes up part of who you are.

"But I bet no one feels that way about you, Sophie."

Oh, only about a thousand people in Cedar Hill. "You'd be surprised."

"Would I?" Nic turned back to me, hovering across the threshold.

"We should go," I murmured, forcing myself to focus on all the questionable things about this boy, and not the way he was making me lose my breath just by looking at me.

If Nic was disappointed, he didn't show it. Instead, he unzipped his hoodie.

"Here," he said, holding it out to me. "We'll have to run to the car." He kept his arm outstretched, leaving him in just a black T-shirt and dark jeans. His jaw tightened, and I felt as if he were daring me to refuse the gesture. "Please."

"Well, if you insist."

I took the sweatshirt and shrugged it on. It was at least four sizes too big. When I zipped it up and shook out the sleeves so that they fell over my hands, the severity in Nic's expression faded. I fought the urge to twirl around so that the hoodie would fan out like a cape. *Don't be weird.*

Nic was smirking at me.

"What?" I placed my hands — which were no longer visible — on my waist. "Have you never seen a drowned rat wearing an oversized hoodie before?"

"None like you," he laughed.

"Well, you need to get out more."

"Clearly."

I shut off the lights, punched in the alarm code, and locked up behind us, following him out into the torrential downpour.

No wonder I hadn't seen Nic's SUV earlier — it was parked all the way across the lot, where even the streetlights didn't shine. We sprinted toward it, wobbling under the force of wind that threw buckets of rain across our faces. When we reached the car, I tumbled in, pulling against the storm to shut the door. I fell back against the cool leather seat, wrapping my arms around me while Nic started the engine. Without the added warmth of his hoodie, his teeth were chattering.

I spent the car ride directing him to my house and running my fingers through my hair so it wouldn't frizz out too much in the humidity. I was just melting into the easy conversation between us, and the welcome feeling of dryness, when he pulled up outside my house.

"Thanks for the ride." I tried not to sound too crestfallen that our time together had ended. I pushed the door open and it flung outward under the force of the wind.

"Sophie." Nic leaned over and gripped my leg, holding the lower half of my body in the warmth of the car. "Wait."

My heart flipped, and I worried he could hear how loudly it was suddenly beating. I tried not to breathe too quickly, or to stare at his hand on my knee. I looked at him and found him studying my arms, my waist, my — *his* hoodie.

"Oh." I shook my hair out, scolding myself. "Your hoodie."

I began to unzip it.

"No, it's not that," he replied quickly, keeping his hand on my knee. "You can give it back to me some other time."

I dropped my hands into my lap and waited, my breath bound up in the base of my throat. I could see he was steeling himself for something else. My brain began to flash with a thousand possibilities and suddenly my heart was ricocheting off my rib cage like it was trying to punch through it.

He inhaled sharply, his expression suddenly uncertain. "The switchblade," he said quietly. "Can I have it back?"

My face fell, and something inside me — it felt a lot like hope — shriveled up and died. I reached into my bag and pulled out the knife, dropping it into his outstretched hand in one hurried movement. "Of course. I forgot."

His fist closed around it and a flicker of relief passed over his features, relaxing them. "Thank you."

"I guess it's for the best. You know, me walking around with a knife isn't exactly a good idea. I'd probably fall on it or something." The words tumbled out in unbidden, high-pitched sentences, trying to distract from the awkwardness I was feeling. "I'd probably end up killing myself or something, and I can definitely think of less embarrassing ways to die." *Could you be any more inappropriate?* I winced right after I said it and then hopped out of the car before I could put my other foot in my mouth. "Thanks again for everything."

"Sophie?" Nic leaned across the passenger seat, his expression serious. "Will you do something for me?"

"What?"

"Don't be thinking of ways to die."

"I won't."

"Good."

He pulled back with a small, controlled smile, and I shut the door.

I stood in the rain, watching the car until it disappeared around the end of the street. Then I thought about the boy with the bruised hand and the inscribed switchblade who had just broken into my father's diner, and found myself wondering why the hell I was feeling so sad to see him go.

CHAPTER TEN

The Artist

There was really only one thing to do with Nic's hoodie.

"This is perfect," Millie said when I called her the following morning to tell her about everything. "Use it as an excuse to go to his house and invite him to the party on Saturday!"

Because of the fight with Alex, Millie wasn't Nic's biggest fan, but she wasn't a grudge holder, either, and given that "boys will be boys," she resolved that she could certainly "see potential" in him and that he should still be invited to her house party. I had a pretty good idea of how Alex would react to Nic turning up, but Millie was adamant. Alex didn't get to veto her guests. Especially since she had so few compared to him.

Besides, she took great interest in my pitiful romantic life, and since Nic was new to Cedar Hill and obviously in the dark about my father's recent past, she saw him as a rare judgment-free opportunity for me to fall in love. Whether he might be bad for me or not didn't weigh into it. It only made her more curious about him and his family, especially considering that Dom had asked her out right after the basketball tournament.

"I'm meeting Dom at six for our date, so try to call me later tonight if you find out anything juicy," she squealed over the phone. "And don't forget to take pictures if you make it inside that house. You owe it to me. I'm too young to die from curiosity."

I decided not to tell Millie that I would not be creepily taking pictures of Nic's house without his knowledge. The idea of inviting him to a party was already terrifying enough. What if he said no? What if he said yes and then found out about my social-pariah status when he got there? "Only if you find out about Dom's scar," I countered instead.

"That's a no-brainer. Good luck today. You won't regret it," she chirped before hanging up.

By the time I reached the Priestly mansion, I was a bundle of nerves. Restored to its rightful regality, the house was like something out of a fairy tale. Beneath the sun's heavy beat, the windows were sparkling like diamonds, and without the ivy that used to slither across the walls, the entire exterior was an unblemished, alabaster white.

Just how was I going to do this? *Hey, thanks for lending me your hoodie. By the way, why don't you come to Millie's party on Saturday? It's coincidentally my birthday, too, but most people there will just ignore me because my dad's a murderer, which technically makes me the devil's spawn. So how about it, will you come?* Smooth. And what if Nic wasn't home and Luca answered instead? *Hey, tell your brother to come to Millie's on Saturday, but make sure you don't show up because you suck.* If Gino answered, I could just distract him with something shiny and hope Nic would come to the door eventually.

With the hoodie draped over my arm and my thoughts spiraling into all the possible ways this could go wrong, I rang the doorbell. When I didn't hear it echo inside the house, I decided to use the brass knocker just to be sure. I waited. I knocked again.

What now? I hadn't come up with any brilliant ideas about what to do if nobody was there. Was I supposed to just leave the hoodie outside the door and let that be the end of it? What an anticlimax. Without thinking, I drifted toward the side of the mansion, where the driveway tapered off into a narrow path that stretched around the house.

When I reached the back, I stopped in surprise. I don't know what I had been expecting — a tennis court or a swimming pool, maybe — but certainly not what I found. Cramped and over-grown, the yard was a far cry from the affluent façade of the house. Around the edges, clumps of weeds tangled into withered rosebushes. The grass was higher than my knees, and was a sickly gray-green color. At the very back of the ruined garden were the remnants of a fountain with elaborate bird carvings etched into chunks of stone; and in the center of the grass, a large wooden table balanced on three termite-eaten legs.

Behind me, double doors inlaid with stained glass panes looked out onto the yard. They were slightly ajar.

I rapped my knuckles against the glass, nudging the doors open, and peered into a sprawling kitchen. The walls and cabinets were a stark white, and the pale wood floors looked new. A black cast-iron stove reached up to a high ceiling, which was studded with spotlights.

"Who is it?" A musical voice came from within, startling me from my snooping.

I hesitated. If I didn't know the voice, the voice wouldn't know me, and so what good would my name be?

"It's Sophie," I said after a beat.

No answer.

"I'm just returning a hoodie."

I opened the doors another crack. More of the kitchen filtered into my view. On the white walls were several ornately framed oil paintings. I recognized one as Da Vinci's *Madonna and Child* — it had been a favorite of my grandmother's — though the others, while also religious in sentiment, were foreign to me. I stared in surprise. I had never seen artwork like this in a home before — it was almost like a gallery, or a church, and I found myself feeling intimidated by the splendor. I considered taking out my phone and sneaking a photo to show Millie after all, but the rational voice inside my head stopped me.

Cautiously, I edged inside.

In the center of the kitchen was a marble-topped island, and beyond it was a glass table covered with several sheets of paper and scatterings of pencils. Sitting at the table was a boy. He was drawing.

"Hello?" I said again, though I could plainly see he knew I was there.

He looked up and his piercing blue eyes found mine immediately. I zeroed in on them, frowning, as my stomach turned to jelly. "Luca?"

He didn't respond. He just put his pencil down and sat in

silent contemplation, his elbows atop the table and his chin resting just behind his steepled fingers, as though he were praying.

I felt my breath catch in my throat. "Oh!"

It wasn't Luca. It was the boy from the window. Just like on that very first night, his eyes grew, but this time in recognition. Set against his olive skin, they were a brilliant, startling blue. They were just like Luca's, but something about them seemed different — warmer, perhaps.

"I recognize you," he said in that pleasant, lilting voice.

I moved toward him, utterly captivated. He had Luca's searing eyes, his golden skin, and his jet-black hair. But while Luca's hair was shaggy, falling in strands across his eyes, this boy's hair was short and clean-cut, combed away from his face entirely, revealing a pointed chin and severe cheekbones. He was thinner, too, and slightly hunched. I couldn't tell if he was older than me — he didn't seem it, but his likeness to Luca made me think maybe he was.

"You were watching my house last week." He lowered his hands and rested them on the table in front of him, but his eyes remained hooded with caution.

I stopped when I reached the table, hovering uncertainly. I realized then why he hadn't moved toward me, and why he hadn't played in the basketball tournament last week. He was in wheelchair.

"Yes, that was me," I replied. I tried not to stare, but he was so like Luca, and yet so unlike him, it was hard to reconcile. "I was just curious."

"I believe you fell rather spectacularly just afterward," he added, but not unkindly.

"That's a point of contention. Your brother actually crashed into me."

He smiled, and it made him seem suddenly very young and boyish. "I hope he apologized."

"He did — eventually." I shuffled a little closer until my hands brushed against the edge of the table. "You're so like him." It was those eyes — they were so unnatural. That they should exist in two different faces seemed unbelievable to me. "Luca, that is. I don't mean to stare, but it's really incredible."

"Well," he said, "we may be twins, but we're not the same."

I was only partly surprised by the revelation. Even though their similarities were startling, all of the Priestly brothers shared the same features, and this boy had an aura of innocence that Luca did not. He seemed sweet, and unblemished by whatever had made his twin such a resounding ass to be around.

"For one thing, he can't maneuver a wheelchair half as well as I can." He tapped the wheel beneath his right hand and released a wry smile. "And for another, I'm smarter."

"I don't doubt it." He seemed appeased by my agreement. "I'm Sophie. But I said that already."

"Hello, Sophie." His smile was a beautiful sight. To think, Luca had the potential to look and act like this and yet he chose not to. "I'm Valentino."

He shifted forward and picked up his pencil again, twirling it between his forefinger and thumb. My attention followed it, and

I gasped as the sheets of paper came to life below me. I tried to study them all at once. "These are incredible."

Valentino waved his hand over the sketches with a casualness that seemed out of place. They were stunning, and surely he could see that. And more than that, he should be *owning* his talent and agreeing with me. I used to think my father was good because he could draw Mickey Mouse, but this artwork was on a whole other level.

I raked my eyes over the drawings and stopped when I found a side profile of Nic. Drawn in pencil, careful shadows swooped across his creased brow line and gathered beneath his cheekbones. His lips were parted in concentration, his hair twisting in strands below his ear as he looked ahead, focusing on something out of frame.

"You make it seem so real."

I glanced at Valentino. He was chewing on his lip, thinking. "I look for the qualities that aren't always apparent at first," he said. "The ones that define part of who we are and how we really feel deep down. I try to look below the surface."

His voice started to bubble with passion, and his hands took on a life of their own. "This life is so complex that we rarely get to be the people we are truly meant to be. Instead, we wear masks and put up walls to keep from dealing with the fear of rejection, the feeling of regret, the very idea that someone may not love us for who we are deep in our core, that they might not understand the things that drive us. I want to study the realness of life, not the gloss. There is beauty everywhere; even in the dark, there is light, and that is the rarest kind of all."

I watched the enthusiasm brighten his features. "I don't know anyone who thinks and talks like that," I admitted. "It's . . . refreshing."

"It's the truth," he said simply.

"Can I see the others?"

He laid his pencil down and wheeled his chair back. I draped the hoodie over the chair beside me and leaned across the table, balancing my weight on my palms.

There was a sketch of Gino and Dom playing a video game; they were sitting on the floor, their legs curled around them like they were little boys again. Controllers clutched in their hands, they were laughing with each other, their shoulders brushing, their heads thrown back toward the ceiling. Their eyes were crinkled at the sides and their noses were scrunched up in amusement. Dom was messing up Gino's ponytail with his free hand.

"It's like the perfect moment," I breathed.

"Happiness," said Valentino quietly, his eyes fixed on the scene.

I returned my gaze to Nic's profile. His jaw was set, his expression focused.

"And that one is *Determination,"* Valentino added.

Beside the sketch of Nic there was a portrait of a woman standing in a kitchen. Her hands gripped the sides of the sink as she looked out the window in front of her. She was willowy and disheveled, dressed in a silken floor-length robe that pooled around her feet. Streaks of sunlight danced along the tip of her nose, and a spill of dark hair fell freely down her back. Her brows were creased at sharp angles. "Is this your mother?"

He nodded.

"She's beautiful," I said.

"She's angry," said Valentino dispassionately.

I reached out and pulled the next portrait toward me. Luca. He was sitting alone on a stoop, dressed in a black suit. His knees came up to his chest, supporting his elbows as he leaned forward. His shoulders were hunched, making his frame appear smaller, like Valentino's. He was looking at the ground, at nothing, and his fingers were scraping through his hair, like he was trying to hurt himself.

I swallowed hard. It was difficult to look at it. I glanced at Valentino and found he wasn't looking at it anymore, either.

"Pain?" I guessed quietly.

"Grief," he replied.

"It must be difficult to look beneath the mask," I said, my throat suddenly tight.

Valentino raised his chin. "No more difficult than it is to wear one."

I pulled my hands back and straightened up as a wave of something unpleasant washed over me. I didn't want to look at the portraits anymore. It was an uncomfortable feeling, staring into the darkest moments of someone's soul without them knowing. "Do you think you wear a mask?"

"I'm wearing one right now." Valentino smiled softly. "We both are."

"It's a sad thought."

"Yes," he said. "But sometimes I wonder about the alternative. Imagine if we had no secrets, no respite from the truth.

What if everything was laid bare the moment we introduced ourselves?"

The idea swirled around my head. *Hello, I'm Sophie. My uncle's a paranoid loon, my father's in jail for murder, and my mother buries herself in work to distract herself from her broken heart. I'm pretty sure I prefer cartoons over real life and I only have one real friend. I'm terrified of storms and I'm deeply suspicious of cats. I obsess over the cuteness of sloths and sometimes I cry at commercials.*

"It would be terrible," I confirmed.

Valentino smirked as though he had just listened to my embarrassing inner monologue. "Absolute chaos."

I nodded, feeling subdued. Somewhere deep down I was trying to fight the sudden urge to burst into tears. As if sensing my inner struggle, Valentino afforded me a moment of privacy. He deflected his gaze and started to rearrange his sketches into a pile, until I could only see the one he was still working on. It was a man in maybe his midforties, dressed impeccably in a glossy dark suit and staring right at me from the page. For a heartbeat it felt as though I already knew him, that I had seen him somewhere before, but the moment passed, and I knew it was his son I was seeing. He was so like Nic it hit me like a punch in the gut. He had the same dark eyes with lighter flecks swimming inside, the same straight, narrow nose, and the same curving lips. His hair was gray in parts and receding, revealing a forehead etched with worry lines. His expression was grim.

"Seriousness?" I ventured.

"No," Valentino said without looking up. "This one is Death."

I watched him smudge the edges. "I draw my father every day so that I'll never forget him. But there's nothing more to find in him now. He's with the angels and he doesn't need to wear a mask anymore. Everything he was is gone."

"I'm sorry," I offered weakly. It really was the only thing I could think to say, and still it didn't seem like half enough.

Valentino shrugged, his expression matter-of-fact. "You can't avoid the inevitability of death. It comes at you one way or another, and takes us all to the same place in the end. To apologize for it is to apologize for the sun shining or the rain falling. It is what it is."

I wanted to tell him he was lucky for his pragmatism, but I didn't get the opportunity. A door opened behind me. I noticed the smell first: a faint sweetness in the air.

"Valentino?" A man's voice, crisp and gentle, followed.

I turned to find a slim, middle-aged man staring at me with surprise. His skin was olive and his hair the brightest silver I had ever seen. His eyebrows were so light I could barely detect them, but by the way they were denting his forehead, I could tell they were raised.

"Oh my," he said in a faint accent. "Hello there."

He advanced toward me like a well-dressed beanpole, his head tilted to one side. I didn't know much about men's clothing, but I could recognize an expensive suit when I saw one. It was black with thin pinstripes, and beneath it he wore a shiny gray shirt and a silk neck scarf. If he was burning up in the humidity, he didn't show it.

He stuck out his hand and I took it; his handshake was cold and firm. The sweet smell was stronger now that he was so close;

it was almost cloying. There was something vaguely familiar about it, too, but I couldn't place it.

"And you are?" he asked, a slow smile forming.

"I'm Sophie, and I just stopped by to — "

"What a pleasure," he said, silencing me with politeness and releasing my hand militarily.

I tried not to stare at the red marks all over his face: not quite pimples, more like pinpricks — hard to spot when far away but difficult to ignore at close range. It was like he had fallen into a rose garden face-first.

"Please excuse my intrusion. I do hope I'm not interrupting anything. I'm Felice," he said, pronouncing the "leech-ay" part with a distinct Italian roll. "Valentino's uncle."

The switchblade buyer. I tried not to curl my lip in disgust.

"You're not interrupting anything," Valentino answered from over my shoulder. There was a hint of indignation in his voice.

Felice rounded the table in wide, graceful strides, taking most of the perfumed scent with him. "I wasn't aware you boys had time to make friends in the neighborhood."

"That's not remotely the case," Valentino replied, his tone acidic. "Sophie is just returning something."

I held up Nic's hoodie in a bid to ease the strange tension that had descended upon us.

Felice looked at it sharply. "Is that Luca's?"

"Unlikely," said Valentino.

Felice shook his head. "Of course it's not," he murmured. "*He* has his priorities in order."

I wasn't sure if that was a dig at me or a dig at the other three brothers.

"Dom's?" Felice asked with a frown, like it was the world's most important mystery.

"No. He's taking out that girl from the diner."

"Ah yes, of course."

My lips parted in surprise. So they already knew about Millie? That news was barely twenty-four hours old! They must have shared everything with each other. And yet they apparently had no idea who I was.

"It's Nic's," I cut in, feeling marginally insulted. "I ran into him at the diner last night and he let me borrow it because it was raining."

Felice stiffened, exchanging a poorly concealed look of alarm with Valentino.

"Nicoli didn't mention that," he said, regaining his composure in a flash of teeth.

His response landed with a blow. How could they know about Millie already but not a single iota about me? Nic obviously didn't think me important enough to mention, even in passing. The thought made me feel stupid for even being there.

"Well, here it is." I dropped the hoodie back on the chair carelessly. I had clearly made too much of it already. "I just wanted to give it back, but then we got to talking about Valentino's artwork and the time got away from me."

"Ah." Felice clapped his nephew on the shoulder and glanced at the pile of drawings. "Exquisite, aren't they?"

"Yes," I said, wishing I had never come in the first place.

"You know," said Felice, to no one in particular, "I've been reading the most incredible things about artistic sensibilities and their connection to great tragedy recently." He moved away from Valentino and began to pace around the table. "Did you know that many artists and composers have been known to create their best works following tragedies in their personal lives?"

He didn't wait for either of us to respond, but continued striding around the kitchen, moving his hands around as he spoke. "Just look at Carlo Gesualdo, a famed Italian prince and widely regarded genius. He murdered his wife and her lover in their bed, mutilated their bodies, and then strung them up outside his palace for everyone to see. And *then* he went on to compose some of the most powerful and dark music of the sixteenth century."

Valentino shifted in his chair.

Felice stopped gesticulating and zeroed in on me for my reaction. "What do you think of that?"

I tried not to think of how horribly awry my plan had gone.

"It seems to me that the composer's tragedy was brought upon himself," I ventured, silently wishing I could just dissolve into the ground and slither home through the earth's core. "So I'm not sure you should count it as something that *happened* to him."

"A debater, I see." Felice's expression turned gleeful. "But surely you could argue that the pressure of having to exact retribution was brought upon him by his wife's actions. To punish her was the societal expectation, but the act of having to do it, for him, I think, may still have been a personal tragedy."

"But surely he didn't have to kill her." If only Millie could see me now — debating the intricacies of sixteenth-century murder. All this and headstones in the last twenty-four hours — the calendar said July, but it was definitely starting to feel like Halloween.

"Well, his wife was unfaithful, and in those days, unfaithfulness carried a high penalty."

"As high as murder?"

"I believe so."

I crossed my arms, feeling offended on behalf of all sixteenth-century women. "I don't feel her betrayal justified his response."

"Ah!" Felice raised his index finger in the air like he had just happened upon the answer to an unsolved riddle. "But seeing as his response led directly to his musical legacy, perhaps, in the grander scheme of things, it did. All in all, I think it might have made the world a better place. And surely there is justification in that."

"Uh . . ." I began awkwardly. I was getting confused, and certainly out of my depth. "I just think the whole thing is pretty messed up."

"Yes," echoed Valentino, clearing his throat. "It *is* messed up. Just like this conversation."

Felice waved his hand dismissively, his attention now resting on the oil paintings behind us. "But the point is, the music *was* glorious. You must consider the possibility of an inverse correlation, which would mean a dark deed leading to a deeper connection with creative energy and, as a consequence, a beautiful composition."

"Hitler was an artist *before* he committed all of his atrocities." That was about the only thing I had gleaned from history class —

and since we were chitchatting about murder, why not throw Hitler into the mix? This day had already hit rock bottom. "So I don't think you can really say murder leads to better creativity or vice versa." I wanted to add something along the lines of: *So I wouldn't go killing your wife just yet.* But I thought better of it.

Felice clapped his hands together. "But isn't it fascinating to think about? That the two parts of one's psyche can coexist like that?"

"There can be light in the dark," I said, echoing Valentino's words from earlier.

Valentino nodded thoughtfully, but I could sense his discomfort. He was gripping the sides of his chair so hard his fingers were turning white.

Ah, weird relatives. There was something quite sweet about the fact that Nic and I shared slightly unhinged uncles. Maybe one day we would get to introduce them.

"Absolutely!" Felice responded to my borrowed maxim after a pause. "And sometimes a dark path can lead to a bright light."

I shuffled awkwardly. He'd lost me again, but I was definitely beginning to see how he thought buying knives for his nephews was a good idea. "I guess it's food for thought."

Felice's phone buzzed, filling the room with an intense flurry of opera. He closed his eyes and swayed to the music before finally pulling the phone out from his breast pocket and answering the call.

"*Ciao*, Calvino!" He covered the mouthpiece. "Excuse me for one moment," he whispered, before leaving the kitchen.

I watched him go. "Well, he's certainly . . . energetic."

When I turned back to Valentino, his expression was unreadable.

"Sophie," he said wearily. "Thank you for returning Nic's hoodie, but I need to be honest with you. He wouldn't want you here."

I felt like I had been slapped. "What?"

"I don't mean to hurt your feelings," he continued in that same soothing lilt. "But we're in the middle of a very private family matter."

Was he referring to their father? His passing was obviously more recent than I'd realized.

"I'll go," I gulped.

Valentino smiled apologetically. "Please don't take it personally."

"It's fine," I lied, turning from him and hurrying across the kitchen. My gaze fell upon a large black frame to the left of the door. It was hoisted midway up the wall and was unmissable from this angle. Inside the frame was the same crest I had seen on Nic's knife — jet-black with a crimson falcon at its center. Below the crest, in cursive red script, it read: LA FAMIGLIA PRIMA DI TUTTO. *Family Before Everything* — Nic's grandfather's words, I remembered.

"It's just the timing of it . . ." Valentino called after me.

I felt tingly all over and I wasn't sure why. Everything felt so intense all of a sudden. Feeling my cheeks prickle as the color drained out of them, I pulled the double doors of the Priestly kitchen closed behind me.

I had barely made it to the end of the block when someone

grabbed the back of my T-shirt. I stumbled backward and bumped against a small cushioned body with a soft *oomph!*

I sprang around, shrugging away from the viselike grip.

"Mrs. Bailey?" The shrillness in my voice alerted me to an octave I didn't know I could reach. "What are you doing?"

The old woman contorted her face like she had just bitten into a lemon. "I could ask you the same question, Persephone Gracewell. What on earth do you think *you're* doing?"

"I'm on my way home. My shift at the diner starts in an hour." I wrung my hands to keep from shaking her. With the day I was having, this was the last thing I needed. "And my name is Sophie!"

"I saw you go into that house," she shot back. "I told you to stay away from that family. You were in there so long I nearly called the police!"

"Are you serious?"

She stiffened. "Haven't you been reading the papers?"

"What are you talking about?"

"I'm *talking* about *several* disappearances and *two* strange deaths in the last two weeks — all of whom were members of *this* community, and *you* haven't even noticed. Open your eyes, Persephone!"

"They are open!" Or so I had thought. I obviously had a lot of Googling to do.

Mrs. Bailey was still ranting, pointing her finger directly in my face. "People don't just drown in their own bathtubs, you know. And they don't accidentally fall off roofs, either!"

"What are you saying?" I asked, folding my arms to keep the sudden chill at bay.

Mrs. Bailey dropped her voice. "I'm saying there's a wrongness in that house and it's *not* something you should be anywhere near."

I didn't make an attempt to hide my irritation. Another day, another rumor. "You can't just go around saying stuff like that, Mrs. Bailey!"

"There's a darkness," she hissed, her resolve unbroken.

I started walking again, quickening my pace so that she had to scurry to keep up. "It's grief! They're mourning their father."

She didn't seem the least bit surprised by my response. In fact, she snorted.

I gaped at her. "Do you find that *amusing*?"

"That man deserves to be where he is."

I skidded to a halt.

She caught up with me, her chest heaving.

"What did you just say?"

"Listen to me very carefully, Persephone." She tugged at my arm, pulling me closer so that she could whisper. "That man deserves to be in the ground. And if those boys are anything remotely like him, then they do, too."

For a long moment I stared at her, my fists clenched at my sides, my nostrils flaring. I was desperately trying to give her the benefit of the doubt, but with the way my emotions had been backflipping all day, I wanted nothing more than to reach out and throttle her. Was that the kind of stuff she said about *me* behind *my* back? Her thoughts on my father had always been crystal clear. "How could you say something like that?" I demanded.

Mrs. Bailey looked over her shoulder, her eyes darting back and forth. "Persephone," she hissed through trembling lips. "There's a reason that man was called the Angel-maker."

The Angel-maker. A wave of nausea rolled over me and I wobbled on my feet. "What does that mean?" I stammered.

"What do you think it means?" she asked. "I've been doing some digging and I can tell you, their father was a very bad man. I doubt those boys are much better, and you must trust me when I say that you should stay away from them. I don't want to say any more than that."

What the hell was that supposed to mean? That she actually had an I-better-not-spread-anymore-crap-today threshold? I regarded her warily. What could she possibly gain from saying this? Then again, what did she gain from saying all the stuff she usually said? She was a notorious drama queen and a one-woman rumor mill, and I started to wonder how many people she had warned away from *me*. Nic *wasn't* bad, I was sure of it. And for that matter, neither were the rest of his brothers. They played basketball and video games. They teased each other and flirted with girls. It wasn't fair to tar someone with their father's reputation. I knew all about that, and I wasn't about to make the mistake a lot of my former friends had. Especially when Nic's father was already gone from this world.

I started walking again.

Mrs. Bailey picked up her pace. "I'm trying to warn you."

"OK." I swerved around the next corner, swinging my arms out in the hope they might bring me home faster. "I appreciate your concern."

"What were you doing inside that house anyway?"

As much as I didn't want to feed her gossip addiction, I figured the truth might keep her quiet. "I was returning a sweatshirt I'd borrowed."

"You smell funny."

"Thanks."

She started to sniff me.

I stopped again. "What are you doing?"

"Each of my six senses is highly developed. I'm trying to figure out what that smell is."

I remembered Felice and his sickly scent. "Is it sweet?" I asked, raising the hand I had used to shake his and smelling it. The faint aroma still lingered on my fingers, but it wasn't as strong as Mrs. Bailey was making it out to be. Maybe I'd gotten used to it.

"Yes," she said, taking my hand and sniffing it. Her whole face furrowed in concentration. "Is it a new perfume?"

"I'm not wearing perfume."

"Ah," she heaved after a moment. Her voice was unbearably smug. "I know what it is!"

I folded my arms across my chest, pretending impatience, but a cold knot had already settled in the pit of my stomach. I couldn't *not* take the bait. "What?"

Mrs. Bailey arched an incriminating eyebrow, savoring her response. "It's honey."

CHAPTER ELEVEN

The Name

The rest of the day passed in a blur of monotony. Uncle Jack finally called the diner to check up on me. He gave me the number of his new phone, but before I had time to talk to him about anything at all, he was hanging up again. I spent the rest of my shift wondering exactly what he was doing and why he hadn't come home yet. I wondered, too, about the honey, and whether Felice's strange scent was linked to the jar I had found next to the register.

Ursula had been pulling twelve-hour shifts to fill the void of competency left by my uncle and by Alison and Paul, who spent more time making out in the kitchen than waiting on tables. Millie, on the other hand, had gotten the day off and been spending it wisely. I called her when I left the diner that evening, and we traded stories about how our days had gone.

"So Valentino basically kicked you out?" she asked through a dramatic intake of breath.

"Pretty much," I said, still feeling a tinge of embarrassment about it. "The whole thing was weird. Did you get a strange vibe from Dom on your date?"

"Nope!" The excitement in her voice fizzed down the line and I felt an unwelcome twinge of jealousy for how differently things had gone for her and Dom. "We just hung out and went on a picnic," Millie chattered away cheerfully. "Can you believe that?"

I stopped when I reached the edge of the parking lot, wondering which route to take. "Seriously? That sounds so — "

"Scripted? I know. It's like something out of a movie."

"And what about his scar?" I asked, crossing the street and opting for the shortcut, unwelcoming Priestly house be damned.

"Boating accident," said Millie through a yawn.

"Really?" I asked, hearing the skepticism in my voice. Dom didn't seem like the boating type. Then again, his brothers didn't seem like the basketball types, either, and I had been wrong about that.

"Yeah, it's a boring story. Something about a fishing hook," said Millie dismissively. "*Anyway*, we got sandwich wraps and smoothies and brought them to Rayfield Park. We just talked for hours. He seemed really interested in me so I guess that's a good sign."

"Definitely." My path home began its slow incline, and my chest started to burn from the effort of walking uphill while trying to explain to Millie everything that had been bothering me at the same time. I mentioned the whole their-dad-might-have-been-a-notorious-murderer thing. Even though I couldn't trust Mrs. Bailey, and when I Googled every possible variation of "Priestly Killer Chicago" on my phone nothing relevant to Nic's family had come up, I wanted Millie to know.

"Do you think we should stay away from them, at least until we find out what's going on?" I ventured.

Millie whined in disapproval. "Soph, Mrs. Bailey is, like, a walking gossip magazine. She thrives on ridiculous rumors. Remember that time she told my mum I was pregnant? She's crazy. There's nothing wrong with Dom or his family, trust me."

"I just think there's something not quite right about it."

"Then let's figure it out!" she urged. "Think of it as a mystery. A sexy mystery."

"What if it's not something we should be trying to figure out?" I asked, thinking again of the cloying honey smell, and the idea that Dom was in a *boating accident*. I just couldn't picture him wearing deck shoes.

"I've seen the way you look at Nic, Soph," Millie said. "Tell me he's not worth figuring out."

Maybe she was right; even if there was something sticking in the pit of my stomach, the way Nic made me feel was undeniable. And Millie knew it. Plus, I didn't want to stomp all over her excitement with hearsay.

"So what did you guys talk about?" I asked instead.

"He told me about how he used to live right in the center of the city with his family, and how the suburbs are boring in comparison. He's nineteen, which is sexy and totally risqué, though he does go a bit overkill on the whole hair gel aspect of his perfection. I mean, Danny Zuko is only a good look on Halloween. Not that that stopped me from staring at him in a daze when he talked. I had to ask him to repeat himself a lot, which was awkward. Anyway, then the conversation turned to me mostly, but I *am* a pretty fascinating topic. *And* we touched on the subject of you as well."

I felt my cheeks grow hot. "Why?"

I turned onto a narrow avenue where gated estates and rows of cherry trees climbed uphill beside me. Halfway up, the street intersected with Lockwood Avenue.

"As much as I *love* talking about you, it was actually Dom who brought you up, by accident."

"Oh?" I didn't know Dom in the least, except that he was obviously less weird than Gino, and that he ranked far below Luca on the I'm-a-smug-ass scale. "What did he say about me?"

"He was asking about the diner and stuff. I mentioned you were probably going to take over running it soon from your uncle and that we're best friends, so you will obviously give me a *huge* pay raise."

"Obviously," I concurred sarcastically.

"Then I went on a bit of a rant about Jack and what a bad job he's doing running the place now."

"Mil!"

I turned onto Lockwood Avenue.

"Oh come on, Soph," she chastised. "A fact is a fact. He's been totally AWOL. I mean, you can't just disappear whenever you feel like it. For one thing, it's rude, and for another, it's weird. This is the exact kind of behavior that gives fuel to Mrs. Bailey's idiotic rumors."

"OK." She had a point and I wasn't going to rile her up about it.

"Anyway, I'm sure Dom will relay the fact that you are going to be sitting on a nice little cash cow someday soon to his brother, and that will no doubt make you seem even more attractive!"

I flinched, thinking of the fib I had told Nic and Luca that first time I saw them, in the diner. Hopefully Nic wouldn't feel cheated by my dishonesty. After all, it *was* technically just my summer job. For now.

As I got nearer, I felt my stomach clench uncomfortably at the sight of their house.

"I hardly think they're gold diggers. You should have seen their house," I said, looking at it.

"Hopefully someday soon, I will." I could tell Millie was wiggling her eyebrows suggestively on the other end of the call. "I'd better go. I'm exhausted from my escapade."

"Wait! Did you kiss him?"

"If I had, don't you think I would have used that as my opener?"

"Too bad."

"But he *did* kiss my hand when he dropped me off. Does that count? It was *so* romantic."

"That definitely counts!" I reassured her as I hurried past Nic's house. "OK, now you can hang up," I said once I was safely on the other side and the mansion was stretching into the sky behind me. I turned left and my path began to wind downhill again.

"Text me when you get in."

"Bye."

"Sophie!" a voice called out just as I was putting my phone back in my bag.

I turned around, feeling a familiar jolt in my stomach. I recognized him immediately, running toward me with his hood up.

I responded with calculated calmness, trying to keep my dreadful enthusiasm from making me burst into an arms-flailing sprint toward him. "Nic?"

He came to an easy stop and lowered his hood. His smile lit up his face. "Hi."

"What are you doing?" I asked.

"You don't sound too happy to see me," he noted. Small dents appeared above his brows and his smile faltered. "Maybe I overestimated how well you would take me chasing after you like a maniac . . ."

"Why? I mean, it worked *so well* the last time," I teased.

His expression turned remorseful but he couldn't hide his smirk. "I should have learned my lesson, right? I didn't mean to startle you."

"It's fine," I assured him. "It's just, you came out of nowhere."

Relief swept across his features. "I was about to come see you at the diner and then I saw you passing by my house so I figured I'd seize the opportunity."

"At least you didn't crash into me this time." I clutched at my chest in feigned relief. "I might have had to kick your ass."

"How terrifying," he said, still smiling.

"Hey!" I punched his arm playfully, reveling in the familiarity that existed between us. "I'll have you know I can be very intimidating."

"I'm sure those tiny fists are very powerful."

I punched him again, but this time he caught my hand beneath his, trapping it mid-assault. "I heard you came to my house today." All of a sudden his expression had turned serious, and his eyes had lost their warmth. "Don't ever come to my house."

I slid my hand out from under his. I turned from him and started walking again. "Don't worry, I won't."

"Sophie." He jogged after me. "That came out wrong, sorry."

"I was just returning your hoodie," I replied, keeping my attention focused ahead of me as I walked. "It was the polite thing to do. Now I see it was the wrong decision, and before you start, don't worry, your brother Valentino already made it perfectly clear I was unwelcome, so you don't need to bother."

"Just let me explain." He sped up, then turned around and began walking backward so he could face me and keep up at the same time.

I blew a stray strand of hair from my eyes and glowered at him.

"I don't mean your presence is unwelcome. I really like seeing you . . . I'm just wary, that's all."

"Of me?"

"No, not of you," he said, pulling at his hair. "Of my family. Some of them are really strange."

So he was embarrassed. Well, that wasn't the worst reason not to want me parading through his house.

"I met Felice," I offered. "If that's what you're referring to."

Nic winced. "I know," he said. "He's very intense."

I decided not to comment on that.

"Does he keep bees?" I asked instead. I had been thinking

about the honeyed scent all day; at times I swore I could still smell it. It's not like it was a crime to make your own honey, but there was something about the way my uncle Jack had reacted to that mysterious jar that kept crashing back into my mind.

Nic stopped walking. "How did you know that?"

"The marks on his face," I said, stopping as well. "They're bee stings, right?"

Nic hesitated for a beat, like he was weighing what to say, then simply answered, "Yes."

"And he smells of honey." I paused, wondering if the next sentence would be offensive, but then I decided to say it anyway. "It's almost like he bathes in it . . ."

Nic laughed. "Maybe he does. He likes to eat the honeycomb raw, and he harvests and extracts the honey by himself. It's . . . his thing." A shadow swept across his features, but he broke into another smile before I could decipher it.

"But there aren't any hives at your house?"

"Thankfully!" he replied, a tinge of relief creeping into his voice. "Felice lives over in Lake Forest. But while my mother's in Europe he makes it his business to check on us, to make sure we're not all killing each other."

"So he makes his own honey?" I confirmed, trying to stay on topic. I thought of the black-ribboned honey jar again, the one that turned up the week Nic's family moved in.

Nic's answer came slower this time. "Yes."

"Does he give his honey away?"

"Why?" His expression changed, and I didn't understand the way he was looking at me. Like he was suspicious of me. Was I asking too many questions about his family? Or had honey just become a universally sore subject for everyone? I had obviously missed the memo.

I shrugged, watching him as carefully as he was watching me. "A jar of honey turned up in the diner not too long ago. It had a black ribbon around it."

"OK . . ."

"We were wondering where it came from, or who it was for."

"Who found it?"

"I did."

Nic's brows furrowed. "What did you do with it?"

"I brought it home and tasted it. It was nice . . . Then I dropped it by accident and it broke," I added. There was no way I was telling him what really happened. It was too weird for even me to understand, and I had known Jack my whole life. One unhinged uncle was enough for this conversation.

Nic's frown deepened, and he shook his head. "Like I said, Felice doesn't live around here."

"So that's not something he would do?"

"I highly doubt it," he said, his attention turning to the stars above us. "Anyway, I wouldn't worry about it."

"But I do worry about it," I said, fighting the urge to tug on his arm so he would look at me again.

As if sensing my request, he returned his gaze to me. "You worry about honey?" he asked, a smile spreading across his face.

I felt myself blush. When he put it like that, it did seem pretty stupid. "I just don't like to feel like I'm out of the loop about something."

"Try being the youngest of five brothers."

We walked on, our hands swinging side by side, almost touching, as rows of beautiful homes on tree-lined streets bled into smaller, boxy houses along cramped, gridlike blocks.

"So you don't mind having an escort home again?" he asked, following my lead as I crossed a deserted intersection.

"No." I felt shy looking up at Nic in the moonlight. There was something about the way his eyes were shining, or how his hair was falling in waves, curling beneath his ears, that made my mouth dry.

"I wanted to make sure you weren't upset about earlier. I know Valentino was rude, but he was probably just trying to save you from the Felice train wreck."

I waved my hand in the air dismissively, even though I felt relieved by his explanation. "I'll get over it."

"Good."

"Speaking of Valentino," I said, letting my curiosity take over, "can I ask what happened to him?"

"You mean why he's in a wheelchair?"

"Well, yeah," I replied, looking at my shoes. "If you don't mind me asking."

Nic didn't seem affronted, and I exhaled quietly in relief. "I take it you've realized that he and Luca are twins," he said. I nodded. "Well, when my mother was pregnant with them, Luca's position in the womb put pressure on the lower half of Valentino's body. He couldn't move properly, his legs became tangled in bands of the amniotic membrane, and when he was delivered he had what they called a 'skeletal limb abnormality.' His right leg was completely crushed and turned in at the hip. The doctors operated on him when he was a kid, but the leg never developed the right way after that. He can walk for short distances with a cane, but he prefers to use the chair."

"Has it made him resentful of Luca?" I wondered.

Nic shrugged. "I think he's just glad Luca didn't decide to eat him in there." He chuckled at my shocked expression. "His words, not mine," he clarified. "I don't think he resents Luca. Valentino has always been the most intelligent of all of us. He has the most creative mind, and understands people really well — a whole lot better than Luca. They're so close that sometimes it feels like they're the same person. They agree on everything, and if you decide to argue with one, then you're arguing with both, and they will steamroll you before you can even think straight." He paused for a second, losing himself in a memory that made him smile. I watched him carefully, trying to figure out what was unraveling inside his head. "I think Luca has always felt guilty about the opportunities he has, but Valentino isn't a victim. They'd die for each other."

"Wow," I said, feeling a familiar sense of loneliness for the siblings I would never have. "Must be nice to have that kind of bond."

"I think everyone can have that bond with someone," Nic said quietly. "Isn't that the whole point of living?"

"I hope you're right." I studied my nails to keep from burning up under his gaze.

Nic stopped walking, and I stopped, too. "I am right," he said resolutely.

I looked at him again, shyly, and before the nerves inside me could bubble up and psyche me out completely, I blurted out, "So there's this party at Millie's on Saturday, and pretty much everyone is welcome, so I thought maybe you might want to come if you're not doing anything?"

Nic raised his eyebrows — whether it was at the sheer speed of my invitation or the actual meaning of it, I wasn't sure. "And I take it her charming brother will be there?"

I inhaled through my teeth. "Yes, but you're definitely still welcome, if that's what you're worried about. They made a rule. They can't veto each other's guests."

Nic's laugh was soft and low. "Saved by the power of disallowed vetoes."

"Exactly," I said, sounding mellower this time. "How could you resist?"

"I don't think I could. I take it you'll be there?"

"Of course. It's actually my birthday, too."

"Ah," he said, smiling. "*Buon compleanno.* I'd love to come."

I enjoyed a brief inner victory dance while making sure to keep my expression relaxed. "Cool."

"I was wondering what kind of stuff you do for fun," he continued. "I was thinking about it earlier."

"So you don't forget about me, then?" I teased. "When you're playing basketball with your brothers or hanging out in your giant mansion and I'm at the diner wasting away from boredom?"

"Absolutely not."

"Good."

"And you're not very forgettable, either," he added, almost as an afterthought.

"I think most people would disagree," I returned.

"I'm not most people."

"You're certainly not," I agreed.

"So tell me about yourself, Sophie. I want to know about you."

"Why?" No one ever wanted to know about me. Especially not bronze, statue-type people. "I'm very boring, I promise."

He laughed again; it was close and intimate this time, and I could feel his breath against my ear as he leaned toward me. "Maybe you should let someone other than you be the judge of that."

Instead of answering, I kicked a stray pebble and watched as it bounced into the street.

"Well, let's start with what we know," he began, rubbing his chin with his hand. "You can be a little defensive . . ."

"Hey!"

"It's endearing," he assured me quickly. "And what else? You don't like storms. You're thick-skinned, and you blush whenever someone looks at you for too long . . ."

I grimaced. So he had noticed that.

". . . which makes it more fun to look at you." He smirked. "Not that it isn't fun to look at you already."

I could feel myself blushing again, and I cursed the timing of it.

"Is it just you and your parents at home?" he continued delicately — seamlessly, almost.

"It's just me and my mom," I answered. "My dad's been gone

for a while, so we do our best not to burn the place down or poison each other with bad food."

I felt guilty about skimming over the part about my father being in prison, but I didn't want to risk everything so soon.

"Do you get along?"

"Yeah, when we're both at home. But we don't see each other as much as I would like, I guess."

Suddenly I felt horribly vulnerable, entrusting my innermost thoughts to this beautiful boy, who probably didn't care about my relationship with my mother.

Nic regarded me contemplatively. "That must be difficult. But maybe your distance makes you closer when it counts?"

"Maybe." I suddenly felt heavy with emotion. What was it with these Priestly boys? Just this morning I was on the verge of tears with Valentino! And now . . .

"So you're going to be a senior?"

Saved by the conversation change. We fell back into step with each other.

"Yup, starting in September. I have one more torture-filled year of high school to go." I sighed theatrically, glad to be moving away from the previous topic. "What about you?"

"Just graduated," he replied with an edge of triumph in his voice.

"And what will you do with yourself now?"

"I deferred college for a semester; I'm working with my brothers mostly."

"In Cedar Hill?"

"No," he replied. "Not exactly. Not all the time."

"Do you like it?"

"What I do or where I live?"

"Cedar Hill." I suddenly felt embarrassed by my association with the place. Especially the part we were in now. It was a far cry from the opulence Nic was used to.

He smiled at me like he could sense my shame. "I didn't like it at first, but I do now."

"What do you do here? What kind of work?"

He shrugged, but kept his shoulders rigid. "Right now? Not a whole lot . . ." he said vaguely, trailing off.

"Do you think you'll miss school?"

Nic shook his head. "It's only one semester. And I like to be active; I want to feel useful, like what I'm doing is making some small difference in the world. I don't think I'll ever need to use trigonometry in real life."

"I know," I concurred enthusiastically. "Or Shakespeare. *Bleugh.*"

Nic reacted like I had slapped him on the side of the head. He stopped and placed his hands on my arms, pulling me toward him until I was right under his gaze. I thought he was going to start shaking me. "Did you really just knock the man who gave us *Romeo and Juliet*?"

I frowned. I had never really considered it at length before; I just knew I didn't like school, and for me, Shakespeare was synonymous with school, a place where I didn't feel welcome. "I guess I'm not a big fan of tragedy."

"What about love?" he said with such intensity I almost forgot to breathe.

Slowly, he moved his hands up my arms, trailing his fingers

across my shoulders until his thumbs were brushing the base of my neck. I felt my skin prickle with anticipation.

"Love is different," I said.

"Love is weakness." He studied his fingers as he moved them up my neck in gentle, butterfly touches.

"Weaknesses make us human," I said, hearing the dryness in my throat.

"And being human makes us fallible." He was so close.

"Are you fallible, Nic?"

His gaze was on my lips now. "Of course I am."

"I find that hard to believe."

"You shouldn't," he whispered. He tucked a stray strand of hair behind my ear, leaving his thumb under my chin.

I rose onto my tiptoes and he pulled me into his body, until my nose was almost touching his. His breathing faltered. Then his hands were around my waist, pressing against my lower back, and his lips were on mine.

I couldn't think anymore. I was undone, and suddenly nothing else mattered but Nic and the way he was pressing his mouth against mine and holding me like he never wanted to let me go. Everything around us dulled and, for a heartbeat, it was as if the entire world were holding its breath.

Then a roaring engine split the silence apart. A car sped up the street, pulling us back into reality and away from our kiss.

As the black SUV screeched to a halt on the street beside us, I felt my insides collapse in disappointment. Nic untangled himself from me and lunged forward to bang on the car's blacked-out window.

"Gino? Dom?" he shouted. *"Cosa vuoi?"*

With a sleek casualness, the window buzzed down and the driver leaned across the passenger seat.

"Luca?" Nic sounded shocked.

Luca, in all his icy-eyed splendor, spat, "Get in, Nicoli."

"What the hell is going on?"

Luca threw his arm out and popped the passenger door so that it swung open against his brother's body. "Get in the car now."

Nic turned back to me, his expression apologetic. "He can be a bit over the top sometimes . . ."

"Without her," Luca interrupted.

"Have you gone insane? Or are you just having an asshole day? I'm not ditching Sophie in the middle of the street!"

Luca rubbed his hand across his forehead and released a sharp sigh. "I don't know what the hell you think you're doing, little brother, but it's not funny."

"What are you talking about?"

"Have you spoken to Dom today?"

"No."

"Vieni qui."

Nic leaned into the open window.

Luca dropped his voice and spoke in one endless, hurried thread. Even though I could tell they had switched to Italian, I stood with my arms folded and listened. And though what I heard was mostly an incomprehensible string of syllables, I managed to glean one word successfully. And that word was "Gracewell."

The second I heard my name spring from Luca's lips, Nic turned around and regarded me with a poorly concealed display of horror. His mouth, which had been soft against mine just moments ago, was pursed in a hard line, and suddenly he was looking at me like he didn't know who I was.

"What's going on?"

"What's your name?" he asked in a strained voice.

"You know my name," I replied, feeling scared by how unrecognizable he suddenly seemed. "It's Sophie."

"Sophie what?"

"Nic . . ."

"*Sophie what?*" he pressed, his voice growing frighteningly shrill.

"G-Gracewell," I stammered, my lips trembling.

He looked like he was about to pass out. "*Cazzo!*"

"What does it matter what my name is?" I heard the desperation in my voice, but I didn't care.

He shook his head. "But it doesn't make any sense."

"What do you mean?"

"I have to go." The words seemed forced, but he pushed them out determinedly.

"What does it matter?" I asked again. "What did Luca say about me?"

Behind Nic, Luca stared impassively at the road, but his hands were gripping the steering wheel so hard, they looked like marble. "Get in the car, Nic. Don't drag this out."

Nic lingered, looking at me like I had just slapped him hard in the face.

"Luca . . ." he pleaded, as if the rug had been pulled from underneath his feet and he had fallen hard on the ground beneath it.

Luca didn't turn his head, and when he spoke again his voice was rough with anger. "Get. Away. From. Her. Now."

I grabbed on to Nic's arm. I didn't know where he was going, but I knew I didn't want it to be without me.

"Now!" Luca bared his pointed teeth like a wolf.

There was a moment of nothingness, when my heart crumpled, and then Nic pulled his arm from me, ripped himself out of our bubble, and jumped into the passenger seat, slamming the door behind him.

I leapt forward and gripped the open window as the engine roared to life beneath me. It was then that I saw there was blood all over Luca's shirt.

"What happened?" I gasped, my stomach filling with dread. If that were his own blood, Luca would have been in the hospital. But he wasn't. He was sitting across from me, seething and unscathed. *Several disappearances and two strange deaths in the last two weeks* — Mrs. Bailey's words rang in my ears. "Where did all that blood come from?"

Luca didn't respond, and Nic spoke instead. "Get back from the car, Sophie."

"Is this about my dad?"

Luca and Nic exchanged a loaded glance, and suddenly I felt like a pariah all over again.

"I want to know what he said!" I shouted at Nic. "Tell me!"

It was Luca who finally responded. Turning his head slowly, he stared at me until his icy blue eyes dominated my worldview. "Gracewell," he hissed, "get off my car, or I will remove you from it myself."

Nic cursed under his breath, but still he wouldn't look at me. Luca, on the other hand, held his hostile gaze until, shattering under the weight of it, I took my hands off the car and stumbled back.

The engine revved twice, and then the Priestly brothers sped off into the night without another glance in my direction. I was left standing alone in the middle of a deserted street as a string of questions exploded inside my brain.

PART II

♥

"It is only in love and murder that we still remain sincere."
FRIEDRICH DÜRRENMATT, *Incident at Twilight*

CHAPTER TWELVE

The Bee

I stood on the street corner, my hands wrapped tightly around Nic's neck as we clung to each other. We watched the pavement crack beneath our feet. The sound of rushing water roared against my eardrums as a chasm split the ground, giving way to flames that climbed out, licking the sky, and then suddenly Nic was gone and I was sinking. I screamed, but my voice caught in my throat. As air turned to sand that filled my lungs, my whole world turned black, like someone had reached into my head and flicked a switch.

And then there was nothing but my heart pummeling against my chest and the smell of Philadelphia cream cheese. Guided by a distant hum, I hurtled back into reality.

"Sophie . . ."

The sunlight was bouncing off my eyelids.

"Earth to Sophie . . ."

I squinted and waited for the ceiling to shift into focus.

"Guess what day it is?"

I cleared the cobwebs from my throat in groggy squeaks and tried to blink away the memory of my dream — this was the second time I'd had it in as many nights. I propped myself onto my elbows.

"Good morning, Birthday Girl!"

My mother was perched on the end of my bed. There were small crinkles at the sides of her eyes, and her mouth was curved upward in a grin that could have put the Cheshire Cat's to shame. I was glad to see her smile like that, even if she was just doing it for the sake of the day. I had missed the way it made her eyes sparkle.

In her lap she held a red velvet cupcake, lavished with cream cheese frosting.

"Good morning," I croaked.

"Happy birthday, sweetheart."

She fished a Zippo lighter from her cardigan, flicked it open, and lit the candle. "Make a wish!" she said, shoving the cupcake so close to my face I could see tiny wisps of smoke rise above the flame.

I hesitated as it danced across my eyeline, taunting me. *Clarity,* I decided at last. *I just want clarity.* I blew purposefully across the flame, extinguishing it in one tiny puff of air.

My mother produced a silver knife from her other pocket. She sliced the cupcake straight down the middle and the two halves fell apart from each other, toppling under the weight of the frosting. She scooped up one half and handed it to me.

"Delicious!" I said, taking a bite. "Thanks."

Setting her half on her lap, my mother reached behind her and fished out a present wrapped in glitzy purple paper. "I made you something."

I smiled as I wiped the residual cupcake grease from my fingers onto my duvet. I already suspected it was the dress she had been working on in secret. Carefully, I unstuck the tape around the edges and peeled away the paper so that the garment slipped out, perfectly folded, onto the bed. I unfurled it. It was structured but delicate, made from light gold silk that fell in soft waves, and adorned with sequins that glinted in the morning sunlight. I brushed my fingers along the thin straps and felt the dress curve in around the waist as I held it up. "It's incredible!"

"And it matches your hair!" My mother smiled. "I thought you could wear it to the party at Millie's later?"

"Great idea." I felt a pinch of guilt knowing my mother was unaware of Millie's parents' absence. Still, what she didn't know couldn't hurt her, right?

She clapped her hands together. "Lunch later?" she asked, bouncing up from my bed. "I want to treat my seventeen-year-old daughter at the Eatery."

"Really?" I reclined and stretched my body out in one long, angular yawn, blinking up at the ceiling. "That sounds great." *And expensive.*

My mother carried the dress across the room with her, hopping over old sweatshirts and unfolded jeans as she went. She hung it inside the closet and, with one final disgruntled — *hypocritical* — look at the floor, she edged back out of the room, leaving me alone with my thoughts, which turned to the strange dream I'd just had. Like a jolt of electricity, the feeling of Nic's kiss took hold of me again and I felt my stomach clench uncomfortably at the memory of how he had left me so suddenly. I hoped I wasn't doomed to relive his desertion in my nightmares, too. There were still so many questions floating around in my head, and no way for me to get the answers I desperately wanted. I clutched at the red velvet uneasiness in my stomach and groaned. Maybe a party was exactly what I needed to take my mind off everything.

The black ponytail stuck out of Gino Priestly's head like a noir mini palm tree. Beside him, the lights were dancing off Dom's overly gelled helmet of hair. What the hell were they doing here?

"What is it, sweetheart? Don't you like the quiche?"

I refocused my attention on my mother, who was sitting across from me. "It's good. I'm just a bit overheated."

"You've been so quiet since we got here. I thought you'd like this place. Is it too fancy?"

As concern etched across her features, a fresh heap of guilt consumed me. I shook my head more vehemently this time. "Are you kidding? This place is great." I gestured around at the Eatery's monochrome décor: The black granite floors were inlaid with intricate floral designs; the tables were covered with expensive white cloths; and all around the restaurant, Romanesque pillars wound toward the ceiling. The walls were decorated with black-and-white photographs of twentieth-century Chicago and dotted incrementally with glass lighting fixtures. "Makes a welcome change from the diner."

My mother smiled and took a sip of her Chardonnay. "Speaking of the diner, I wanted to talk to you about that . . ."

I let my attention fall on Gino and Dom again — or rather, on the backs of their heads — and wondered about the odds of us being at the same restaurant. It was miles away from Cedar Hill, right in the center of Chicago, *and* since it was one of the best restaurants in the city, it was more of an eye-wateringly expensive, special occasion kind of place. The karma gods must have been enjoying the show.

At least Nic and Luca weren't with their brothers. I tried to remind myself of how horrible Nic had been the other night, but it was difficult to forget all the other things about him: the softer, funnier, kinder things. The way he smiled, the way he had pressed his lips against mine . . . the way he drove away from me in the middle of the night without a second glance. I flinched.

"Sophie?"

"What?" I took another bite of my quiche Lorraine, wondering why I had ordered it. Then again, I didn't understand the majority of the fancy menu and I wasn't convinced I would enjoy "truffle-infused fries" as much as normal ones.

"I want to talk to you about the diner."

"OK, shoot."

Behind my mother, Gino was recoiling from something the bald man sitting across from him had said. Dom sat on his brother's right and there was a narrow, taller man on his left, his back half-turned to me. It was Felice — I would have wagered my meal. Even though they were at the other side of the restaurant, curled around one another in a secluded corner booth, the faint smell of honey was hanging in the air. I was sure of it. Or I was going crazy.

I averted my eyes.

My mother was still talking, her hands flailing animatedly in front of her. ". . . placed unfair expectations on you. You need to get out more and spread your wings, don't you think?"

A buzzing sound tugged at my attention. A bee had found its way inside the restaurant and was circling the table next to us.

"Get out of where?" I asked, dragging my gaze back to my table and scolding myself for being so distractible. I could still see it, though — a small blur of yellow and black in my peripheral vision.

"The diner."

I jabbed my fork into my quiche. "What about the diner?"

The man I didn't recognize got up from the Priestly table. He was tall and bald, with a high forehead and a thick black mustache that dominated his angular face. He grunted as he passed a waitress, and then disappeared through the restroom doors.

"I think you should quit. It's too taxing on your energy and you barely have any free time."

Now that I had heard it in its entirety, I was surprised by her suggestion. I set my fork down and swallowed the mouthful of quiche in one overzealous gulp. "But it's Dad's. I thought the whole plan was for me to run it until he gets back." I didn't know why I was fighting against her idea — the thought of running the diner when I turned eighteen had never excited me; I had always known it wasn't my calling.

The bee whizzed past my face, missing my nose by an inch. My mother dropped her fork and released a small yelp.

"Sorry," she explained sheepishly, regaining her composure. "They always give me such a fright."

"I think bees are kind of cute," I said, trying to put her at ease.

Across the restaurant, the bee was zigzagging toward the Priestly table. *Probably returning to its "master,"* I thought, registering the back of Felice's silver head again.

"What's going on with you today? You're all over the place." My mother grabbed my wrist, tugging at me.

"Sorry." I shook my head in a futile attempt to settle my wandering attention, and pulled my hand back. "What were you saying?"

"Why not let your uncle continue to manage the diner after you graduate next year, until your father comes back. That way you can give college your undivided attention — and go to school in Chicago instead of staying here in the burbs. There's a whole world out there, you know."

I shoveled another forkful of quiche into my mouth. "I'm still saving for a car. I need the money," I said ineptly, covering my mouth as I chewed.

I flicked my gaze again. The bald, mustached man had come back from the restroom and was rejoining the Priestly table, sitting down with an audible grunt.

"I can give you a little cash every week to put toward a car. You wouldn't even miss the tips from the diner," my mother was protesting.

"I don't want to put that strain on you," I said, my mouth still half-full. "I know we don't have that kind of money anymore."

My mother pushed a square of feta cheese around her plate with her fork. "Sophie, I'd really prefer it if you left."

"Did Uncle Jack say something to you? Have you heard from him?" I was starting to get an uneasy feeling in the pit of my stomach again. My mother was acting strange, like just about everyone else in my life.

"No, but maybe we should put some distance between you two. He seems a little more unhinged than usual lately."

"I think he'd take it pretty badly if I ditched him now. Especially after his friend just died."

She shrugged and skewered a thin slice of red onion, popping it into her mouth. "Jack's not even around anymore. And he can't always get what he wants."

My eyes slid across to the Priestly table again. Dom and Gino were arguing with the bald, mustached man. Felice — yes, it was definitely him, I could see now — was sitting perfectly still, his hands clasped on the table in front of him. He was quietly observing the bee that was now swirling perilously close to their table. As the others argued, their voices swelled and traveled through the restaurant.

"What is going on?" My mother swiveled around so she could catch a glimpse of the commotion, but it died down almost as quickly as it had begun and she lost interest.

"Mom?"

She looked at me expectantly.

"Is there something you're not telling me about Dad and Uncle Jack? Or you and Uncle Jack? I get the feeling I'm missing something."

She leaned onto her elbows and knitted her hands under her chin. "What do you mean?"

"Well, I don't know what I mean. That's why I asked . . ."

There was an almighty *clap!* We jumped in our seats.

"Calvino!" A scream so high it sounded like a woman's. But it hadn't come from a woman, it had come from Felice, who had sprung to his feet and was clasping his hands to his face. Now everyone in the restaurant was looking at them. The bald man — Calvino — sat back in the booth, casually lifting his palm from the table and wiping it with a napkin, his face placid. He had killed the bee.

Felice's chest was heaving. He said something in amplified Italian, but Calvino didn't bat an eyelid. He tried to wave Felice back into his seat. The calmer he acted, the more incensed Felice became. He began to spit vitriol as he gestured futilely at what I assumed was the squished bee carcass.

I gaped. I had never seen someone so calm flip out so quickly.

Felice reached into his suit jacket, prompting Gino and Dom to pull back in their seats. Calvino shot to his feet and held his hands up, like he was surrendering. He spoke quietly and quickly.

Felice pulled his hand from his pocket and clenched it into a fist by his side. He ran his other hand through his hair, stopping to squeeze the back of his neck, pinching at it.

Slowly, and without taking his eyes off Felice, Calvino sat down.

Felice remained on his feet. He raised his chin so that he appeared even taller than usual, and with one final curse word directed solely at Calvino — but heard by everyone within a one-mile radius — he stormed out of the restaurant like a graceful, seething skeleton.

"What a strange man," my mother whispered, her hushed words mingling with everyone else's.

"Strange family," I muttered, watching Gino and Dom resettle themselves at their table, falling back into conversation. Maybe in this one case I was actually *lucky* to have been ostracized. The Priestlys obviously had a lot going on, and I had already reached my drama quota for one lifetime. It was probably for the best. Even if it didn't feel like it.

I shifted back to my mother and found her chewing up her bottom lip. "Sophie, there's a lot you don't know about your father and Uncle Jack," she said, returning to our conversation like the dramatic interlude hadn't happened at all. "Sometimes I can't help but think Jack deserves to be in jail more than your father does."

This was the first time I had ever heard my mother play the blame game about that night — or speak about it willingly, for that matter. It was one of those unsaid, defining moments that was always bubbling beneath the dynamic of our relationship but rarely openly acknowledged by either of us.

"But Jack wasn't even there."

"I know that," she conceded. "But your uncle has always made friends with the wrong people, the sort of people who care more about money than family, and who encourage his paranoid delusions. When your father came to Cedar Hill, it was to make a new life with you and me — a better life than the one he had growing up. He was respectable and successful, but then Jack started coming around. He didn't have a family of his own and so he looked at us like we were his, too. It had always been just him and your father growing up, those two boys against the world, and I think your father felt like he owed him a piece of our lives, too, so he wouldn't be out on his own.

"But then Jack started putting these thoughts in your father's head. The same thoughts I can see him trying to put in yours — ones designed to make you afraid and anxious. It got to the point where Jack would question everything and everyone who came into the diner, and soon he was making your father paranoid, too. The more I think about it, I can't help but feel that if Jack hadn't been getting under your father's skin, then he wouldn't have been so quick to believe that man was a dangerous intruder that night at the diner."

"And he wouldn't have shot him," I finished coldly. "I don't know if you can blame that on Jack."

"He gave your father the gun."

"He wanted him to protect himself," I countered. "They've always looked out for each other."

She scooped a tomato wedge onto her fork. "You're right," she replied quickly, shaking her head. "Never mind. I shouldn't have brought it up on your birthday. This day should be about all the good things in your life."

Suddenly the air between us was awkward and strained. I took a gulp of my Diet Coke and let my eyes wander back to the Priestlys, who had become uncharacteristically silent. Gino sat with his head in his hands, and Dom was leaning back, staring blankly at the ceiling. I knew how they felt.

CHAPTER THIRTEEN

The Party

I examined myself in my bedroom mirror, making sure my mother's tinted moisturizer had blended into my skin. I applied some of her bronzer to the high points of my face and added some blush to my cheeks. I rifled through her makeup bag and fished out a deep kohl powder, sweeping it across my eyelids, before applying gooey black mascara to my lashes. Then I stood back and appraised my reflection, marveling at what the wonders of modern cosmetics could do for sun-starved skin.

My mother shuffled into the room and my gaze fell on the gift in her hands — a large rectangle covered in Disney princess wrapping paper. "Is that from Millie?"

My mother put the gift on the bed. "She dropped it off when you were in the shower. Open it. The suspense is killing me."

I didn't have to be asked twice. I ripped open the wrapping paper to find a gray shoe box. CARVELA was scrawled across it in neat black letters.

"How did Millie afford those?" My mother echoed my thoughts.

I shook my head in disbelief. How was it possible to have such an amazing best friend? I eased the lid off the box and pulled the tissue paper away to find a pair of patent leather nude stilettos. The heel, which was at least five inches high, was coated in a subtle gold gloss, while the front of the shoe slanted downward into a perfectly rounded peep-toe.

"I think I'm in love," I groaned.

My mother sighed. "I've never been so disappointed to have smaller feet than you."

I slipped my bare foot into the left shoe and teetered upward. "How am I going to walk in these without falling on my face?"

My mother grinned as she handed me the second shoe. "No one really *walks* in high heels. They just get by."

After fifteen minutes of practicing, I shimmied into the gold dress. Twirling in front of my closet mirror, I pulled out the pin that I'd wedged into my hair so that it tumbled down my back in waves. I barely recognized my reflection, but I had a feeling she was going to have a whole lot of fun.

When we pulled up outside Millie's house, I could hear music blaring through the walls. Cars lined the streets and crammed into the driveway. I climbed out onto the curb.

"Are you sure Millie's parents are OK with this?" I watched my mother survey the cars warily.

"Yup." I turned away from her so she couldn't see my brazen, lying face.

"OK . . ." she relented. "Have a blast."

I watched the car until it shrank to a small blue dot.

When I turned around, Millie was standing at the front door,

wearing a short black dress that accentuated her bust and ban-
daged her in around the waist.

"Mil!" I exclaimed, making my way toward her in high heel–
induced slow motion. "Thank you so much for the shoes!"

"Holy crap," she shot back, her red-lipsticked mouth agape.

I hunched my shoulders and covered my dress with my arms.
"Is it too much? Should I change?"

She gestured at my dress, moving her finger up and down in
several slow flicks. "That dress *really* shows off your best assets!"
She made a botched attempt at a wolf whistle and then wiggled
her eyebrows suggestively.

"Pervert," I teased, reaching her.

"What?" She raised her hands in a gesture of feigned innocence. "I meant it really brings out the blue in your eyes . . . So
vivid . . ."

"Who are you talking to?" Alex arrived behind Millie at the
door. His blond hair was styled in perfect spikes and he wore
dark-rinse jeans paired with a tight blue shirt. He was smiling
goofily and clutching a red plastic cup. When he noticed me hovering in the doorway, he let his jaw drop so that, side by side and
wearing the same expression, he and Millie looked like twins.

"Sophie Gracewell," he spluttered.

"I know," Millie murmured. "I know."

Millie and I danced like maniacs across her hardwood floors,
throwing our hands in the air and whipping our hair in circles,
both of us teetering precariously on our respective sky-high heels.
All around us, couples gravitated toward each other like magnets,

pushing up against one another or peeling off to other rooms to make out. I barely recognized most of the people — the majority were Alex's college friends, and those who heard about it from Millie were ignoring me, as usual. It didn't matter. Everyone was laughing and having fun, and it was contagious — I was relaxed and energized. But more than that, I was eternally grateful to Millie, who had converted the entire downstairs of her impressive family home into a hub of energy, which meant I could spend my birthday having some much-needed fun.

The front living room had been cleared of its picture frames, knickknacks, and creepy porcelain dolls, which usually peered out from glass cases in the corners — an obsession of Millie's mother's. The lights had been dimmed so low that the features of anyone standing more than two feet away were foggy and indiscernible, and the leather couches and upholstered armchairs were pushed back against the wall. Above the fireplace, a fifty-inch TV was blaring music through surround-sound speakers.

"Where's Dom?" I asked, ignoring the dull ache in the balls of my feet.

"He's not coming." Millie's face crumpled, but she waved her explanation away as though it didn't matter. "I haven't heard from him since our date. He didn't even return my text."

"I'm sorry, Mil!" I shouted above the music. "That sucks!"

"It's fine," she returned loftily, but I could tell it wasn't. She had been hopelessly obsessed with Dom after their date, and the fact that he hadn't bothered to follow it up was strange, not to mention incredibly rude.

"I hope it's not because of me," I suddenly realized, feeling the color drain from my bronzed and blushed face. "Maybe Nic said something to him."

Millie's expression soured. "If it *is* because of you, then Dom is as spineless as his brother and they should both be shunned for judging you for your father's *accident*. I don't want to be with someone like that anyway!"

"It's his loss," I offered, feeling her anger ignite my own. "He's an idiot."

"They both are! I hope they have a really boring time styling their stupid hair and overspending on their stupid Italian clothes while they all grow old together in that creepy mansion!" Millie threw her head back and started swaying her hips, putting an end to the topic of Dom and his brothers for good.

Following her lead, I closed my eyes and let my body melt into the music. But deep down in my private bubble, I couldn't help but imagine Nic's hands around my waist; that he had shown up to apologize for his strange behavior and that there was a reasonable explanation for his sudden callousness. But when I opened my eyes and twirled around again, I saw a collection of faces I didn't recognize, all red-faced and panting.

After a while, my feet started to throb. I stopped dancing and slipped through the double doors that led into a large marble-fitted kitchen. Inside, a bunch of guys were leaning around a keg, chugging their drinks. At the table, two skinny brunettes in short skirts were squealing their way through a game of beer pong.

I squeezed by a red-haired girl who was inking a henna tattoo on her friend's back, and made my way toward the fridge just as

Alex slammed his beer cup across the counter and backed away from his friends with his arms up in victory. "Losers!" he shouted. "You can't beat the champ!"

I smiled. Alex had been so uptight at the basketball tournament; it was nice to see him in a lighter mood — even if he was still being abnormally competitive.

When his eyes fell on me, he stuffed his hands down by his sides and hunched his shoulders, adopting a sheepish expression. "Beer?" he offered, gesturing at the keg behind him. "Or we have some harder stuff, too?"

I pushed the matted hair away from my forehead, feeling beads of sweat underneath my fingers. "Maybe later," I said. I was already having a hard time standing up in my heels. I figured I better practice some more before adding alcohol to the mix.

"You sure you don't want one?" Alex prompted with a smile that I used to daydream about in school. But something was different now.

"Yeah, I'm sure." I opened the fridge, pulled out a can of Diet Coke, and cracked it open while the boys behind me laughed among themselves. I wondered if they were laughing at me, but I was too chicken to confront them about it. Feeling myself blush, I moved away and shimmied past the girl with red hair, who was inking a dolphin on her own hip now. A Ping-Pong ball soared past my head and bounced off the marble island in the middle of the kitchen.

I made it back to the living room in one piece, squeezed by a couple who were making out against the door, and danced around someone doing the worm, to get to the nearest couch. When I reached it, I found Millie chatting to Paul and Alison from the diner.

". . . and then I thought, whatever, I'm going to have fun without him — hey, birthday girl, come sit." She patted the sliver of space beside her.

"Hey." I squeezed in between Millie and the armrest, feeling instant relief in the balls of my feet. "When did you guys get here?" I followed Millie's gaze to Alison's lap and saw that she and Paul were holding hands. They had obviously made it official.

"Just now. Ursula let us off early."

"Happy birthday, Sophie," Paul added cheerily. "Great party."

"Thanks." I shrugged. "It's not mine. I don't know most of these people."

"Oh, sure it is," Millie interjected, waving her hand dismissively. "And if Alex's friends didn't know you before tonight, then they definitely will now, thanks to that dress." She drained her drink and sighed satisfactorily.

"Yeah," Paul agreed, causing Alison to dig her nails into his lap. "Ouch!" he yelped. "Sorry, I was just saying."

"Time for a refill, I think." Millie sprang to her feet and sauntered through the parting crowd with more attitude than Beyoncé. I envied her ability to walk so effortlessly in her heels without experiencing the urge to lie down and chop her feet off.

I went in search of a bathroom. The sound of vomiting from downstairs prompted my journey to the second floor, where, after knocking three times, I swung the door open and came face-to-face with a half-naked couple. It was a traumatic moment for all of us.

I quickly shut the door and made my way farther along the upstairs hallway, stopping outside Millie's parents' room and rapping my knuckles against the door. When there was no answer from inside, I eased my way in, praying I wasn't about to encounter another scarring scene. The bedroom was empty.

The narrow door beside the wall of closets meant my memory had served me correctly and that they did have an en-suite bathroom. But as I approached it, the handle was yanked downward from the inside and it swung backward on its hinges. I jumped back and landed against the bed. I shot my hands up and covered my eyes. "Sorry, I didn't know anyone was in here."

My explanation was met with a deep laugh. "Relax, Sophie. I spilled some beer on myself and all the other bathrooms were *ocupado*."

I unsheltered my eyes and found Robbie Stenson leaning against the doorway, holding a red cup in each hand. "Do you want one? I've got a spare."

"Um, thanks." I was glad to know Robbie wasn't holding our basketball tournament debacle against me. "I'm not sure if I should drink — it's hard enough to walk in these heels while sober. I don't want to risk my life by doing it drunk."

He flicked his floppy hair across his forehead and smirked. "It's just cranberry with seltzer, but it'll give you a nice buzz. I think it's the sugar content or something."

"Cool." I reached for the cup in his outstretched hand, feeling hot all of a sudden. "I am pretty thirsty."

"No kidding." He sat on the bed with a plonk and arched one of his perfect eyebrows at me. "You were dropping some killer dance moves earlier. Why didn't you use some of that talent on the court? Then we might have had a snowball's chance."

I smiled into the cup. "I'm not sure I could have dribbled the ball and done the robot at the same time."

Robbie snorted with amusement. "It might have intimidated our opponents." He stared unblinkingly at me as I drank. "You look great, by the way."

"Thanks." Suddenly I had a feeling our conversation might mean something different to him than it did to me. What *was* it about this dress?

"I should get back downstairs," I said, setting the empty cup on the nightstand.

"I thought you had to go to the bathroom?"

"Not really anymore. I think I was just feeling overheated." I rose and teetered to the door as my feet began to ache again.

"Maybe I'll catch you later," he hollered after me.

"Yeah, maybe," I said, gripping the banister and lowering myself carefully onto the stairs.

Back in the kitchen, I found Millie cuddling up against a boy with a questionable goatee. She was leaning into his shoulder and giggling like a little girl. Her attempts to forget about Dom were obviously going well.

"Sophie." She grinned broadly and stood up when she saw me. "Come meet Marcus. He's so great." She shuffled closer and dropped her voice. "*So* much more fun than *boring* Dom. I don't know what I was thinking with that guy. Obviously we're not compatible, he's *way* too serious."

Suddenly she was looming back and forth in front of me, and I was starting to feel funny. "Can you stand still?"

"Have you been drinking, Soph?"

Her eyes grew too big for her face and her mouth was hanging open at an unnatural angle. I shook my head and felt it spin.

"You sure?" She came up close until I could see every freckle on her face. They moved around like a puzzle and then disappeared.

"C-course." I slumped backward against the wall. "I don't feel very well, though." Alarm bells started to go off inside my head, but they got fainter and fainter.

"You sure you didn't do a shot of something?"

The music was thumping against my skull. "No, I-I just . . ." I paused and scrunched up my face. "I forgot what I was going to say."

"I think someone should take you home." I wasn't aware of much, but I could tell the amusement had drained from Millie's voice, and the guy with the goatee had disappeared.

"I have a headache. C-Can you get me something for that?" I heard myself falter over the words and grimaced. They sounded so clear in my head.

"What's going on, Sophie?" Out of nowhere, Alex had appeared and was standing in front of me, holding me up. Suddenly I realized that, if he let me go, I would crumple into a heap on the ground. I fell into him, stubbing my nose on his chest.

"I think she's had too much to drink," he said, holding me steady again.

"I didn't," I slurred as the room started to fade into darkness.

And then I was lying down in a quiet room at the back of the house, staring at the crystal chandelier above me. Nausea gathered in my stomach. "I want to go home."

"Crap," Millie muttered from somewhere far away. "Celine is going to kill me if she finds her like this."

"I'll take her home," someone suggested.

"You sure, Robbie?"

"Yeah, I know the way. She can't go on her own. Not like this."

"I don't know." Alex's face contorted above me, his eyes spinning like little rainbow wheels. "Maybe we should just call her mum."

"Alex, I'll take her. I haven't been drinking. You don't want to get this whole rager shut down, do you?"

I groaned and clutched my sides. "I don't want to go with him," I whispered into a cushion. "Get Nic."

The cushion didn't reply, and Nic never came.

"OK, Sophie, let's go." Alex placed his arms under mine and lifted me off the couch until I teetered unsteadily against him. The world spun around until the faces of Millie, Alex, and Robbie blurred into one strange mosaic of humankind.

"Hang on," Millie said. "She can't walk home in those."

Suddenly there were only two faces in front of me and I couldn't remember who was who. I thought Alex had blond hair, but the other guy was wearing his blue eyes. I shook my head back and forth to get rid of the fuzziness.

"How much did she drink?"

"I bet she polished off that tequila, man."

And then I was at the front door, wearing a pair of Ugg boots that didn't belong to me. My chin got stuck to the top of my chest, and the ground started pulsating up and down.

"Robbie, get her to call me when she's home, OK? Don't forget."

And then we were galloping down the driveway and rounding the bend into an empty street that loomed ahead of me like a black river. Suddenly my head was swelling like a balloon.

"I'll fall in."

I jumped across the cracks in the pavement.

Robbie slid his arm around my waist and scooted me forward in a straight line. "Just chill out. You're a little buzzed right now, that's all."

At the mention of the word "buzz," I felt something in my ear. I jerked my head and slapped my hand against my face. "Get off, get off, get off!"

And then I was outside a row of small box houses that looked like they had been punched in.

"They look so sad," I moaned into Robbie's shoulder.

I blinked my eyes, and when I opened them again I was gliding along the sidewalk and squinting into the overbearing starlight. The Priestly house climbed into the sky ahead of me, like a castle.

"There's a princess in there." I felt an urgent need to rescue her. And then I forgot what I was thinking about. "I'm exhausted," I realized as the world around me became silent and still.

We had stopped walking.

"I know." Robbie propped me against a wall. I was vaguely aware of the uneven stones scratching against my back.

"I haven't slept for nearly a hundred years," I remembered. My head lolled until I was looking down at the pavement.

He lifted me back up like a rag doll and squeezed his hands above my waist. "I've got you."

"Am I home?" I asked wearily. Everything was so hard to concentrate on, and I had a bad feeling that any minute now, I would vomit.

"Yeah, just relax, Sophie. Everything is fine." I felt a finger under my chin, nudging my head. My eyes rolled back as the sensation of warm breath tickled my face. I struggled against my drooping lids, forcing them open. When I did, I found myself staring into two hawklike gray eyes an inch from my face. And just as my body relinquished control of my limbs completely, I felt his hands start to inch up my dress.

CHAPTER FOURTEEN

The Dark Knight

Somewhere deep inside me, panic was rising.

"Stop," I heard myself gasp.

Robbie's eyes shrank to slits in his puffy face. "Just relax."

"I don't want this." I tried to shake my head, but could only make a sideways figure eight.

He chuckled. "Then why would you show up to a party wearing *this*?" He tugged at the fabric of my dress. I tried to speak again, but I couldn't conjure up enough energy to push the words out. He moved a rough finger against my lips and I moaned, feeling saliva pool at the back of my throat. He inched closer. Spittle gathered at the sides of his cracked lips as he said, "Stop playing hard to get."

His hand moved below my hips and settled on my bare leg, and suddenly it was all I could focus on. He tapped his fingers across my thigh and pressed himself against me, sandwiching my body between his thick frame and the cold wall. He started to run a hand through my hair, tangling it and jerking my head backward.

I struggled to remember how far I was from home, but

everything was a blur. The panic grew and pulsed against my skull until it throbbed. I tried to move my arms, but they were unresponsive, crushed beneath his weight as he walked his other hand up toward the hemline of my dress.

My eyes fluttered back in my head as he pushed his salty lips against my mouth. Fleetingly I thought of Nic: how he had tentatively pressed his lips to my mine like he was trying to savor every part of the moment; how excited butterflies had exploded inside me as his hands gently curled around my waist. But these were not his hands, or his lips. Coarse and dry, they mashed against my mouth, pulling it open beneath the force of a snake-like tongue until I collapsed into Robbie, falling farther into the maw that probed mine so relentlessly it began to hurt.

And then the sound of an engine punctured the horrifying silence, and tires screeched to a halt somewhere nearby. Robbie froze with his lips still on mine, and moved his hands back onto my waist. In my dazed state, I imagined we looked like two wooden puppets, propped against each other in the night.

I don't know how long I leaned against the statue of Robbie Stenson, but I rejoiced in the welcome rush of cool air when his body was ripped away from mine. He let out a strangled yelp as he sailed backward, taking the pressure with him so that my chest expanded again.

Someone was shouting. My body slumped against the wall and slid to the ground beneath legs I could no longer feel. Faraway gravel shifted, and a deep cry rang out. There was a resounding crack and an earsplitting wail that sounded like a dying cat. Shoes scraped against the ground. High-pitched sobs descended into desperate pleas. I tried to understand, but the words became garbled and indistinct as my body slid toward the ground and my head connected with the concrete.

"Get out of here before I rip your heart out."

Is he talking to me?

More shuffling.

Why is it so dark?

The sound of footsteps — farther and farther away.

Am I still alive?

Another set of footsteps, steadier and quieter than the last, moving toward me.

"Sophie? Can you hear me?"

Something gripped my shoulders. My whole body shook gently, but there was no strength left to open my eyes. I was dead to the whole world. Dead to everything, except his voice.

"Sophie? Come on." More gentle shaking. A finger pressed up against my neck. I could feel my pulse throb against it. There was a sigh — long and relieved. "Come on, Sophie. Wake up."

I struggled for the energy, but I was spent, like a deflated balloon. Silence followed, and I found myself trying to remember where I was and what was going on. Had I left the party? Did I fall down?

"Can you try opening your eyes?"

Why couldn't I place that voice? It was so familiar yet so far away. An arm slid around my shoulders and another underneath my knees, lifting me away from the cold ground. My head drooped onto something hard, and I could hear a steady heartbeat drumming against my ear.

I sailed through the air, and into a warm place. The muffled sound of a car door gave way to the comforting hum of an engine, and soon I was rocking back and forth against something soft. The minutes bled into one long stretch of darkness until I was soaring again, through a realm of a hundred distant voices, flashing lights, and groaning beeps.

A lone finger trailed along the side of my cheek.

A faraway voice invaded the moment just as I was piecing together where I was, and the thought fluttered away from me before I could pin it down.

"I located her mother. Don't you want to stay until she gets here?"

"I can't."

Footsteps clicked against the floor, getting softer, until I could hear nothing but the sound of my own breathing as it rattled through my chest. Feeling safe in the complete absence of everything, I fell into nothingness, where half-forgotten memories mingled with harrowing nightmares until I forgot what was real and what was imagined.

I woke to a ceiling entirely different from the one I was used to. It was big and tiled, with fluorescent lights that stung my eyes. The smell of disinfectant hung in the air, and the open curtains of a faraway window were a dull, unfamiliar green. I tried to wriggle my body, but it was constricted under the weight of overly tucked-in sheets. And yet, despite the warmth that clung to me, I felt a cold stiffness rippling through my left hand.

The bed was edged with bars and the walls beyond were a blinding shade of white. I flexed my fingers against the thick bandage just above them and noticed, with a pinch of horror, that there was an IV drip invading my hand.

"Mrs. Gracewell, she's awake."

My bed shook from the other side. I rolled my head and flinched against a sudden onslaught of pain in the base of my skull. The un-made-up face of my mother was the first thing I saw. Beside her was an exhausted-looking Millie, wearing an oversized hoodie and last night's lipstick, which was just a red stain now. She scooted her chair forward. "How do you feel?"

Trying my best not to completely freak out, I wiggled each of my limbs in turn and was relieved to find them unbroken. I checked my body for bandages and found none. Then I dragged my hands through my matted hair and all around my face to make sure there were no stitches.

"What happened?" I croaked. "This is the worst headache I've ever had."

"That's OK, sweetheart." My mother stroked my hand reassuringly. "That's to be expected."

Millie looked like she was about to burst into tears. Her foundation was streaked with tear tracks and there were dark smudges of mascara beneath her eyes. She dropped her head into her hands and pulled at her disheveled brown hair. "I'm so sorry, Soph."

My mother squeezed my hand until it stung. "It looks as though you were drugged at the party."

It took several seconds for the meaning of the words to connect in my fuzzed brain. Then my heart plummeted into my stomach. "Drugged?"

"We had no idea," Millie sniffled. "One minute you were fine and then the next you couldn't stand up. You kept forgetting where you were and you kept saying you wanted to go home."

I tried to find them but the memories would not come. "So you brought me here to get my stomach pumped?"

Millie frowned and traced shapes in the hospital blanket. "We thought you were just drunk. Someone said you had taken some shots of tequila or something. So we sent you home with Robbie Stenson."

My mother's features scrunched into a display of disapproval. "Though Millie now knows she should have called me," she said. "Whether you were drinking or not, I still should have been called to make sure you were OK."

"I'm so sorry, Mrs. Gracewell! If I thought for a second someone had slipped her something, I wouldn't have just sent her home like that . . ." Millie broke into sobs that shook her frame with every heave.

My mother rubbed her back in large, circular movements. "I know," she said, trying to comfort her.

"What happened?" I felt like I was trying to recall something on the tip of my tongue, but the more I struggled, the more I seemed to forget.

"Robbie hadn't been drinking and he said he knew the way." Millie was holding back, skirting around something; I could sense it.

My mother cut in, "I got a call to say a young man had brought you to the emergency room. When I arrived they ran some tests and discovered traces of Rohypnol in your system."

The word fell into the air like a ton of bricks. "R-Rohypnol?" I stuttered. "I was roofied?" Immediately my hands flew to my underwear.

"No, don't worry," Millie interjected hurriedly. "He got to you in time."

"Robbie?"

My mother exchanged a glance with Millie. "No, not Robbie. The nurse said a young man with tanned skin and dark hair brought you in. She says he wouldn't give his name."

My head throbbed so hard I could barely think. Where did Nic come into all of this? And why was he being so secretive about his involvement?

"I don't understand . . ."

"He told the nurse he found you with a boy who looked as though he was trying to take advantage of you. He raised his concerns and the boy left. Then he brought you here when he realized what bad shape you were in."

I felt my hand pinch beneath the drip. "Where is Nic now?"

"He was gone when we got here," Millie answered this time. "The nurse said he stayed for almost an hour, though, while they tried to reach your mom. He wanted to make sure you were OK."

My mother sat back in her chair and seemed to relax a little. "Millie and I tried to contact the Priestlys, but they're unlisted. It would be a good idea to have a talk with that boy when we get out of here."

"So where did Robbie Stenson go when Nic showed up? Was he the one trying to take advantage of me?"

Millie shrugged, her eyebrows knitting themselves together in confusion. "I guess Nic thought he was trying to kiss you. I thought Robbie might have a crush on you, but I didn't think he'd do something like that when you were so out of it. I mean, you'd vomited twice before you left my house."

I winced — I didn't remember that.

"Alex has been trying to call Robbie all morning to find out what happened," Millie continued. "Maybe Nic just freaked out when he saw the two of you together."

Memories of how Nic had reacted jealously to Alex at the basketball tournament tugged at my brain, but I was still washed out and confused. I couldn't remember meeting Robbie Stenson last night, though I had a vague recollection he had been at the party somewhere among the crowds.

"So who was it?" I asked, growing hot with anger. "Who put the Rohypnol in my drink?"

"We don't know, Soph. You were the only victim, as far as we can tell." Millie could barely look me in the eye. "Alex says it might have been a cousin of one of his friends. He was mixed up in something like that a couple of years ago. He wasn't even invited in the first place, and now we can't track him down." Millie's voice turned quiet. She rubbed her eyes, smudging her eye shadow until she looked like a panda. "It's all my fault, Soph. I'm sorry for letting the party get so out of hand."

"It's OK," I offered, hoping it would ease her guilt. "It could have been worse, right? I didn't come to any harm."

"Yes, thankfully," said my mother.

I clamped my eyes shut and concentrated. I was dancing. I was in the kitchen. I was with Millie. And then, nothing. "I'm trying to remember."

My mother rubbed my arm. "Sweetheart, the doctor says it's unlikely you'll regain your memory of last night. There is a possibility of flashbacks, but they probably won't have all the answers to what happened. We're determined to get to the bottom of it, though. The police will want to speak to you now that you're awake, and we'll talk to this Robbie boy when he surfaces, too, I promise."

"We'll figure it out," echoed Millie.

I glanced at the needle in my hand and felt a heightened awareness of the cold liquid entering my body, drip by drip. "When can I get out of here? Hospitals give me the creeps."

As if right on cue, a heavyset nurse with short ash-blond hair sashayed into the room. "How are you feeling?" she asked.

I had the vaguest feeling I had heard her voice before.

"Confused and headachy," I surmised.

Without looking up, she launched into what seemed like a perfectly rehearsed speech. "The Rohypnol is leaving your system and the worst of its effects have subsided. You're going to experience residual headaches and possible nausea for another day or two, but after that you should be back to normal. The doctor says you're ready for discharge when you feel strong enough."

"I'm strong enough."

The nurse pulled the corners of her plump lips into a frown. "In the future, I would caution you to keep your drink with you at all times and to have it covered when you're around people you don't know well."

I opened my mouth to argue, but stopped myself. I was furious, but not at her. I was angry at everything: at the person who'd drugged me, at the boy who'd tried to kiss me when I was so out of it, and at Nic for leaving me here with my mounting confusion.

First, he speeds away with his brother, ditching me in a deserted street, and then he turns up out of nowhere to rescue me, but leaves me with no clue about what happened. Even in his absence, he was still playing games with my head, and one way or another, it had to stop.

CHAPTER FIFTEEN

The Warning

I sat with my elbows on the table, watching my phone. It vibrated against the wood and made the peas on my plate quiver. The number on-screen was Jack's.

"He's not going to stop calling." My mother's words squeezed themselves out through a mouthful of dried pork chop.

"I'll deal with it tomorrow." I wanted to talk to my uncle, but it was late and I could barely keep my eyes open, save for the hunger. I swallowed the mountain of mashed potatoes in my mouth and scowled. "Why did you have to tell him so soon anyway?"

"I didn't tell him. I told Ursula because I don't want you going into work tomorrow, and when he called the diner, she told him about it." My mother shrugged and popped a forkful of peas in her mouth.

My phone started buzzing again, exacerbating the headache that still lingered at the base of my skull. I picked it up and swiped my finger across the screen. "Hi, Jack."

"I'm outside, let me in."

"What?"

"Open the back door."

He hung up. I crossed to the kitchen window. He was just a shadow lingering by the bushes, carefully out of range of the motion detector so I could barely make him out at all. Where did he come from?

"Is he here again?" My mother's voice was teeming with bewildered disapproval. She stood up. "What is he doing?"

I unlocked the door and he slid inside, shutting and locking it behind him.

"Sophie," he panted, his cheeks blotted with circles of pink.

"Where did you just come from?"

He waved my question away and crushed me into his shoulder so hard I thought I would lose my breath. I hadn't hugged Jack since I was a child. I was used to him showing his affection in other ways — expensive presents, a shift off at the last minute, or random phone calls. But there was something about the hug that made it better than all that — I felt protected. "I'm so glad you're safe," he huffed into my hair.

He released me and I stumbled backward, my hand clutching my chest. I was getting a tight feeling in the base of my throat. I swallowed it, hoping it would go away, but the way Jack was looking at me with my father's eyes, so full of worry and relief, made me want to cry.

"If I had let anything happen to you, Mickey would have broken out of prison just to kill me," he said, trying and failing to lighten the mood.

"What are you doing here?" I mushed the words together to distract myself from the lump rising in my throat. Behind me, my mother was hovering. I could almost feel the suspicion seeping through her skin.

Jack rubbed the buzzed hair on his head. He was unusually disheveled, his typical suave suit replaced by loose-fitting jeans and a nondescript black sweatshirt. He didn't look half as important, or affluent, as he usually did. "I've been calling you all day, Persephone."

I grimaced. He must have meant business. "I was in the hospital."

"I heard. I was going out of my mind with worry."

"You and me both," said my mother. She drifted over to the sink and started to fill the kettle for tea.

"How are you feeling?"

"Where have you been?" I asked at the same time.

Jack rubbed his eyes. "All around the state," he replied wearily.

"Doing what?"

"Business things."

He was being curt. He never talked to me about his other business ventures. I knew it had something to do with investments and interest rates, which was why I never bothered to press him about it. The boredom would have overwhelmed me.

"Are you back now? In Cedar Hill?" I was surprised at how childlike the hopefulness in my voice sounded, and felt embarrassed because of it. I had obviously missed him more than I'd realized. He was the only real male presence in my life, and without him, it felt emptier than it should have been.

He shook his head grimly. "Not yet. Not completely."

My mother had been busying herself at the stove. She passed a mug of peppermint tea to Jack. He took it with an arched eyebrow for good measure.

"Thank you, Celine."

"Before you ask, there's no booze in it."

I winced. It had been going so well. He took a sip without breaking eye contact with her, leveling whatever his response would have been for my benefit.

"Couldn't this visit have waited until a more reasonable hour, Jack?" My mother's voice was edged with disapproval. "Do you always have to do things in the dead of night?"

He ignored her this time, setting his mug down on the table. "What happened last night was really serious," he said to me. "And on your birthday, no less!"

"I know," I said, biting my lip to stop it from wobbling.

"Do they know who spiked your drink?"

"No," I responded, feeling tired of the same question already. The police had already interviewed me at the hospital, and that hadn't exactly been helpful. It's not like there were any leads, and I was pretty convinced I would never regain full memory of the night. I knew, too, that Robbie Stenson, whenever he resurfaced, was going to avoid me forever. He had finally texted Alex back to say he was out of town for "family reasons," and that he didn't realize how out of it I had been. He actually thought I *liked* him and *wanted* to kiss him, and he was sorry my "boyfriend" got so angry about it and interrupted us. If he was so apologetic, he could have texted *me*, but he didn't even bother. And the only other person who had any knowledge of the forgotten parts of my night was my "angry boyfriend," Nic, who was already doing a trophy-worthy job of avoiding me.

"Was it someone at the party who spiked it?" My uncle Jack continued his pointless interrogation.

I gave him the same answer I gave the police. "Yeah, but there were so many people there, it could have been anyone."

Jack nodded thoughtfully. "Was there anyone you didn't recognize? What about that new family on Lockwood Avenue?"

"No," I replied resolutely. "In fact, if it wasn't for that family, I might have ended up in way worse condition."

"What?" he snapped, the softness in his voice disappearing.

"One of them found me on my way home and brought me to the hospital." I left out the part about Robbie Stenson; I didn't want my uncle thinking about me kissing a boy. Besides, I could barely think about it myself without feeling my skin crawl.

Jack set his mouth in a hard line, squaring his jaw. "How do you know he wasn't the one who drugged you in the first place?"

"What are you talking about?" I didn't bother to keep the mounting irritation from my voice. I would not let Jack taint this good deed with his preconceived notions of Nic's family. "He didn't drug me. He wasn't even at the party!"

"I don't know," Jack grumbled. He looked to my mother, but she was staring past him, evidently fed up with his visit. She had done her best; she had lasted four minutes.

I released a sigh that turned into a yawn. "Even if he *did* drug me by *magical intervention*, then why would he bring me to the hospital and get them to call Mom?"

"I'm sure there are ways he could —"

"Please," I labored. "Just stop. You're being paranoid."

"It's exhausting," added my mother, her voice clipped. She folded her arms across her chest and moved closer to me.

I covered my mouth, stifling another yawn.

"OK," Jack conceded. "I'm just worried, Sophie. Can you understand that? I want to make sure you weren't targeted."

I may have been tired, but I wasn't too exhausted to register the oddness in my uncle's statement. "Why would someone target me?"

My mother bristled beside me. Her tolerance for Jack's paranoid mutterings had run out a long time ago. After all, it was this habit that had led my father into the mess that had gotten him thrown in prison. "What are you talking about?"

"I don't know," he said, more to himself than to us. He dragged his hands across his face and through his hair. I surveyed him: his bloodshot eyes, his week-old stubble, his blotchy skin. Even his lips were pale.

"Sophie's OK, Jack," my mother said, biting back whatever else she might have wanted to add. It was clear he was troubled about what had happened to me, and there was no point antagonizing him for it. "I think you need to get some rest. We all do."

"OK," he relented to my mother. "I'll go."

He smiled at me then; it was a sweet, hopeful sort of smile with just a shadow of something darker.

"When are you coming back?" I sounded like a child again, but I couldn't help it. I wanted my uncle close by. He was the unpredictable, wilder half of my calm, measured father, and right now he was doing his best to be both of them for me. He might not have been succeeding very well, but we were still bonded, he and I. And even though my mother would never dare admit it, without my father, we all needed each other.

He ruffled my hair. "Soon," he said gruffly. "I'll call you."

He paused with his hand on the door. "And remember what I said. Keep to yourself."

"I will." I lied easily this time. Jack's paranoia had only made me more determined to find out exactly what was going on around me. And I suspected some of those answers were in the Priestly house.

CHAPTER SIXTEEN

The Misunderstanding

After two days, I had almost fully recovered and was ready to begin my investigation.

I wasn't surprised that Nic hadn't tried to contact me after I was discharged from hospital, because nothing Nic did or didn't do surprised me anymore.

I walked to his house in the early afternoon. Pausing outside the wrought iron gates, I surveyed the mansion with a growing sense of foreboding. There was only one car in the driveway, and suddenly I felt horrified at the thought of coming face-to-face with any of Nic's other family members. After all, I was still a Gracewell — whatever terrible thing that meant to them — and there was nothing I could do to change that.

Steeling myself, I marched through the open gates and crunched along the gravel driveway. When I reached the red front door, I rapped on the knocker and edged back into the driveway, waiting nervously.

After what seemed like an eternity, the door was unbolted in three metallic thumps, and heaved open to reveal a statuesque figure, darkened by the shadowed hallway behind him. But I knew that outline almost as well as I knew his voice.

"Sophie?" Nic hovered in the doorway, immaculate in faded jeans and a white T-shirt. His feet were bare.

"Hi," I ventured, watching him clench and unclench his jaw. "I want to talk to you."

Anchoring his hands on either side of the door frame, he leaned out at an angle and searched the emptiness behind me. "Sophie," he said again, but softer this time. "What are you doing here?"

By the way his eyes searched mine, I knew there was still something between us. The air around us pulsed, and I decided to cut to the chase before it consumed me. "You don't have to play dumb about the other night."

His expression turned, his eyes growing. He stepped forward, slowly, then stopped, wavering, like he was fighting the urge to come to me. "What are you talking about?"

"The nurse told my mother about you. I know you asked her not to, but she did, so you don't have to lie about it."

He wasn't stalling anymore. He came toward me, bare feet on the gravel. He dropped his voice to a whisper and placed his hands on my arms, gently pulling them — and me — into him. I watched his hands on my skin and my lips twisted in confusion.

"Sophie." His eyes locked on mine. "I have absolutely no idea what you're talking about."

"What? You didn't bring me to the hospital the other night?"

At the mention of the word "hospital," confusion burned up

into anxiety. "Why were you in the hospital?" He scanned me up and down. "Did someone hurt you?"

"You really didn't rescue me?" I asked, suddenly feeling embarrassed.

"*Rescue* you?" he said, horrified.

"But the nurse told my mother . . ."

"Sophie." He moved his hands to my waist as his voice grew harder. "Please tell me what happened to you."

For a second, I could see the Nic I'd first met, standing in front of me. He was right there, within reach, until another figure appeared in the doorway behind him.

"Nicoli?" That was all Luca had to say to make his brother leap away from me like I was on fire.

"What is it?" I demanded. "What's wrong?"

"I can't," he half-pleaded, backing up. "I just can't."

"I don't understand." I shifted my gaze to Luca, who was leaning against the front of the house, folding his arms across his chest.

He looked through me. "You should go back inside, Nicoli. Valentino's looking for you." The last part sounded like a veiled threat, but I couldn't tell why.

Nic hesitated, his fists clenched tight. "Luca, I'm not leaving until I make sure she's OK." He was angry, and I was reassured by that, but not reassured enough. "Something happened to her. She was in the hospital, and I need to know why.'"

"I know," Luca said, striding carelessly toward his brother so they could face each other straight on.

Luca was taller than Nic, but Nic was broader. I wondered

who would win in a fight. And then I wondered how Luca knew I'd been in the hospital.

"How?" Nic and I asked him at the same time.

"Because I brought her in."

"You what?" I spluttered.

"Are you kidding me, Luca? Why the hell didn't you tell me?" For a second I thought Nic was going to lunge at Luca; take him down, and do us all a favor. But he didn't. He just stood there, seething. I watched his chest rise and fall.

Luca grabbed the back of Nic's neck, bringing him closer so he could mutter something in his ear, and when he pulled away, some of his brother's defiance had shifted.

"You'd better handle it," Nic snapped before turning back toward the house. "Because I can't be expected to stand by and do nothing . . ." His sentence died alongside his sudden retreat.

"Um, bye, Nic!" I called sarcastically to his departing figure, scolding myself for letting his desertion hurt me again.

"What a family of *oddballs*," I muttered, making sure it was loud enough for Luca to hear.

His eyebrows disappeared under messy strands of his raven hair. "Is that what you came here for? To call me names like a child?"

I crossed my arms. "I thought I was coming here to see Nic."

He pursed his lips. "Sorry to disappoint you."

"You're not sorry."

"You're right, I'm not."

I fought the urge to stamp my feet.

"So did you launch yourself on an express mission to thank him and only him? Or do I, the actual person who helped you, merit some kind of gratitude?"

I bit back several curse words. "This can't be happening."

"Well, it is." Suddenly Luca was pulling me by the arm until we were standing on the other side of the SUV, sheltered from the street's view and most of the house's windows.

"Get off me!" I snapped, shrugging him off. "What's your problem?"

"What's *my* problem? Are you kidding?"

I stepped back, pressing myself against the SUV, and suddenly a memory flashed against my brain. *I was being mashed up against a stone wall.* I shook my head and it flew away. "Why do you have to be such an ass?"

Luca lessened the gap between us by another half foot. "Why did you drink yourself into that state the other night?" he countered viciously. "Have you no regard for your own safety?"

"How dare you?" I snapped. "You have no idea what you're talking about, so just shut up!"

"I was the one scraping you off the sidewalk!"

"For your information, I wasn't drinking!"

Luca curled his lip, and anger, like a shot of hot metal, rose in my bloodstream. Before I could stop myself, my hands were against his chest, shoving him so hard that he stumbled backward. I landed against him, pushing him farther and farther. "I was roofied, you ass!"

For a moment, we stood against each other, bound by the force of my anger and the sound of our mingled heavy breathing. Then, with exaggerated slowness, he grabbed me by my shoulders and pushed me away from him with ease.

I tried to focus on my breathing, to steady myself, but I was panting hard.

"I see," he said at last. "I didn't know."

I shrugged, feeling deflated. "I guess I should have been more careful."

He scrunched his nose in disgust. "And he should have been a lot more respectful, regardless of what state you were in."

I felt a lump form at the bottom of my throat, but I had been keeping it at bay for the last two days and I wasn't about to give in to my tears now, especially not in front of Luca. "I don't remember anything," I said, setting my jaw and looking at the patch of grass behind him. "I'm still struggling to."

"Don't." Luca stuffed his hands into the pockets of his jeans. "Some memories hurt when they hit you."

"Are you saying it will hurt me to know what Robbie did?"

He shook his head. "He didn't hurt you, OK? He was just some idiotic drunk guy trying his luck with a pretty girl."

My eyes widened at the inadvertent compliment.

"I was just making a point about that guy," Luca went on quickly. "He was dumb, OK? He shouldn't have tried to take advantage of you."

"Wh-Where was it? Where were we?" I hadn't imagined talking about the night would be this difficult — and I definitely never thought I'd be talking about it with the obnoxious Luca Priestly — but I had to know.

"A couple of blocks away. I saw him with you sometime

before . . ." He stopped abruptly and changed the direction of the sentence. "I didn't like the look of him, so I drove around to make sure he wasn't doing anything he shouldn't be doing. And when I found you guys, I could see you were pretty out of it, so I decided to intervene."

"What happened to him?"

"You don't remember?"

"No."

"I just asked him to leave, and he did," Luca said simply. "He was very obliging."

"So he just walked away in the middle of the night and left me with you, a person he barely knows?"

I studied Luca carefully, waiting for him to elaborate. The sun was making his blue eyes shine, so that he seemed almost friendly, but there was nothing friendly about the edge in his voice when he answered me. "When I ask someone to do something, I usually don't have to ask twice."

"That almost sounds like a threat."

Luca just rolled his eyes and shrugged. "Do you know who roofied you?"

"No."

"I'd be interested to know, if that information comes to light."

"Why?" I asked, feeling a bout of uneasiness.

"You're asking why I want to know the identity of someone who thinks it's acceptable to poison girls' drinks at neighborhood parties?" His reply conveyed the *duh* sentiment.

"I don't see what difference it would make to you," I told him plainly.

"No," he said. "You wouldn't."

I could sense the hostility again, the chill I had gotten the night he ordered Nic away from me, and I couldn't stand it. He was so infuriating. "What have you said to turn your brother against me?"

He shook his head. "I'm not getting into this."

"I deserve an explanation."

"You should leave now. I think I've done enough for you, Gracewell," he returned evenly. "I'm not interested in helping you walk off into the sunset with my brother."

Gracewell? So I wasn't even worthy of my first name now. "What have I done to make you hate me so much?"

He rolled his eyes again. "I don't hate you. I *nothing* you."

His retort stung more than I thought it would. "You're horrible, do you know that?"

He didn't even flinch.

"And arrogant," I muttered. "And smug."

"Are you done now?" In an instant he had pinned me between his arms against the SUV. "Let's get one thing straight, OK?" There was a savagery in his eyes. "This is the last time I want to see you anywhere near this house, got it? When you walk home from work, cross the road. Don't look inside. Don't come in this direction. Don't even *breathe* in this direction. I told you I don't ask twice. If I see you around Nic again, even if you're just saying hi or trailing after him like a lost puppy, then I'll come for you, that chatterbox British best friend of yours, and your mother, and believe me, you're not going to like it. Do you understand me?"

I felt the horror infiltrate my features. Now I saw it. I finally saw the danger that Jack and Mrs. Bailey had been warning me about. Not to mention the kind of attitude that must have put blood on Luca's shirt before. Maybe my paranoid uncle and the old busybody had been right about this family all along — certainly about Luca, at least. I wanted to say something defiant and witty, but he was looking at me like he was going to eat me, so instead I nodded like a zombie.

"From here on out, we go our separate ways. *Capisce?*"

My voice shook with anger and fear. "You can't talk to people like that."

He moved his hands away from the car and stepped back from me again. "Do you understand everything I just said, Gracewell?"

I wrapped my arms around myself and nodded.

"So we are clear?"

"Crystal."

"Do I frighten you?" He tilted his head.

"Yes," I said weakly. "Are you proud of yourself?"

He looked at me for a long moment before replying. "No, I'm not," he said, so faintly I had to strain to hear him. Then he turned from me and made his way back to the house.

"Wait!" I called as the rational part of me screamed in protest.

Luca turned around slowly.

"You make a point of keeping your brother away from me and then you bring me to the hospital to make sure I'm OK. And you don't tell the nurse who you are in case I would think you are a *semi-decent* guy. I don't get it."

"You don't have to get it. You just have to deal with it."

"Why did you bother *scraping me off the sidewalk*, then? Why do you even care if I was roofied or not?" The question hurtled across the space between us. He blinked twice and his mouth dropped open into an O. For a second, he looked young and innocent, like his twin.

"Are you kidding?" He was dumbfounded. "I'm not a monster."

"You could have fooled me."

He pinched the bridge of his nose and inhaled like he was about to say something. But then he didn't. Instead, he just shook his head. "You should go, Gracewell."

"I have a name, you know!"

He laughed, looking up at the sky, like the maniac he clearly was.

"It's Sophie. S-O-P-H-I-E."

He continued to laugh, but when he returned his attention to me, his voice was utterly flat. "Are you sure about that?"

I blanched. "What do you mean?"

"You know what I mean."

Before I could process the uneasiness grumbling inside me, he spoke again. This time his voice was disturbingly quiet. "Don't you get it? You're a *Gracewell*. That's all you'll ever be to us."

"What does it matter to *you* if I'm a Gracewell?" I demanded.

For an interminably long moment, he regarded me pensively. When he finally relented, it was with a determined exhale, like some internal decision had finally been made. He crossed the driveway and reached me in four strides.

"You really have no idea why you're not welcome here?" he hissed. "Are you seriously that ignorant?"

I swallowed against the sudden dryness in my throat. "What are you talking about?"

Luca frowned. I didn't understand his question and he didn't understand my response.

"*Cazzo.*" He studied me with an almost violent confusion — it pinched the hollows in his cheeks, making them gaunt. "I'm not dealing with this."

"I want answers!" I protested.

"You won't get them here."

"Then where?" I said half-pleadingly, exasperation sinking into my voice.

Luca ground his jaw in slow clicks, whatever shred of patience he had for our conversation rapidly diminishing. "Go ask your father, Gracewell. You probably owe him a visit."

A familiar feeling of dread crept up my spine. *My father.* Everything always came back to my father. Of course it had something to do with him — I would never outrun what he'd done. I would never live it down. But there was something more to Luca's words, something deeper, and it was twisting my stomach. What had my father done to the Priestlys? Before he was arrested he never put a foot out of line. As far as I knew, at least.

Luca wasn't about to wait until I figured it out. He turned away from me once again, storming into the house, and slamming the front door with a deafening bang.

Feeling my cheeks prickle and burn, I looked up and caught sight of Valentino where I had seen him that first night. He was utterly still, his elbows perched along the windowsill as he looked down on me — on everything that had just happened. His face was solemn. Did he hate me, too? Did he think it right for his twin to act like that?

He raised his hand and held it up, like a salute. I waved back, my arm feeling as heavy as my heart, and he smiled at me. It was a small moment of kindness — a soft tug at the lips, nothing more.

Then he was gone. And I was left bound up in the realization that if I really wanted answers, I would have to seek them from somewhere I had been avoiding.

CHAPTER SEVENTEEN

The Memory

The following day I called in sick to work and took a bus to visit my father at the Stateville Correctional Center in Crest Hill. I didn't tell my mother — she had been stressed out ever since the incident at Millie's party, and I figured my father's incarceration was the last thing I should bring up. Besides, I was going there for answers to a problem she seemed to have no knowledge of and, if it was as bad as I was anticipating, I wanted to keep it that way.

The correctional center encompassed several concrete cell blocks and one roundhouse building fenced in by a perimeter with ten walled watchtowers. Beyond the walls, over two thousand acres of barren landscape surrounded the prison, keeping it far removed from anything that might have once resembled normal life for its nearly four thousand inmates, one of whom was my father.

It was the sixth time I had seen him since he had gone to prison almost eighteen months ago, and each time was harder than the one before. I tried not to dwell on the fact that I still had four more years of these visits ahead of me.

After presenting my identification and passing through the security check, I met my father in the visiting room. Around us, other prisoners sat on metal stools at white tables with their families; kids as young as one and two mingled with heavyset grannies and Gothic teenagers. Prison guards lingered by the walls, eyes narrowed in pursuit of a forbidden embrace or any other illicit exchange, above or below the tables.

My father was paler than I expected and there were new dark creases under his eyes. I knew it could have been a lot worse. Since my father wasn't gang-affiliated, he was technically, in prison parlance, a "neutron," which meant the violent inmates mostly left him alone. He could not, however, avoid the effects of meager food and limited physical exercise. He was losing weight and losing sleep.

"How are you?" I began to chew on my pinkie nail — a nervous habit that usually returned in his company.

My father shook out his scruffy gray hair so it fell across his forehead and hid the faint bruises above his eye — they only *mostly* left him alone. "Getting by, Soph." He tried to smile, but it was crooked and yellowed. "It's so good to see you."

It took everything in me not to crumple in my cold metal seat. How did my father end up in this place? He was a shadow of the man who had raised me on sweeping fairy tales, swashbuckling adventure movies, and faraway hiking trips. The worst things he ever did were yell at me when he lost his temper, forget to wash the dishes, or stay out too late with Uncle Jack every once in a while. He didn't belong in here with murderers. Even if he had killed a man.

"Dad, you don't look so good."

"We don't get lots of fruits and vegetables in here," he teased, but the joviality didn't reach his eyes. He leaned forward and took my hand in his; I could feel his rough, calloused skin against mine. "Happy belated birthday, Soph."

"No contact across the tables!" shouted a nearby prison guard. I resisted the urge to slam my head against the table as we pulled our hands apart. I kept my gaze on my fingernails instead. "Thanks, Dad."

"So how is everything at home?" His eyes lit up with interest, brightening his face and pulling my attention away from the new lines that had formed around his mouth.

"Boring, as usual," I lied, purposefully omitting the part about me being drugged at Millie's house party. I knew he would hear it from Jack or my mother soon, but it wasn't going to be from me.

"I started a new book yesterday . . ." he began.

I listened as he told me all about the books he had been reading. When he finished, I traded some of my own safe topics, including how my mother had gained some new clients in Lincoln Park and Millie's recently formed harebrained intention to go Greek-island-hopping after high school. We spoke about Mrs. Bailey's weekly visits and touched briefly on my fast-approaching senior year. My father smiled and contributed at all the right times until the conversation drew to a natural close. As much as I wanted to pursue less threatening topics, I knew I had to prioritize my true intentions, because the visit would soon come to an end. As it was, I hadn't even scratched the surface of the real reason I had come to see him.

"Dad," I interjected before he could launch into another ambling conversation. "I have a question."

He perked up in his chair and regarded me seriously. I loved that about him — he had always treated me like an adult worthy of respect, even when I was a small child. I knew that meant he would answer me as best he could. "What is it, Soph?"

I decided to dive straight in. "Remember I told you how a new family moved into the old Priestly place? There are five of them and they're all boys."

His eyelids fluttered, but he kept his mouth closed in a hard line, waiting for me to finish.

"Well, I think you might know them."

"Have you spoken to this family?" he asked, rubbing the stubble on his chin. "Have they approached you?"

"Yes," I said. "I've spoken to them."

My father buried his face in his hands and released a heavy sigh. "Jesus," he said, half-muffled. "Jesus Christ."

That horrible sinking feeling came over me again, pricking at my eyes and sticking in my throat. "Dad?"

"Sophie," he said, but this time it was weary, and heavy with disappointment. He uncovered his face, letting his hands fall to the table with a heavy *thunk*. "I thought Uncle Jack told you to stay away from them?"

"How do you know that?"

"Because he came to see me when he found out they had moved in. And we decided — "

"Hold on," I cut in. "What do the Priestlys have to do with our family?"

My father double-blinked, his mouth twisting to a frown. "The Priestlys? Who are the Priestlys?"

"The — " I stopped abruptly. My whole brain shifted. *Think.* Who *were* the Priestlys? We had all just assumed the connection between Nic's family and the old house. After all, it had never been put up for sale, which meant it was inherited or passed down, surely. Even my mother hadn't questioned it. But now . . .

"Sophie," my father said, his voice so quiet I had to lean toward him. "I don't know where you got that idea from, but they are definitely not Priestlys. They're Falcones."

He might as well have punched me square in the face.

I slumped backward in my chair. How could I have been so stupid? So ignorant? Luca was right. I was wrong. I had been wrong all along. They had never identified themselves as Priestlys — I had plucked the name from an old neighborhood legend and never thought to check whether it was true. The realization came upon me in a succession of lightning bolts. The Mediterranean complexion, the Italian dialogue, the Falcon crest. Nic's face. *Those damn eyes.* The sudden *hatred.*

"Falcone," I repeated, *Fal-cone-eh,* my voice sounding very far away as I tripped over the word that had just changed everything.

"Yes." There was a heavy pause, and then, delicately, my father asked, "Do you remember who Angelo Falcone was?"

It was a painfully unnecessary question. The name was seared in my brain forever.

"Of course I remember." I rested my head on the cold metal table. I had looked at Angelo Falcone's picture fifty times, and yet it hadn't clicked. I had studied Valentino's portrait of him and hadn't even made the connection between his face and the man in all the newspapers when it happened. The man with Nic's eyes. *Oh God.*

I lifted my head. "He's the man you killed."

"That's right." My father had placed his hands in his lap so I could no longer see them, but I knew he was fidgeting. If I concentrated hard enough, I could see the vein in his temple pulse up and down against his skin. He started to grind his teeth — it was a habit he had picked up in prison. For a long moment, neither one of us said anything, but every time his molars rolled against each other, I winced.

I would never forget that name or that day for as long as I lived. But we had never talked about it, not properly. Maybe it was time.

"It happened on Valentine's Day," I said, breaking the silence. I had gotten a card from Will Ackerman that day at school. He had slipped it into my locker during recess, with his phone number scrawled on the back. It had a teddy bear holding a big heart on the front, and on the inside, a short poem about how he liked my hair. It wasn't the most impressive literary offering, but I could have died and gone to heaven right then. He had been my crush since forever, and all my friends were burning up with jealousy.

"Yes," he said. "It was Valentine's Day."

"There was a storm," I continued, my thoughts lost in another time and place. "I had a headache so I took some aspirin and went to bed early. I was just falling asleep when Mom burst into my room. She was crying, and I couldn't understand what she was trying to tell me . . ." I trailed off. I could see it was hard for him to hear it. It was harder for me to say it, but I was going to, because someone had lost his life that night, and I was only beginning to understand the true gravity of it. Nic's father was dead. And all I had ever fixated on was how my father had been thrown behind bars because of a mistake he made when he was in the grip of fear during a dark, stormy night at the diner. "Mom said you had been closing the diner on your own when a man ran out of the shadows and started yelling things. You thought he was going to try and rob the place, so you took out the gun Jack gave you for Christmas and you shot him."

"And he died," he finished.

"Yes," I echoed. "He died."

"And it turned out he wasn't armed."

God. "Right."

"And the gun I used didn't have a permit."

It gets worse. "Oh."

"I shouldn't have been carrying it," he said, frustration spilling from his voice. "But it was late and I was nervous. Your uncle had warned me about the gangs around Cedar Hill at that time and I thought I needed the extra protection. I thought that man was going to attack me."

"So you shot him." My expression was unreadable. Inside, I was ice-cold. "And now you're doing time for manslaughter while Angelo Falcone's sons — "

"Are living in Cedar Hill beside my daughter," he finished, biting down on his lip before a curse word slipped out.

I was clenching my fists so hard my nails were digging into

my palms. "And you didn't think to *share* this *massive* piece of information with me?"

"Jack and I didn't want you or your mother panicking about it."

I almost laughed at the absurdity of it. "So you thought it would be better if one of Angelo Falcone's *sons* filled in the blanks?"

"I thought Jack would make sure you stayed away from them!" he countered, his mounting anger beginning to match mine. If we kept this up, I'd be asked to leave by one of the prison guards.

"You should have told me," I said, lowering my voice. "I wouldn't have freaked out. I could have handled it." *Probably. Maybe. Eventually.*

"OK, what if you weren't afraid, then?" he countered. "There was always the chance you might approach them, to try to apologize or make amends for what I did. I know you, Soph. You've got a good heart. It's not foolish to expect something like that from you."

"That's crazy, Dad!" Maybe it wasn't, but I was so riled up I wasn't going to consider the chance he might be right. "And what about them staying away from me?" I hissed. "They came into the diner right after they moved in! A less cryptic heads-up would have been nice. I thought Jack was just being weird!"

My father shook his head and sighed, his expression defeated. "Maybe we should have gone about it differently," he conceded.

"Yes," I said. "You definitely should have."

He watched me quietly for a moment. His eyes grew big and round until they dominated his weathered face; there was barely any blue left in them now, just stormy gray. "Sophie, now that you know the truth, please stay away from the Falcones, like Jack told you. There's no knowing how deep their resentment toward me runs, or why they're back in Cedar Hill again."

"OK" was all I could muster. I was too spent to argue any more. And besides, it's not like the Falcones were clamoring to hang out with me anyway.

"They're a dangerous family in their own right," he continued, his breath hitching.

"What's that supposed to mean?" I vaguely remembered something from the time it happened — Angelo Falcone wasn't exactly a stand-up citizen, but I could do with a refresher course on the details, considering I had deliberately avoided reading anything in-depth about my father's victim.

"It means I don't like any of this," he said, and now there was panic pouring from his expression. Panic I could tell he had been trying to hide from me. "I don't like that they're near my daughter and there's nothing I can do about it."

You've already done enough, a part of me wanted to say, but I couldn't be cruel. "They're just boys," I said. "They're the same age as me."

"Five minutes!" shouted a stocky prison guard standing three tables over.

My father started wringing his hands. "Will you stay away from them? Please be careful. I'll speak to Jack about this."

"They're just boys," I repeated.

He closed his eyes and made an attempt to calm himself. "This is what prison does to you." When he opened them again, his face was still creased with worry.

I nodded, feigning understanding. "Do you think they're back for something?"

"I don't know," he said quietly. "I honestly don't know."

Out of nowhere, the memory of the black-ribboned honeypot dropped into my mind. I shook it away.

CHAPTER EIGHTEEN

The Angel-maker

When I got home, I told my mother I was going to bed with a headache. Fighting the urge to ignore everything and force myself to sleep, I pulled out my father's old laptop and typed "Angelo Falcone, Chicago" into Google. I found an article from the *Chicago Sun-Times* dating from two Februarys ago, and clicked on it, and suddenly I was drowning in a sea of nausea and incredulity.

A "WHO'S WHO" OF AMERICA'S INFAMOUS FAMILIES ATTEND FUNERAL OF MOB BOSS ANGELO "THE ANGEL-MAKER" FALCONE

The funeral of notorious mob boss Don Angelo Falcone took place on Tuesday, February 18, at Holy Name Cathedral, Chicago. Falcone, who was dubbed "The Angel-maker" due to his alleged position as a prolific Mafia career assassin, was gunned down at 11:00 p.m. on February 14.

Falcone was outside Gracewell's, a local diner in the Cedar Hill suburb of Chicago, when he became involved in an altercation with the owner of the establishment. Falcone, who was unarmed, was shot twice in the chest. He died instantly. Michael Gracewell, proprietor of the diner, remains in custody and is awaiting trial. Despite Falcone's position as a Mafia don, police do not suspect underworld involvement in his death.

Angelo Falcone has been well known to police since his ascendancy to the head of the Falcone crime family in the mid-1990s. Despite his arrest on several occasions, he proved questionably fortuitous in avoiding prison when key witnesses either disappeared or retracted their statements before trial. He is believed to be responsible for the recent brutal murders of two pivotal members of the Golden Triangle Gang, an infamous drug cartel based in the Midwest, among others.

Plainclothes police officers and members of the FBI were among the crowds outside Holy Name Cathedral on Tuesday. While trouble was not expected due to a tradition of respect shared by Mafia families during funerals, law enforcement officials attended to ascertain who might succeed Angelo Falcone as head of the Falcone Mafia dynasty. The identity of the underboss was unknown at the time of Falcone's death.

Police believe that Angelo's younger brother, Felice Falcone, may now succeed him. In a move that seemed to support this assertion, Felice Falcone (pictured above) briefly spoke to reporters while other mourners remained tight-lipped after the service.

The suspected current boss of the Falcone Mafia family said about the deceased: "Angelo was a true soldier of God. There is no doubt in our minds that he will be rewarded in heaven for his good work here on earth. He goes to Our Savior with honor and dignity, a clear soul, and a noble heart. We will miss him dearly, but he will never be forgotten."

"The Angel-maker" was laid to rest in a black marble coffin in the family mausoleum in Graceland Cemetery.

He is survived by his wife — daughter of the rival Genovese mob clan — Elena Genovese-Falcone and their five sons, Valentino, Gianluca, Giorgino, Dominico, and Nicoli (pictured below).

I stared, unblinking, at the final image. In the foreground was Nic: a slightly younger, glassy-eyed Nic, wearing a black suit. His hair was shorter than it was now, absent of the stray, curling strands that fell across his forehead. He was less filled out, making his cheeks seem almost gaunt, and his mouth was pressed into a hard line. He was balancing the front of his father's coffin on his left shoulder.

Luca was supporting the other side of the coffin, the same concentrated expression on his face, his eyes a haunting blue. Gino and Dom stood behind them on either side, their faces crumpled with grief. At the back, I recognized the tall, bald man from the restaurant and the unmistakable Felice, who wore a dark gray scarf and an equally grim expression. Valentino was at the bottom of the cathedral steps, his expression blank, his eyes empty. His mother — the tall, dark-haired woman from his portrait — stood beside him, a netted black veil covering most of her face. Her hand was clenched firmly on Valentino's slumped shoulder as he watched his brothers carry their father away.

I clasped my hand over my mouth to try to keep from vomiting. There was so much to take in, but it was coming at me all at once, like bullets of reality. My father had killed the man in that coffin; he had widowed that weeping woman; and he had taken Nic's father away from him forever.

But Nic's father was a killer — a notorious mob boss, the

angel-maker — whose legacy hung over his family like a black cloud. And now Felice was in charge, whatever being "in charge" even meant, and suddenly he didn't seem harmless or quirky, but terrifying.

My thoughts began to spiral and before I knew what was happening I was sprinting to the bathroom. I stayed there for a long time — curled around the toilet, gasping as every heave shook me violently, as if trying to remind me that my understanding of life in Cedar Hill had changed forever.

CHAPTER NINETEEN

The Ugly Truth

I stood on the sidewalk, trying to pull my feet away from the mush that rolled over them. I was sinking. A falcon dropped from the sky, circling at close range. It pecked at my eyes until blood began to pour from my pupils, blinding me.

Ping! I blinked hard, and in the sudden darkness I saw my father, crumpled in a heap, his head cradled in his hands. I called out to him, but he was fading from me, and the harder I tried, the more my lungs burned.

Ping! I woke up, sweating and gasping for air. Behind my curtains, something was bouncing off the window. I grabbed my phone from the nightstand and lit up the screen. It was 1:48 a.m.

Ping! I slipped out of bed and crept up to the window. A tall, dark figure bent low to the ground and picked something out of the untended grass. He lifted an arm into the air, taking aim at the spot where my head was. He paused when he saw I was standing where the darkened curtains had been just seconds before, then dropped the pebble from his hand.

I opened the window and a rush of warm summer air hit my face.

"Sophie?" He came closer, setting off the light sensor above the kitchen window.

"Nic?" I closed my eyes and flinched, remembering everything at once. The memory of the funeral photo flashed inside my head, along with the word "Mafia." Nic's father had killed people, and my father had killed him.

I wondered what good would come of me going to Nic, looking him in his dark eyes, and seeing the hurt behind them. Hurt he must truly hate me for.

"Sophie," he said again. "I need to talk to you."

I swallowed hard, hoping my voice wouldn't crack. "OK — I'll come down."

I flicked on the bedroom light and unearthed a pink cardigan from the floor, wrapping it around me before skirting downstairs. When I reached the backyard, Nic was standing at the back of the garden in the dark, waiting for me.

The light flickered back on as I walked toward him. His expression was inscrutable, his gaze fixed on me.

"Hi," I said, reaching him. I cradled myself, waiting, as the darkness enveloped us.

"You're probably wondering what I'm doing here," he said.

"Among other things." I didn't look at him directly. There was too much guilt inside me and if I looked him in the eyes, I knew it would explode right out of me.

"I had to make sure you were OK. Luca told me what happened . . ." He trailed off, then cursed under his breath. "And I didn't want to leave things like this, not the way my brother made them. He was wrong to say that stuff to you, Sophie."

I chewed on my lip until it stung. "I'm not sure what else there is to say."

"Will you at least look at me?" He inched forward until I could see his feet.

I shook my head, keeping my attention fixed on the grass. There were too many emotions bubbling inside me. I had to keep it together or else I would lose it entirely. I had to focus.

"Sophie, please . . ."

"I can't." My throat bobbed up and down. I shut my eyes to stop the tears, but I could feel them welling up, ready to fall. I didn't have enough resolve to hold it all in, not anymore.

"Why not?" he murmured.

"How can I look at you knowing what I know now?" I lifted my chin and stared at his chest.

"Sophie . . ."

"I visited my dad today," I continued shakily. "I know he killed your father. I know that's why you hate me."

Nic reached out and pressed his index finger under my chin, nudging it softly until I lifted my head and met his eyes.

And then the dam that had been holding my tears for as long as I could remember burst completely. They fell hard and fast down my cheeks, shaking my body with every heave as my breathing hitched, gasping out for air.

Everything I had suppressed — my father's incarceration, my mother's pain, Jack's desertion, the Falcones' disdain for me, and my burning desire for Nic — was bound up in those heavy tears as they fell away from my face and rolled down my neck. I sank to the ground and pulled my body into a ball, hunching over and cradling my head in my hands as I wept uncontrollably for the first time since my father's arrest, not caring about anything but the pain that was springing free from my body at last.

In an instant, Nic was beside me, curling my huddled body into his and enveloping me in his arms until he was all around me. He rested his head on mine and whispered into my hair, "Please don't cry, Sophie. Please don't cry."

He held me for a long time, until the rage of tears subsided into quiet streams, and I began to catch my breath again. Then he guided my head into his chest and I buried it in his neck, inhaling his scent.

"How could you not hate me?" I mumbled into his skin. "You'd be inhuman not to look at me and see what my father did."

He stroked the back of my hair, his words soft against it. "It's not like that, I promise."

"He didn't mean it, Nic. It was an accident," I sobbed quietly. "He wouldn't hurt a fly."

"I know," he whispered. "Please don't cry."

"I'm sorry." My words were so garbled I could barely understand them.

"You don't have to apologize."

"Yes, I do. Luca said —"

"Look at me . . . Please just look at me."

Slowly I raised my head, which was dizzy and heavy all at once. He wiped the wetness from my cheeks.

"Listen to me, Sophie. I want to be very clear about this. Luca had no business saying whatever he said to you. It has nothing to do with you or him, and he knows that. What happened with my father was an accident. It's over now."

"But it's not over." I thought of Valentino's drawings, and my father's gaunt, tired face. It would never be over.

"Well, it's not raw anymore," he replied carefully. "And it's not something I blame you for. When I look at you, I feel happy." He nudged my chin with his finger again. "I don't care where you've come from or who you're related to, I knew from that first night when I held you that I didn't want to let go of you. But then you jumped away from me, so I had to . . ." He trailed off and smiled. "And I felt empty."

"I don't understand," I whispered. "Why would Luca say it if it wasn't the reason you were avoiding me?"

"Because he was trying to get rid of you," he admitted. "And he knew that would work."

"I've never done anything to him," I protested weakly. "How could he hate someone he hardly even knows?"

"I know things changed when Dom told him who you were, but Luca doesn't hate you. He's just protective."

I rolled my eyes, which were damp and sore from crying. "What's he protecting you from?"

"It's not just about me." Nic stroked my cheek again. I swallowed hard. I had never wanted to be kissed so badly in my life, and yet I had never felt this desperate for information before.

"Do you always do what he says?" I heard the bitterness in my voice.

Nic tightened his lips; it accentuated the shadows beneath his cheekbones and the circles under his eyes. "Mostly."

"Why?"

He pulled his hands away, knitting them together. "It's complicated."

"That's why you can't be around me anymore," I pressed, watching his hands and missing their warmth on my skin. "Because he said so?"

Nic's expression turned rueful. "You make it sound so simple."

"Isn't it?"

"No."

"I don't understand."

Nic shook his head. "I know you don't."

Edging away from him until our bodies were no longer touching, I steeled myself and regarded him coolly. When I spoke again, I said the words as slowly and as clearly as I could so he would understand I knew more than he thought I did, and that I didn't need to be protected from it.

"I guess it must be a Mafia thing."

The silence that followed was resounding. Nic reacted like I had hit him; his chest was rising and falling unsteadily, his mouth twitching uncertainly. I watched him carefully, keeping my expression blank.

"What do you mean?" he said at last, but the words barely made a sound.

I kept my voice steady. "I think you know what I mean."

He glanced over his shoulder, like he was afraid someone was going to jump out of the bushes. He turned his gaze to the grass beside me. A click of his jaw and then — "I don't."

"The Angel-maker." It was a statement, not a question, and it made the balmy summer air seem colder once I'd said it.

He blinked hard. It had wounded him like I knew it would, and I instantly regretted it.

"So it's true, then?" I asked, fearing and yet needing to hear him say it. "Your family is part of the Mafia?"

He plucked a long, thin blade of grass and tried to split it in two. "I do not deny it."

A familiar wave of nausea rose in my stomach, but it was weaker this time. I had come to terms with most of my horror before falling asleep, and now, his confirmation of something I already knew was more like a dull punch in the gut.

When I didn't answer him he grabbed my hand with violent speed, like he was afraid he had lost me in that one quiet moment. I left my hand in his and pressed on, as carefully as I could.

"Does Felice tell you to hurt people? Do you answer to him the way you answer to Luca?"

"Of course not." He seemed affronted by the implication, and I was glad of that. If he didn't answer to "the boss," then he must not be involved in the things his father was accused of.

"What does it mean," I asked, "for you and your brothers to be part of the Mafia?"

Nic hesitated, and I could see he was trying to formulate his answer. "Infamy."

"And notoriety?" I remembered the article and shivered.

"Yes," he said plainly, like it didn't bother him the way it would bother me. "From birth we are stamped with our family's reputation, named after bosses from past generations, and raised with a strong sense of loyalty and honor . . ." He trailed off.

"Do you hurt people?"

He ran his hand through his hair until it hung loosely around his eyes, shielding them. "It's not like that."

"What is it like?"

Nic took both my hands in his. "Sophie, there's a lot I can't say to you. I've taken a serious vow, and to break it would mean violating a code of silence upheld by every member of my family. But if you can trust nothing else, trust this: I am a good person, with good morals. My brothers and I are loyal, to the death. We have been raised with an understanding of right and wrong. We protect and serve our mother so that she may be happy every day of her life, we mourn the death of our father, and we attend church every Sunday to pray for his soul. I want to protect those I love and those who cannot protect themselves. But most of all, I want to make the world a better place by being in it."

I felt a surge of relief. I didn't know what I had been expecting him to say, but this was so much better.

"You were born into your way of life," I said, almost as if I were speaking to myself, "but that doesn't mean you are part of it." Nic inhaled like he was about to say something, but then he stopped himself. "We are both living in the shadows of our fathers," I said, realizing for the first time that it was true.

"I would never hurt you," he said quietly.

"I know." I laced my fingers through his. I had seen those hands hurt Alex, I had seen purple bruises along the knuckles, but I had to believe it was different with me. I studied our fingers, his olive skin against the paleness of mine, his grip sure and strong. It felt different. It felt right.

For a while, neither of us said anything. A lot of bandages had been ripped off our psychic wounds and we were both weary with emotion.

"Do you know why I can't be with you?" Nic said at last. "I want you to know that it's not my choice to walk away."

I was starting to understand that. "When Luca found out who I was it changed everything, didn't it?"

"What's in a name, right?" Nic's expression turned rueful. "It's not a good idea, our being together. Not with what's happened. I don't want to draw any unnecessary attention to you."

"Am I in danger? They warned me about that . . ." I thought of my uncle, and I understood his concern. A Mafia family moves up the street from the family responsible for their boss's death. I inhaled sharply.

"Jack warned you?" The faintest undertone of animosity tinged Nic's words.

"And my father."

"You're not in danger." He tried to sound casual, but there was something new creeping into his voice now, straining it. "But we think it's best that you're kept far away from us and some of the more . . . unhinged members of our family . . . at least for the time being."

Nic fell quiet again. He moved his hands to my arms and began to rub them. I hadn't even realized I was cold until I felt the warmth in his touch.

"Should I be scared?" I asked.

"You don't have to be scared of anything," he said quietly.

I smiled weakly. I was scared of losing him, but I couldn't say so. It wouldn't do any good.

He flicked his gaze to my lips. "If I knew that night would be the last time I got to kiss you, I wouldn't have stopped."

My smile faltered. Why couldn't he be someone else, *anyone* but a Falcone?

"I should go," he said, like he was convincing himself and not me. But he wasn't going, he was leaning in to me. Our fingers were entwining and he was pulling me closer, sliding his arms around my waist.

Slowly, like he was fighting the urge to do so, he nuzzled his forehead against mine. "But what if . . . What if, in this one moment, you're not Sophie Gracewell and I'm not Nicoli Falcone . . ." He trailed off and let his lips find mine.

Desire raged through me as I pressed my lips against his. His mouth was firm against mine, hot and unyielding, and when our tongues met, I lost myself, wholly and completely, in the passion of his kiss.

All too soon, in the heat of something so intense I found it hard to pull my lips away to breathe, the distant sound of a strange hum dragged us back into our earthly bodies. Breaking away from me and panting heavily, Nic fished his buzzing phone from the pocket of his jeans.

He placed a hand over his heart and clutched at his chest. "Valentino," he answered in a shaky voice. "I'm on my way." He clicked off and returned his attention to me, but the softness in his eyes was gone, and I realized with a jolt that I was looking at a very different version of Nicoli Falcone.

"You have to go," I said, still breathing hard.

"I'm sorry." He took my hand in his. "Sophie, please don't speak about this with anyone. I've taken a vow and my family wouldn't be pleased with me breaking it, even just a little."

"I won't," I said without having to think about it. I could still feel the warmth of his kiss on my lips, and I might have promised him anything just then.

He lifted my hand to his lips, brushing them against it. "*Riguardati*, Sophie," he murmured. "Be safe."

In a fleeting moment of madness, I considered running after him and pulling him back to me, but then I remembered Luca's warning. I didn't want him anywhere near Millie or my mother.

I trudged back upstairs and crawled into bed, thinking of that brief moment in the backyard when everything in my life was heady and blissful. It was just as I was dropping off into nothingness that I remembered something Nic had said.

Jack warned you . . . ?

How had he known my uncle's name? I had never mentioned it to him — I *knew* I hadn't.

I started to remember other things then, things that were only just beginning to make sense: Luca's strange questions in the diner the first time we met; Dom's interest in Millie's place of work, and how he'd dumped her once he'd gotten information about me; how Nic had been lingering around the diner that night we broke in, his car parked far away in the shadows, as if he was waiting for something or someone.

Suddenly I had a horrible feeling in the pit of my stomach that this certain something or *someone* was the very person who had been avoiding Cedar Hill since the Falcones first arrived — my uncle Jack.

That's when I realized there was more to the Falcone-Gracewell story than I'd thought. And that while Nic may have had feelings for me, they certainly weren't interfering with his ability to lie, and lie hard, to my face.

CHAPTER TWENTY

The Movie

The initial aftermath of my nighttime good-bye to Nic was harder than I thought it would be. The things he said had turned my world upside down and made me question everything I thought I knew about my family, and my heart. Every so often, sneaky memories of his dark eyes, the way his tousled hair fell, or how sometimes his smile tugged more to one side would creep into my consciousness and twist the knife deeper into my gut until it felt almost like a real pain threatening to split me in half.

I tried to ignore the unpleasant flickers as much as possible by doubling up on shifts at the diner, coming in early and staying late to cash out. A small part of me hoped Nic might come in, but I knew, deep down, that he wouldn't. I made sure to take the longer route home after work so I wouldn't have to pass the Priestly — or *Falcone* — house and risk the horrible sinking feeling I had come to associate it with.

Things with my uncle had gone from strange to entirely bizarre. He was completely AWOL. I kept trying his new number, but he never answered. I texted him constantly, but he replied

only once, and when he did, it was with two irritating words —
I'm fine. More lies.

There was something wrong with him, I could feel it, but I
still couldn't pinpoint it. He knew I had questions for him and he
had no intention of answering them, through text or otherwise.
Now, not only was he avoiding Cedar Hill, he was avoiding me,
too, and it was making me increasingly anxious. I was beginning
to feel like I was screaming into a void and there was no one
around to hear me.

"So you really haven't heard anything from him?" Millie asked
as we made our way through the stone archway at the entrance
to Rayfield Park. It was outdoor movie night, and she had convinced me to go with her. She wanted me to at least try and put
everything out of my mind for a few hours, before I went insane
with worry. "That's really unlike Jack."

"I know." Jack had made a promise to my father that he would
always look after me, and the fact that he wasn't responding to
my attempts to contact him was not a good sign. "Something
must be really wrong if he's avoiding his whole life," I said.

We followed one of the winding stone pathways that looped
around an expanse of open greenery bordered by puffed-out
chestnut trees. Ahead of us, a group of pimply teenagers were
carrying an array of blankets, picnic baskets, and fold-up chairs.
"What if he's actually just run away with all the diner money?"
asked Millie.

"What money?"

We both laughed.

It felt good to unwind with Millie after everything. Even

though she knew what my father did to Nic's father, I tried not to feel guilty about neglecting to tell her certain details — *Mafia* details — about the situation. I had made a promise to Nic, and I didn't want to be someone who didn't keep promises. Plus, having Millie in the dark was better for her anyway; I didn't want to risk putting her in danger, especially after Luca's threat.

Millie tapped her chin. "Well, your uncle must get the money for those fancy suits from somewhere."

"Trust me. I've seen the books. It's not from the diner."

"Dammit," Millie lamented. "And I was still holding out for that pay raise."

We slipped in behind a throng of people who were following a connecting pathway that led to the park's central square. Up ahead, Erin Reyes and three of her vapid clones were flirting loudly with a bunch of guys from school. She caught my eye and smirked before flipping her hair in her customary I'm-so-much-better-than-you way. Her giggling intensified.

"That has to be a fake laugh."

"Then it matches her nose," said Millie, before dragging me away. She trailed her hand along the bark of a nearby oak tree as we walked.

"Trying to reconnect with nature?" I teased.

She nudged me and I teetered off the path, into the mud that lined it. "Hey!"

"Just trying to get your mind off everything."

"You're a real gem."

"Thank you, Sophie," Millie said, giving me a ridiculous curtsy.

Finally, we entered the square: generous patches of grass divided by crisscrossing stone paths and bordered on all sides by towering trees. At the north end, a huge screen had been erected.

"They have a taco truck this year!" Millie squealed, dragging me by one of the belt loops on my denim cutoffs. "Let's sit somewhere around here."

Scores of people were already relaxing on chairs and blankets in front of the giant screen. Families had come out with their children, who were running around with careless abandon, while others were arriving as couples sewn together at the hips and hands and elbows, carrying everything from cushions and picnic baskets to cans of beer and bottles of wine.

"Whoa, people must really love Monty Python," I observed as Millie fanned out her blanket in a spot equidistant from the screen and the taco truck. She smoothed down all four corners, making sure it was perfectly straight.

"I still can't believe you've never seen this."

When we were comfortably sprawled out, I emptied the contents of my bag until our makeshift feast was scattered across the quilt in streaks of sugar and chocolate.

Millie ripped into a bag of sour gummi bears and stuffed four into her mouth at once. "I love these," she said with swollen cheeks. "Even though I'm not allowed to eat them." She grinned, revealing tiny slivers of jelly that were now anchored to her invisible braces.

I laughed at her, and felt good about it. Since the night I fell for Nic, I had been tormenting myself with questions and wallowing in self-pity, which was doing more harm than good. I had to stop before I drove myself insane thinking of things I knew I couldn't change.

I broadened my smile and then felt it falter at the sudden look on Millie's face.

"But I thought he was out of town," she mumbled, her voice was unnaturally subdued.

"Huh?" I followed her gaze and squinted into the growing crowds. "Who are you talking about?"

"Robbie Stenson. He's here."

CHAPTER TWENTY-ONE

The Gun

I poured all of my concentration into the back of Robbie Stenson's stupid round head. Even though I still couldn't remember anything from that night, I felt angry just looking at him. It was like my skin was burning at the memory and my brain was struggling to catch up. Beside me, Millie's raucous laughter was buzzing in my ears. She was blissfully glued to the movie.

"Why aren't you laughing?" she asked.

I scanned the screen, where a bunch of British knights were harping on in comical French accents. *Strange.* "I'm distracted."

"What are you trying to accomplish by staring at Robbie's head like that?" Millie shoveled another handful of caramel popcorn into her mouth. "Are you trying to make him explode with your mind?"

"I don't know." I scrunched up my face in an effort to find the memory that was hovering just outside my realm of consciousness. "I'm trying to remember."

Millie stuffed another handful into her mouth and chewed thoughtfully. "Don't," she said, letting sticky kernels spew across the blanket. "Just try and forget about it. You're here to unwind, remember?"

I did my best to follow her advice, but still, something wasn't right . . .

After almost an hour, the screen blackened to text, which signaled a short intermission. "Taco?" I offered, feeling the need to stretch my legs.

"If you insist," Millie replied, reclining. "Get me two, please."

I brushed the crumbs off my clothes and walked across the grass, taking my place at the end of the taco line; soon after, I was wedged between a girl with bright pink hair and an overweight man.

"This register is open!" a pubescent voice shouted. A slew of people from behind me parted and shuffled into a second line, and suddenly I was standing almost side by side with Robbie Stenson.

He glanced at me and then quickly looked away, but not before I caught sight of the yellowing bruising around his eye sockets and along his thick jawline. What the hell happened to him?

The register chimed and the line moved forward, taking me with it. Robbie caught up on his side; he was swirling a red cup in his hands, making the liquid slosh back and forth. He lifted it to his lips, smacked them against it, and began gulping down its contents greedily. The more I saw the red cup bobbing back and forth toward his mouth, the more I fixated on it.

Then it all came flooding back to me.

I remembered going into Millie's parents' room and coming face-to-face with Robbie Stenson. *I spilled some beer on myself—*

wasn't that what he had said? But he had been holding two full cups in his hands. And he told me he hadn't even been drinking. I grimaced as the memory of the sweet, fizzy liquid glided into my mind, reminding me of how he had urged me to drink it and how, as we sat on the bed, I had become uncomfortable with the way he watched me. And then everything in my memory went dark. I realized, just as the register rang again — echoing the alarm bells in my brain — that Robbie Stenson had drugged me that night and then orchestrated our walk home together so that he could assault me. There was nothing innocent or naïve about it.

And worse, I felt sure that if Luca hadn't intervened when he did, things would have gone from bad to awful.

The line pushed forward.

"Move," the fat man behind me whined, but I couldn't move. I was rooted to the spot. "Hey, come on." He prodded me.

Bile rose in my throat. Beside me, Robbie was shuffling forward, dangling the empty red cup back and forth in his hand. It had become a pendulum hurling explosive memories at me, one by one, and before I knew what I was doing, I was shoving him out of the line.

"What the hell?" His stocky frame stumbled sideways. He tripped and landed on the grass, clutching at his ribs.

"How could you?" I lunged again, but this time he was prepared. He pulled himself up and backed away from me, away from the crowds. I followed him.

"What the hell is your problem?" he spat through gritted teeth.

"You tried to assault me!" I hissed.

"No, I didn't," he returned so evenly that I might have doubted the memory if it wasn't pulsating against my brain. "I was walking you home when your boyfriend beat the crap out of me for no reason. You're lucky I didn't report him."

So Luca *had* caused Robbie's injuries, and by the looks of things he hadn't held back. But stranger than Luca's likely status as a psychopath was the realization that somewhere beneath my conscience, I felt a wisp of satisfaction. Robbie Stenson hadn't gotten away with trying to violate me.

"I know you drugged me." I was vaguely aware of hysteria rising inside me. Thanks to Luca Falcone, Robbie might have paid for what he did, but he hadn't paid for what he'd planned to do. "You set up the whole thing! I remember what you gave me."

Robbie snorted and his features shrunk into his face. "Do you?" Still holding his sides, he rounded on me like a vulture circling its prey. "Well, I doubt that would stand up in court."

"So you admit it?" I returned furiously.

He shrugged and then I was hurling myself at him again. A sharp pain rippled through my left shoulder as I landed against his chest with a thud. He grabbed me, his hands digging into my rib cage.

"Stop it!" His face contorted in pain. His hands squeezed tighter in warning. "You're making a fool out of yourself. Let it go."

I struggled against his arms. "Get off me!" I shrieked. I dug my nails into his fists as hard as I could until they snapped away.

"Fine," he replied. "Just get out of my face."

I jumped back, widening the gap between us. "You're a sick

freak!" I shouted, raising a fist at him as adrenaline pumped in my veins. "How could you do that to me? To anyone!"

Robbie's grin stretched into his bruised cheeks. "Oh, come on. You must know that banging Michael Gracewell's daughter means serious novelty points."

"You mean *raping*," I spat, circling him.

"Don't tell me you're going to try and fight me?" he sneered.

He was the ugliest person I had ever encountered. "I hate you."

"Relax, Sophie. I wouldn't even touch you now."

The way he said my name like it was some dirty word made me feel physically ill. "You'll pay for this!" I watched with satisfaction as the color drained from his face. His eyes grew wide and he hugged himself tighter. But I was wrong to think my words had suddenly started to scare him, because Robbie wasn't looking at me anymore; he was looking over my shoulder.

Out of nowhere, a third voice joined our conversation. It was eerily calm in contrast to our heated exchange.

"*Ciao*, Robert. Long time no see." I would have mistaken the dulcet tone as familiar — friendly, even — if I weren't so sure it belonged to Luca Falcone. I watched Robbie throw his hands up and recoil as Luca stepped out from behind me like he had just sprung up out of the grass. How long had he been there, listening? I turned around, searching for his brothers, but he was alone. "I couldn't help but overhear your conversation," he said calmly. "I hope I'm not intruding."

"Get the hell away from me, dude, or I'll call the police." Robbie's voice quivered an octave higher than usual and the smugness rapidly vanished from his face.

"Robert," Luca said. "I think you need to calm down. You seem very highly strung."

"You broke my ribs!"

"Only a couple," said Luca dismissively.

"What do you want?"

Luca's fake-friendly voice was almost more harrowing than his threatening one. "I just want to talk to you about something, is that acceptable?"

He took another step forward and Robbie stumbled backward. "I don't know you. What the hell would we talk about?"

"Doesn't your dad own a furniture business?"

Robbie's eyes widened. "How do you know that?"

Luca took another step, closing the gap between them. "It's common knowledge, right?"

"I guess."

"And you work for him, don't you?"

By now I could only see the back of Luca's head as he made his way forward, ignoring my presence completely.

"Yeah, I do," Robbie said, sounding fractionally more confident.

"Good." Luca crossed his arms. "Let's put our little bit of history aside for just a second, OK? The past is the past, and I think we should move on from it. This is really none of my business anyway."

Robbie nodded like one of those bobble dogs on car dashboards.

"I'm in the market for some new furniture, believe it or not."

"Really?"

"And I thought, to make up for our unfortunate run-in a little while ago —" Luca pointed his finger at Robbie's bruised face, twirling it round and round for added effect. "Do you remember that?"

"Y-yeah."

"And that?" He indicated toward his rib cage.

"Obviously," Robbie hissed, cradling himself with his meaty arms.

"Well, I thought, to make amends, that I might send some business your way. I need a lot of stuff."

Robbie relaxed his shoulders.

"I'm not a bad guy," Luca continued, and I got the sense he was smiling — an event rarer than a solar eclipse. "So why don't we talk some stuff over?"

"Now?" Robbie cocked an eyebrow. "The movie's about to start again. Why don't we do it when I'm at work?"

"The matter is time-sensitive, so let's talk now." Luca clapped his hand on the back of Robbie's neck. "Come on." He pulled him away from the park and toward the trees. "Wave good-bye to Gracewell," he prompted. "She's going to be staying here."

I sensed the warning in his words, but as I watched them disappear behind the taco truck, I found myself contemplating an unexpected dilemma. *The movie's about to start*, I reminded myself, yet my feet were leading me toward the trees and not back to where Millie was sitting on the lawn, waiting — impatiently, no doubt — for the tacos I now had no intention of buying her.

The way Luca draped his arm around Robbie's shoulders made them seem almost like friends, and I had to admit there was something undeniably convincing about the way he had spoken to him. I, unlike my assailant, was not dumb enough to fall for it. I knew, better than most, that Luca had no need for friends. Or furniture, for that matter. Whatever was going to happen in those trees was unlikely to be a business transaction — for Robbie, at least. But like a bona fide *idiot*, he let Luca lead him away, and I couldn't *not* follow them.

Hurrying my pace so as not to lose them completely, but keeping far enough behind that they wouldn't notice me, I slipped around the back of the taco truck just as the movie flickered to life over my shoulder. Up ahead, I could see Luca and Robbie disappearing between two overhanging trees. I hung back again, tiptoeing across twigs and dry leaves as I followed their voices.

After I spent several minutes of sneaking around, their conversation reached me through a small clearing. They had stopped walking, so I did, too. Between the break in the trees, they were standing across from each other; Robbie had his hands folded around his ribs, while Luca's were resting casually by his sides.

I crept closer.

"But I thought you wanted to know about furniture," Robbie was protesting.

"I just remembered," Luca replied. "I don't need any furniture."

"Then why are we —" Robbie's breath was knocked out of him before he could finish his sentence.

I watched in muted horror as Luca slammed his fist straight into Robbie's stomach, making him crumple in half onto the ground. He rolled over onto his side and moaned into the dirt.

"We're here, Robert, because I heard what you said to Sophie." Luca's voice was eerily calm. He stamped down on Robbie's foot, but the dirt muffled his scream. "And if there's one thing I hate, it's drug pushers." He rounded on him, obscuring him in his shadow, and kicked him hard in the shoulder. "*Especially* someone who drugs *a girl* and then tries to *rape* her." He pulled his foot back, and this time he hurled it into Robbie's stomach. There was an audible crack. Robbie screamed into the dirt as Luca used his shoe to roll him onto his stomach. "I mean, it was bad enough when I thought you were just trying to hit on her, but now?" He stamped down on Robbie's back so that he was spluttering into the dirt and weeds. "Now you're the *lowest* of the low. You are *scum*."

I started to stumble forward, half-paralyzed by fear yet determined to do *something*. But my attempt to assist the sobbing bundle of cracked ribs was short-lived as another figure entered the clearing.

"Get up!" he roared, and his voice stopped me dead.

"Nicoli, I told you to stay behind!"

But Nic wasn't listening to Luca; he wasn't even looking at him. He was looking at Robbie's crumpled frame, his eyes full of hate as he charged.

"Get up, Stenson!" he yelled in a voice I barely recognized; it was like glass, and edged with a kind of rage I had never known. "Stand up and look me in the eye, or I'll come down there and cut you open!"

Slowly, Robbie heaved himself off the ground. He managed to half-lean against a tree by sticking his fingers into the bark and bending his knees in front of him. He puffed hard as Luca moved away from them, clasping his hands behind his back and tilting his head like he was watching a puppet show.

I tried to move, but I couldn't. My legs were shaking violently beneath me and I had to claw against a tree to stop myself from falling to the ground in fear.

"I said *stand*," Nic seethed.

"Nicoli," Luca cautioned, but he didn't move. "Be careful."

Groaning, Robbie pulled himself up, the strain contorting his face. "My ribs," he sobbed. "Please."

Nic grabbed him and shoved him into the bark. Robbie's face was beginning to bleed. He closed his hands around Robbie's throat. "Do you think it's OK to put your hands on someone who doesn't want your hands on them? How is this for you?" He tightened his grip on Robbie's thick neck.

"Nicoli," Luca muttered. He stepped closer and put his hand on his brother's shoulder, like a chaperone. *"Stai attento."*

"What is that?" Robbie gurgled as his face began to turn purple. "Is that a —"

A flurry of rushed movements followed, so I could only discern two things. The first was the appearance of a black metal object against the side of Robbie's head. The second was the sound of a click.

And then, in a measured reply, I heard Nic confirm everything I had just witnessed: "It's a gun, you fucking idiot."

Robbie tried to scream, but Nic moved the barrel into his mouth so fast it choked it right out of him.

"Listen up, you piece of scum," Nic snarled. "This is your final warning. I'll be watching you. If I ever hear of you attempting to handle drugs again, then you're dead. If you try to give a girl any kind of drug, requested or not, you're dead. If you attempt to force yourself on anyone ever again, you're dead. And if you so much as *glance* at Sophie Gracewell again, I'll rip your heart out and stuff it down your fucking throat. Do you understand?"

Robbie nodded.

"The police might not have enough to go on to convict you of attempted date rape, but I do. And I'm not a big fan of trial by jury, Stenson. So I'd advise you to use this final warning as a gift from God. Change your life. And if you so much as breathe a word of this to the police, you'll be shot by one of my brothers before you fall asleep. That, I can *guarantee*." Nic leaned forward in what felt like slow motion. "Or maybe I'll just shoot you now and do the world a favor."

I pushed my jelly legs forward, intent on stopping whatever was about to happen, but Luca got there first.

"*Basta!*" he said, pulling Nic's hand away from Robbie's mouth; Nic let it drop willingly, but he didn't relinquish the gun, and Luca didn't force him. Instead, he kept his hand on his brother's shooting arm, so he couldn't raise it again. I stood frozen in my new spot, half in and half out of the clearing, watching Nic's chest rise and fall as he stared unblinkingly at Robbie's whimpering face.

Nic finally moved his arm away from Luca's hand, uncocked the gun, and stashed it in the waistband of his jeans. The movement looked like second nature, and I found myself wondering whether he had been carrying a gun the last time he held me in his arms. He shook out his hair and stepped back, gripping his chest, and turned away from Robbie. "Luca, get rid of him before I change my mind."

Luca stepped forward and slapped Robbie on the cheek in a bizarre show of camaraderie. "You get all that, Robert?"

Robbie started to wipe the tears from his face with the back of his hand. "I p-p-promise," he faltered.

"Good." Luca lifted his arm and pointed behind Robbie to where the rest of the sprawling park continued. "Now run like your life depends on it. Because it does."

And that's exactly what Robbie did. Without sparing another second, he pitched himself forward and hurtled clumsily through the trees until he was just a dot hobbling into the darkness. When the sounds of his uneven footsteps had disappeared entirely, Luca removed his attention from the space between the trees and settled it on Nic.

"I told you to stay behind." He sounded weary rather than angry, like he was used to this kind of behavior.

"You told me he tried to take advantage of her. You didn't tell me he had *drugged* her!"

"I didn't know that then. And you shouldn't have been eavesdropping."

"You shouldn't have expected me to stay out of it."

"*Sei un pazzo*, Nicoli."

"This is different."

"You always say that."

"This *is* different."

"She's not yours."

"She's mine to protect."

"You would have *killed* him," Luca hissed.

"He deserves it," Nic returned evenly — casually, almost.

"What happened to laying low? You could have ruined everything. And I told you, it's not your concern."

"She is my fucking concern!"

"She won't want to have anything to do with you now anyway," Luca continued, a sudden airiness in his voice.

Nic snapped his head up; his eyes were frantic. "Why not?"

I felt my heart constrict in agony as I realized what was about to happen; and it was too late, there was nothing I could do to stop it.

Luca raised his arm until he was pointing directly across the clearing. "Because she's standing right there."

Nic followed Luca's finger until his gaze found mine and, just like the night he had discovered my name, horror possessed his features, warping them as we stood apart from each other, both of us heartbroken for different reasons.

"Sophie . . ." he whispered, but it was too late.

I couldn't speak. I couldn't even open my mouth I was so petrified. I started to back away.

He stumbled forward.

"Let her go," Luca cautioned. "She's terrified."

I faltered back into the shadows between the trees. My retreat turned to reckless abandon. I careened through the park, racing toward the flickering of the screen. When I passed the final scattering of trees, I sprinted around the taco truck, where I collided with Millie.

"Careful, Soph!" she screeched as I tumbled backward and landed on the grass beside the taco I had just knocked from her hands. Groaning, she hoisted me up from the ground. "Where the hell have you been?"

"We have to go," I explained, springing forward. "If you knew what I just saw . . ."

"What's going on?"

"Come on!" I pulled her toward the grass. I threw everything back into my bag, watching the trees every few seconds for the reappearance of Nic and Luca. "I'll explain everything when we're out of here." And then I was off again, dragging Millie as I raced down the winding paths.

"What's going on?" she whined in between heaves. "I'm. Too. Out. Of. Shape. For. This."

"Just come on!" I navigated our way back through the walkways until the entrance to Rayfield Park edged into view.

Before we passed through the arch, Millie stopped and clutched at her sides like she had been punched in the stomach. "Stop," she wheezed. "I need. A minute."

"Can we please just keep going?"

"I think. My feet. Are bleeding." She brushed her hair away from her face, which was glistening with a fresh sheen of sweat. "What's going on. With you?"

Before I could answer with an explosion of everything I had just witnessed, someone grabbed onto my arm and yanked me away from her.

"Hey!" I protested as Nic pulled me into him.

"Whatever you're about to say to Millie, don't," he urged in a voice so low only I could hear it. He tightened his hands around my wrists and held them against his. "Please."

Behind us, Millie was noticing the sweat stains pooling out from under her arms and the bleeding along the straps of her sandals. "Gross," she moaned as she sank to the grass, panting.

"You can't tell me what I can and can't tell my best friend," I snapped, shaking him off me.

"You promised," he said quietly. "That was supposed to mean something."

"I promised when I thought you were an *inactive* member of the Mafia, which you *clearly* are not! This is completely different. I will not be bound by that!"

"Sophie," he said, his voice full of strain. "I really need you to be quiet about what you just saw."

I could feel my face growing hot with anger. I grabbed his shirt and pulled him around the side of the arch. "You lied to me!"

His hands shot up in surrender. "I didn't lie, Sophie. I just . . . left out certain things. Let me explain."

I shoved him. "You made me believe you were good!"

"I am good!"

"No, you're not!" I shoved him again. "You made me think you were innocent. You made me believe you weren't part of all that crazy Mafia stuff!"

Cautiously Nic removed my hands from his chest. "I never said that."

"You had plenty of time to set the record straight." I wanted to slap him. It took every ounce of my self-control to curl my hands by my sides instead.

"I know."

"But you didn't."

Purpose and defiance flashed in his eyes. "I didn't have enough time to explain everything. But I didn't lie to you. Everything I said was true, just not in the way you might have taken it."

"I asked you if you hurt people! You said no!"

He came closer. "I said it wasn't like that. And it's not. Everything I do is about protection."

"Protection," I scoffed. "Is that what you tell yourself when you put your *gun* in someone's *mouth*?"

He pulled me into him. "Listen to me."

"Don't," I cried, feeling the tears swarm behind my eyes. "I'm scared of you."

He recoiled like I really had slapped him. "I told you I would never hurt you."

"How do I know that?"

He stared at me so hard it took my breath away, and after an agonizing moment, he responded quietly, "Because you're a good person."

I glowered at him. "That makes one of us."

"I'm a good person, too."

"You just put a gun in Robbie Stenson's mouth," I hissed.

"I'm sorry you had to see that, but it was inevitable."

"*How* is an assault like that inevitable?"

His eyes darkened, but he didn't respond.

"You must know how totally unacceptable that was. I have to report it to the police."

"Sophie, it was for *you*. How could I let him walk away from me after I found out what he tried to do to you?"

I backed away from him again. "Are you insane, Nic? You know you can't just go around *pulling guns on people* for me. I can take care of myself!"

He pinched the bridge of his nose and sighed. "That was a service to society. Stenson is the type of character who won't stop at just one girl. It was everything I could do shy of actually blowing his head off."

I gasped. "Can you not be so graphic?"

He scraped his hands through his hair. "Sorry."

"I don't think you are."

He wasn't looking at me anymore and I knew I was right. He wasn't sorry; he was sorry I had seen it. "I know I have no right to ask anything of you," he said, "but please don't tell anyone about what you saw. It will make trouble."

"No kidding. I witnessed a crime. And even if the victim was someone I hate, it still doesn't make it right. I won't keep it a secret. I won't be your accomplice."

"Then wait at least." He grabbed my hands and closed his around them before I could pull them away. I tried to avoid his dark eyes. "Sophie, I'll break the vow. I'll tell you as much as I can," he whispered urgently. "I need you to understand who I am. Please just give me the chance to show you."

"It's too late," I said, but my resolve was as unsteady as my voice.

He moved my hand to his heart so I could feel it hammering in his chest. "I'm not a bad person. I know you can feel it. I admit I lied to you by letting you believe what you wanted to. I needed you to feel happy and secure, and I didn't want to take that feeling away from you after everything you had discovered about our fathers. I'm not ashamed of who I am or where I come from, but I was afraid of you knowing about it and not giving me the chance to help you see what it really means. I was terrified that the truth would change the way you look at me. But you deserve it all, and I'll give it to you if you'll let me."

My defiance was crumbling and we both knew it. I pulled my hands from him and folded them. I *knew* there had to be more answers, but I didn't think he would admit it so freely after lying to me for so long. Now, the way he was convincing me was working — he was pushing all the right buttons. He had me right where he wanted me. I hated it and I burned for it.

"You get one chance."

CHAPTER TWENTY-TWO

The Falcone Calling

Nic offered me a ride to his house from the park but I decided to walk with Millie instead.

"Ah, a lovers' tiff," she had assumed on our way home. She wasn't half-wrong, but she wasn't completely right, either. I didn't tell her the truth about the argument in Rayfield Park for the same reason I didn't tell her why I was going to Nic's house after we went our separate ways at Shrewsbury Avenue. I wasn't ready to organize my thoughts about everything, and until I did that, I wanted to make sure she would be safe. The less she knew, the better.

When I turned into his driveway, Nic was already standing in the doorway. "You came."

I approached him in silence. He stood against the open door so I could sidle past him. I tried not to notice when I brushed against him, but I could see it register on his face.

The front of the house was entirely different from the modern kitchen at the back. Now, I was hovering in the setting of every horror story I'd ever heard, and it was exactly how I'd imagined it.

A crystal chandelier, still covered in spiderwebs, hung from the high ceiling. The wooden floors in the large foyer were discolored and uneven, creaking with each step. Ahead, a grand staircase lined with a thick burgundy carpet turned sharply to the right and up toward the second floor, while paneled wallpaper fell away from the walls in tattered strips. The hallway continued down the left side of the stairs, branching off into a line of closed rooms with narrow doors. The right side was distinguished by huge, newly varnished doors with heavy brass handles.

"Sophie?" I turned to find Nic looking at me expectantly. "Do you want to follow me through here?" He led me into a large sitting room, where two dark red leather couches rested around a stately fireplace.

I seated myself on one of the couches; Nic chose the other. I noticed, without an iota of surprise, that there was no TV, just a leather footstool, an old clock on the grand mantelpiece, and a built-in bookcase that spanned the entire length of the far wall. It was filled to the brim with Dickens, Defoe, Twain, Swift, and every other great or intimidating novelist I could have imagined. Above the fireplace, an oil painting lorded over the room. It was some kind of avenging angel, rendered in sweeping dark colors and framed in gilded gold. It stretched the entire width of the mantelpiece.

"That's one of Valentino's," Nic said, following my gaze.

"It's incredible."

"It's kind of dramatic."

Dramatic. The thought of Nic holding a gun to Robbie

Stenson's head flittered across my memory. "Well at least he puts *his* time to good creative use."

Nic cleared his throat awkwardly.

"Well, I'm here," I said, keeping my thoughts focused on what I needed to know. "Start talking."

He leaned across the corner of his couch, pinning me with his dark eyes. "What I'm about to tell you is not for the fainthearted," he said. "Discussing my family like this is not something I do lightly, and I need to know that you won't use it against me. Against us."

I hesitated, and he seized my silence.

"Once it's been said, I can't take it back, and I'm risking a lot already."

I thought about it for a long moment, really considering what he was asking of me, and what he was offering me in return: the unvarnished truth. I didn't want to betray his trust, but I was afraid to offer my silence if what he told me was too big to handle. But I had to know. He wanted to let me in, he wanted to trust me, and despite everything, I wanted to let him.

"OK," I said. "I promise."

"It won't be everything. It can't be."

"I just need enough to understand, Nic."

He watched me for a moment more, like he was trying to read something in my eyes. Then he leaned back and sighed, finally, after all this time, surrendering. "Sophie, my family and I are in the business of protection. And what that means is, sometimes we have to hurt people, and sometimes we have to kill people."

And there it was — out in the open at last. My unspoken fear had come to fruition. Like father, like son: Nic was an Angel-maker, too. I covered my mouth with the back of my hand and concentrated on steadying my breathing. I couldn't speak. I felt sick.

"Let me explain," Nic said. He reached out to me, but I edged away and he dropped his hand. And then he hit me with a fresh bombshell: "We only go after people who deserve to die."

I gaped at him. "Is this some sort of sick joke?" I managed, my mouth still covered by my hand. "Because it's not funny."

He just looked at me — defiantly standing by the craziest thing I had ever heard come out of his mouth.

"You mean you go after people like Robbie Stenson?" I pressed after a beat.

He nodded — calmly. Too calmly.

"Would you have killed him if Luca hadn't been there to stop you?"

He didn't miss a beat. "Without hesitation."

I thought about getting up and bolting, slamming the door behind me and running far away. But I didn't, I couldn't — not when there was more to know. "Can't you see how crazy that is?"

This time, Nic looked away from me, his expression twisting. "He deserves worse than what he got . . . If Luca hadn't been there . . ."

"You'd probably be in jail," I finished dryly.

"And he'd be six feet under."

I dropped my hands and ground them into the leather to keep

my anger at bay. "That's what the police are for, Nic. Not normal gun-wielding citizens like you and Luca."

There was a chasm between us. I studied my lap as the bitterness stung my throat. Even though Nic had never owed me anything, I felt betrayed, wounded by the truth of his character, and afraid of the feelings that still lingered for him deep down in spite of it.

I thought about leaving again. As if sensing my unease, he slid onto the couch beside me so that his leg brushed against my bare thigh, and I felt charged by his nearness. He rested his elbows on his knees and turned so that all I could focus on was the passion in his voice and the fire in his eyes. "Do you think Robbie Stenson would have never tried to hurt someone again just because his attempt didn't work on you?" he asked, his voice subdued. "Because I don't. Someone had to put him in his place before he did what he tried to do to you to someone else. Someone who might not have been as lucky as you were. This is the kind of thing we do, Sophie."

"What do you mean, the kind of *thing* you do?" I reeled. "Are you trying to tell me your family is some sort of self-righteous vigilante force?"

Nic laughed unexpectedly; it was a foreign, misplaced reaction, and I wondered how he could be so lighthearted considering what we were talking about. "When we decide to combat a certain problem, we don't do it within the confines of the law. For us, it's that simple. There's an entire underworld of crime that can't be accessed by the police. Criminals who won't hesitate to kill anyone who gets in the way of profit — the kind of people who have more judges and lawyers in their pockets than cash. They don't play by the rules. *They're* the kind of *things* we deal with."

I fell back against the couch, groaning under the weight of everything I was being asked to understand. "But why do you go after people at all? What does it have to do with you?"

Nic dropped his voice, and quietly, like he was revealing a great and terrible secret, he said, "This has everything to do with us, Sophie. It's in our blood."

"The same way managing the diner is in my blood?" I would have laughed if I wasn't so full of horror.

"Sort of." Nic smiled. "My people are descended from Sicily. From the very beginning every member of my family has been born into the Mafia. Not inducted. *Born*. For us there is no other choice, no alternate way to live."

I felt a pang of uneasiness in my stomach. Did that mean he was stuck in this life? Did being a Falcone mean he was destined to kill, the same way being a Gracewell made me bad at math? How was that even possible?

He continued, undaunted by my silence. "The Falcone traditions are unique, our membership confined to blood, and our actions informed by honor and solidarity. We are on earth to make the world a better place. We give everything for the family, and in turn, everything in the pursuit of good."

"That's all very poetic," I said after a moment of consideration. "But when are you going to explain the killing part?"

"Now." Nic reacted with formidable calmness. He didn't even

blink, he just dropped his hand on top of mine and tangled our fingers together on his knee. I let him do it, and I don't know why, but I was trying to look at him as a product of his ancestry and his upbringing, and I wasn't sure whether I could punish him before I understood what that truly meant. I didn't even know if I was safe or not, being here with him, but I felt comforted by his touch, and despite everything telling me to run, I didn't.

"In Sicily, the Mafia came about from the need to protect the local townspeople. It wasn't anything like it is now, different families governed by ruthless behavioral codes and illegal money-making schemes. The true and real Mafia, *La Cosa Nostra*, was different." His voice twisted, turning wistful, like he was remembering something he had once been part of. Maybe that's how he felt. "After Italy annexed Sicily in the nineteenth century, the lands were taken from the Church and State, and given to private citizens.

"Trading grew and so did commercialism, and out of commercialism came the ugly side of profit: greed, crime, murder. There was no real police force. The townspeople didn't have anyone to protect their homes, their businesses, even their families, so they looked elsewhere. My grandfather used to say it was a simple case of supply and demand. First, small groups of men started to spring up across Sicily; in return for money, they ensured safety by killing those who threatened to destroy it. Word spread, and after a while these groups were hired by wealthier families to settle personal vendettas or offer additional protection."

"So these groups — these early members of the Mafia — were just a law unto themselves?" I asked. *Sounds familiar.*

"And that was the problem," Nic replied. "With no law, apart from their own, temptation got the better of many of them; some organizations turned against the people they protected, falling into violence for violence's sake, extortion, money laundering, and racketeering — all the things that make the Mafia as infamous as it is today.

"After that, many of them, who had become formidable families in their own right, emigrated to America. My grandfather's family were among the first immigrants in the early twentieth century." Nic paused for a moment before continuing with quiet surety. "But the Falcones never chose the corrupt path of those around them, not in Sicily and not here. We have always tried to protect those who can't protect themselves, to stay on the right side of right and wrong. And sometimes, the right thing is to kill the wrong kind of man."

Suddenly he seemed so much older. A part of me wanted to cry for him and for the innocence he never really had, but another part wanted to shake him and scream at him for being so idiotic, for not seeing his life's calling as I did — as an insane death wish.

"What are you thinking?" he asked.

I shook my head. "That you could die at seventeen because you're chasing down vendettas that have nothing to do with you, and I still don't really understand why."

"It's my job," he said simply. And then came four horrifying words: "I'm a career assassin."

I lost the ability to blink. Suddenly there wasn't enough space in my lungs to fill them with the air I needed to breathe. If I had remembered any curse words in that moment, I would have used them all at once. Nic just waited, politely, while I connected the word "assassin" with a seventeen-year-old boy who had big, beautiful brown eyes and an easy smile.

"How many?" I stammered, as numbers ran through my mind — five people? Ten? Fifty?

He slow-blinked at me, but I knew he understood. I spelled it out for him. "How many people have you *killed*?"

"I don't know." *Lie.*

"Ballpark," I demanded, but my voice wavered. Did I really want to know? Would it be worse than my guesses?

"Not that many." His eyes grew, and I caught myself noticing the flecks of gold inside them.

I refocused. I was not about to let him smolder his way out of this. "Anything over zero is 'many.'"

Nic had the good sense to look away from me, even if he *was* feigning the shame he should have been feeling.

"So how many?" I asked again.

"I can't discuss it, Sophie. I'd get in trouble," he said, almost pleadingly. "Just know they were bad people. People a lot worse than Stenson. And it's my job."

"*How* could that be your job?" I finally managed, though it came out with an eye-watering shrillness.

"It couldn't be anything else," he replied simply.

"It could be lots of things, Nic!" I was screeching without meaning to. "You could be a teacher, a doctor, a barista, a fishmonger, an accountant, a — "

"Sophie," Nic interrupted softly. "Just calm down . . ."

I clamped my mouth shut until the hysteria subsided, and when I had finally calmed my breathing down, I conceded, "I'm scared."

"I told you I would never hurt you," he said quietly. "It's just a job."

"No," I said, shaking my head. "How could it be?"

"The Falcones have earned our position as one of the most honorable and respected lineages in the American Mafia. The other families always come to us, for one reason or another, and we always respond. That has been our calling within the underworld. And it is how we operate within *omertà*." The last word rolled off his tongue.

"What's *omertà*?" My tongue stumbled over the word.

Nic smiled at my botched attempt. "It's a code of silence. Our people don't speak to the law, but we speak to each other, and that's how we get things done. How we solve certain . . . problems."

"You mean people," I pointed out.

"People," he confirmed.

"So your family is like a special branch of the Mafia?" I ventured.

He considered it for a moment before conceding with a soft smile. "I suppose it has become that way. We are the part that takes care of the people who shouldn't be dealing on the streets, or trafficking, or killing innocent bystanders . . ." His voice grew hard. "We take care of the scum."

He studied me intently as I started knitting the pieces together in my head so I could see the picture he was creating. His family hurt and killed people whose aim in life was to hurt and kill innocents. That was his job, but it was more than that, too: It was his legacy. But how could he justify it to himself, and how could I justify his understanding of it? The idea that I was sitting beside an assassin made me dizzy, and yet when I looked at Nic, I didn't feel afraid, I felt . . . confusion. "And you get *paid* to do this?"

"Yes, we do."

"By other families in the Mafia?"

"Yes."

"Handsomely, I'm guessing."

"That's not important." He was right, the answer wasn't important. The mansion spoke for itself.

"Wait." There was something not quite right about his explanation. "Don't members of the Mafia break the law, too? I know they're not exactly law-abiding. I've heard about horse heads and secret murders and money laundering and brutal family feuds . . ." I trailed off, hoping Nic wouldn't notice I had just listed a bunch of things I had seen in movies over the years. After all, those stories must have come from somewhere.

He inhaled through clenched teeth. "Yes, the families are not exactly *angelic*."

"Well, how do you have their protection if you have to go after at least some of them, too?"

Nic regarded me like I had suddenly sprouted horns. "Sophie," he said, his tone affronted. "We *never* go after members of our own culture, whatever they have done."

All of a sudden I was back on my own planet, watching him

from afar and resisting the urge to shake him until all the stupidity fell out. "Is that a joke?"

"No."

I pulled my legs underneath me and fell back on my haunches so that I was hovering over him on the couch. "So you just go after the ordinary, run-of-the-mill criminals? Not the ones on your side?"

"We can't," he said, looking up at me through thick, dark lashes.

"Why not?"

"Because we'd all have died out by now." He said it so matter-of-factly it surprised me less than it should have.

"But don't mob families fight with one another all the time?" Another movie-based assertion, but I had a feeling I was right about that.

"Yes, but not with us. We are untouchable."

"Because most of the time you're doing their bidding, right? You provide them with a service and in return they keep you living in the lap of luxury," I shot back. "That is so messed up."

Nic shifted so that he was sitting up straighter, putting us at the same height again. "We are eliminating the worst kinds of people in society. Can't you see that?"

I shook my head. How could he be so naïve? "You only kill their competition, Nic. The Mafia can still do whatever they want."

"It's still a service to society."

"It's a selective one."

"Better than none at all."

"Doesn't it bother you? Don't you think about the hypocrisy of it all? Murderers paying you to murder other murderers?" My mind was starting to spin again.

"I try not to think about it."

"You should."

"What?" he asked, his voice wounded. "Consider that my whole family are going to hell for trying to make Chicago a better place for people like you to live in? Consider that no matter how much freedom and protection we have, our hands are still tied by others in our culture?"

"Yes!" I urged. "Think about that!"

"Sophie, there's nothing I can do about it!" His voice escalated with anger. "This is my life. It's everything I've ever known. It's what I know is right. It's *all* I know."

I settled my hands in my lap and fell back from him, recognizing the losing battle I was fighting. "It shouldn't be all or nothing."

"I know," he conceded, exasperated. "But what can I do?"

"You could walk away."

"The only way to leave this way of life is in a coffin," he said with chilling finality.

Silence descended. Part of me understood. I wanted to cry for him and the future he was bound up in, but I didn't. I was too numb, too afraid to consider the possibility that maybe Nic didn't *want* to walk away from his way of life, that he enjoyed the feeling of punishing people, of watching them quiver and beg before him. I studied my cuticles while he studied me.

"It's suicide," I muttered.

Nic sat back and smiled, and for a second he looked like the teenager he was supposed to be. Happy and carefree, not dark and hardened. "My brothers and I, we have been training for this life since we could walk," he said. "We can read situations unlike anyone else. We can break a man's neck ten different ways. We have the knowledge to infiltrate gangs and the skill to shoot their leader from a hundred feet away." He spoke like he was listing a set of everyday skills on his résumé, and not reeling off his special mob-related activities.

"Do you have to answer to the boss of your family?" I asked.

"Yes," Nic said slowly, as though he was starting to realize something. "We follow his instructions."

"Who is he?"

He shook his head like he was coming out of a daze. "Sophie," he said hesitantly. "I've already said far too much. I got carried away . . . I always seem to with you . . ." He trailed off. "You could ruin me now."

"I won't," I said automatically. I hadn't even thought about it, but my heart already had an answer. Despite everything, I didn't want to ruin him. He was already being ruined by the people around him. By his own family. If only he could see that, maybe I could get through to him.

"I can't say anything else," he said.

It didn't matter; I already knew who the boss was.

How could their father have OK'd this when he was alive? My father saw me pretending to smoke a candy cigarette once and nearly grounded me over it. But Nic's father probably bought him his first gun, taught him how to load it, how to aim it, how to kill with it. And now Felice? Surely he had a responsibility to look out for these boys, not use them to kill people.

I fell back against the couch, suddenly feeling exhausted. "You don't have to say anything else," I said softly.

Nic leaned down so that the height of our noses was aligned when he looked at me. "Are you frightened, Sophie?"

I did my best to ignore how close he was. "I don't know."

"You didn't run away."

"Not yet."

His smile was a soft tug at the lips.

I was beginning to feel intoxicated again; dizzy with desire. "You do bad things," I reminded myself aloud, making the mistake of looking into his eyes. How many people had spent their last seconds on earth looking into those eyes?

"Only sometimes," he said quietly.

"Do you have to be so casual about it?"

"I don't feel bad about what I do." He brushed his finger along my neck, and my spine started to tingle. How many necks had he broken with those fingers? "But I feel bad that you dislike this part of me, and this part is almost all of me, Sophie."

"But there's so much kindness in you, Nic," I whispered.

"Kindness for the right people." He watched my lips as he trailed his finger beneath them. "For people like you."

I felt a familiar rush in the air. *Don't get distracted.* What were all those things I'd wanted to say? Suddenly I couldn't remember a single one. "You shouldn't break the law."

He pulled my chin toward him and brushed his nose against

mine. "I know," he hummed against my lips. His breath was as unsteady as mine. *"Bella mia,"* he moaned softly into my mouth, and that was all it took to make my resolve implode.

This time, our kiss was deeper than before. Nic tangled his hands in my hair, pulling me into his body and molding my shape to his. He dragged his mouth along my skin, intoxicating me with his kisses. "Staying away from you is too hard," he groaned into my neck. "I don't want to be good anymore."

"Then don't be," I said, clutching him tighter and feeling the muscles in his back flex against my fingers. Gently, he dipped my head back and found my mouth again, parting my lips with his tongue as he pushed me down across the couch, holding me beneath him.

When the sound of the front door slamming against its hinges made the couch jump under us, we were shocked back into reality. I pulled myself up just in time to see the look of unbridled horror on Nic's face. He shot up, his cheeks flushed with pink, his eyes darting.

CHAPTER TWENTY-THREE

The Underboss

Luca stalked into the room.

"Nic, have you heard from Val — What the hell is she doing here?" The beginning of his sentence differed drastically from its end, which grew substantially in pitch.

Nic raised his hands in the air like he was surrendering to a police officer, positioning his body protectively in front of me as though Luca might lunge and tear my throat out.

He came to tower over us. Fury and shock mingled in his eyes, but there was something else there, too, something I couldn't place. "Nic, I am going to rip your heart out and make you eat it, you stupid . . ." His sentence descended into the worst combination of expletives I had ever heard in one single breath.

Nic jumped to his feet and squared up to his brother. "I had to explain what she saw."

Luca's icy blue eyes flashed with fury. "So you *brought her here?*"

Nic balled his fists. "Don't start."

Feeling dangerously close to losing it, I sprang to my feet and pushed past Luca. I couldn't handle being on the edge of a conversation that would undoubtedly slide right over my head, but still be close enough to drive me insane with questions. I shouldn't have been there with them anyway, and now that my clarity was back, I was going to use it. "I'm going to get out of here."

Nic reached for me, but Luca slapped his hand away. "Let her go," he warned. "Unless you want this whole thing to get worse."

Nic didn't protest, and I wondered why. I stepped away from him, sliding across Luca's stiffened frame without another look at either of them and banging the front door behind me in my own display of hostility.

As I crunched through the gravel of the driveway, my mind revolted with questions about how I had gotten back into the same situation all over again. I had just begun to move on and now I was back at square one, feeling confused and jilted by a *mafioso* who was as good for me as a syringe full of poison.

I started to run, skidding over the gravel, but I didn't get far before something wrapped around my arm and I was twirled unceremoniously into the unyielding frame of the last person I wanted to see.

I removed myself from where I had landed against Luca's chest. He gripped my shoulders and pushed against me until I was backing up against the stone wall at the end of the driveway, pinned between his hands just like before. His face adopted the angry, feral appearance I was already so familiar with. "I thought I told you I don't ever want to see you in my house again." He was so close I could see a small white scar above the right side of his lip. It occurred to me, pretty inappropriately, that I was probably one of very few people alive who knew it was there.

I blew a stray strand of hair from my eyes, rustling his in the process. Now armed with the knowledge that he wouldn't hurt an innocent girl, I felt fractionally more confident about how I could speak to him. "Nic invited me."

"I don't care if the Pope invited you. You're not welcome here."

"Well, take it up with your brother. I don't respect your authority."

My reply provoked his temper, which was etched above his eyebrows in deep dents. "You know you shouldn't be with him."

"I can handle it."

"You can't."

"I know you won't hurt me."

Luca's eyes flashed in warning, but when he spoke again it was quiet — gentle, almost. "That doesn't mean you won't get hurt." He scrunched his eyes in frustration, and when he opened them again they were blazing. "Just tell me what I need to do to get rid of you, since rehashing your father's crime didn't help!"

I pushed my face forward and clenched my jaw. "Tell me what you're doing in Cedar Hill."

Luca regarded me warily, hesitating, then — "No."

"Then I guess I'll just stick around here."

"I wouldn't do that if I were you," he threatened.

"What are you going to do, Luca?" I clenched my fists at my side. "Pull a gun on me?"

"If that's what it takes."

"How brave!" I exploded. We were so close to each other now. "You can't use your words, but you're more than happy to use your gun."

"I'm not going to be responsible for ruining your innocence!"

I tilted my face toward him to show I wasn't afraid, or as innocent as he clearly thought. "Go ahead," I whispered. "Shatter it." We were nose-to-nose. "It *almost* worked last time, when you told me about my dad."

"I don't care," he replied resolutely. "I'm not punching Bambi in the face."

I raised my voice again. "Tell me what you're doing in Cedar Hill!"

Luca moved his unblinking stare from my eyes to my lips and then shook whatever thought was forming out of his head. "No," he said calmly.

I prodded him in the chest, pushing him away. "I know you're in the Mafia. If you think I can't handle that, then you're wrong."

He shook his head again, in disbelief, his voice pulsing with a level of anger that far eclipsed my own. "Of course he told you. That idiot. And you're still here, which doesn't make you any smarter than him."

I glowered at him. "I know you don't hurt innocent people. You're all about 'honor' and 'morals' . . . skewed as they are," I added venomously.

He pulled back, his expression suddenly unreadable. There was a beat of silence and then, in a cold, calculated voice, he said, "And revenge."

"What?"

He narrowed his eyes. "You forgot about revenge."

"What about revenge?" I faltered, thinking about my father. His father. Our history.

Luca's sudden smile sharpened his cheekbones. "Oh, Nicoli left that part out? Figures he'd be selective."

I started to chew on my lip, searching internally for the bravery I had just summoned, but I had spent it all screaming in his face. "He said you're different from the other families."

"Yes." Luca remained perfectly still, watching me like a hawk circling its prey. "Except when it comes to revenge. Like the other families, the Falcones *always* exact revenge, regardless of whether it's morally sanctioned."

"No," I said, jutting out my chin and shaking my head.

"No?" Luca laughed freely; I gathered it was his real laugh, and it was a strange, silvery sound. "Gracewell, you really are something else. What did you think?" he asked bemusedly. "That we're gun-toting, knife-wielding avenging angels without fault or sin? You saw Nic put that gun in Robbie Stenson's mouth. You heard him cock the trigger. Do you really believe that the idea of revenge is above a dynasty of temperamental, hot-blooded, territorial assassins who have appointed themselves the underworld distributors of a kind of karma that shouldn't be policed by anyone else on this earth? Do you think that everything we do is the right thing?"

He shook his head disbelievingly, and I cursed my naïveté. I had been stupid to get swept up in romantic notions of Nic as some sort of vigilante; he was a killer, plain and simple, prone to the same tempers and temptations as the rest of us.

I slid along the wall so I was out from under Luca. He let me, and I felt a pinch of relief. "You're not going to hurt me . . ."

"No," he replied. "I'm not."

"Then why are you being so dramatic about it?"

Luca's voice grew dangerously quiet. "Listen very carefully to what I'm about to say." I had to watch his lips as he spoke because the shards of turquoise in his eyes were suddenly too intense. "I am the underboss of the entire Falcone dynasty, and if I'm telling you to keep your head down and stop coming around here, then you'd better believe I have a damn good reason. You need to get away from this house and as far away from Cedar Hill as you can. Nic might have deluded himself into thinking he can shield you from what's going to happen, but he can't. My father was a made man, and that means your family owes us a blood debt, Sophie."

A blood debt. The air left my lungs in a swift gasp. Luca's expression faltered, but he twisted away from me before I could catch the real emotion behind it. When he reached the door again, he turned around. I was rooted to the same spot like he knew I would be.

"Do you know what that jar of honey meant?" he asked.

My stomach twisted at his tone, at his knowledge of the honey. Although I think I had always known, deep down, that there was a connection, it suddenly felt more sinister now than I ever could have imagined.

I shook my head.

"It wasn't a gift."

"I didn't think it was," I lied.

There was nothing in Luca's voice or on his face now; it was completely void of emotion. He looked past me into the night sky. "There's a reason people in the underworld call my uncle Felice 'the Sting,' you know."

I didn't respond. I just stood there, trying to get my legs to work, as memories of his uncle's bee-stung face crept across my mind.

"When Felice Falcone gives someone a sample of his black-ribboned honey, it means he's going to come back for the jar."

I tried to swallow the tightness in my throat, but it was unyielding.

"And when he does, he brings his gun. That jar of honey is the Falcone Gift of Death." Luca shifted his gaze again, pinning me beneath his stare. "Let that be your final warning. Get out of here while you can."

I blanched, my mind whirling frantically. I had all the pieces, I just had to make them fit. "But what are —"

"Talk to your uncle, Gracewell," Luca cut in. "Or should I say, *Persephone?*"

Before I could respond, he was slamming the door in one deafening bang, leaving me shaking from head to toe.

CHAPTER TWENTY-FOUR

The Intruders

I started home, pulling out my phone and dialing my uncle's number. It rang and rang and went to voice mail. *Come on.* I could have smashed my phone in frustration. I called four more times in a row and still, nothing. I left two voice mails and finally I sent a text:

I know what the honey meant. We need to talk about the Falcones. Call me ASAP.

I was almost home when my phone started ringing.

"Jack," I answered. "I think I'm in danger."

"Sophie, I just read your text. Is everything OK?" His voice was edged with panic, and it was taking hold of mine, too.

"Where the hell have you been? I've been calling you!" I exploded.

"Focus, Sophie," he snapped. "I'll explain all that later. Where are they now?"

"I don't know," I said. There were so many of them they could be anywhere, doing anything. I told him about Luca's threats —

about the blood debt and the honey, my words catching between breathless gasps as I spoke.

"Where are you now?" he asked once I had finished.

I skidded up my driveway. "I'm home," I said.

"Go inside, lock all the doors. I'm sending someone for you."

"Uncle Jack?" I was struggling with my keys. I only had three on the chain, but they kept frittering from my shaky grasp. "Are they going to hurt me?"

"No," he answered too quickly. "Of course not," he added after a beat.

"What's going on?" The million dollar question, and I still hadn't put all the pieces together.

"There really isn't enough time to explain, Sophie." I could hear him barking orders at someone in the background.

I slotted the right key into the lock. The click inside flooded me with relief. "If you knew I'd be in danger, why would you take off like that?"

Now that my fear was ebbing away, I was getting angry. Jack had been avoiding Cedar Hill like the plague for his own safety and he hadn't bothered to tell my mother and me to do the same. So much for that promise he had made to my father. I made a mental note to call my mom after I was done with Jack. She was in the city at a series of bridal fittings until tomorrow evening, but I knew she'd freak out at being left out of the loop. Especially this one.

"Sophie," Jack was saying, his words edged with one big, constant sigh, "they're not going to hurt you. I wouldn't have left you behind if I thought that. Those boys are just shooting their mouths off. That family love the sound of their own voice."

"They want revenge, Jack." I slammed the door behind me and fixed the chain in place. "They want a blood debt for what Dad did. Luca told me himself!" I skirted into the kitchen and climbed onto the countertop. I clamped the phone between my shoulder and my ear so I could lock the windows shut.

The phone line buzzed with Jack's defiance. "Ignore what Luca said. He's just trying to frighten you."

I slid off the counter. "But why?"

"Listen. The Falcones' problem is with me. *Just* me. Not you."

"What do you mean with you?" I jiggled the back door handle to make sure it was locked.

"I can't go into it now. I've sent Eric Cain for you. He'll keep you safe. You've met him before, at my birthday a few years ago."

"I remember," I said, vaguely recalling a small, effeminate man with enviable dark-red hair. How exactly was he supposed to keep me safe?

"I'll meet you somewhere outside of Cedar Hill and we'll talk about it."

"What about Mom?" I asked.

My uncle had the audacity to laugh. I balled my fist until my nails dug into my palm.

"They wouldn't go near Celine," he said dismissively. "She's got nothing to do with me. It's common knowledge your mother loathes the ground I walk on. And they're not interested in punishing your dad, Sophie. Have you locked the doors?"

"Yes." I was in the hall again. I took the stairs two at a time, deciding to lock all the second-floor windows just in case. "Why are you taking me away if I'm not in danger? At least tell me something so I can be prepared."

"It's a precaution, Sophie." He labored over the word "precaution" like it would make me feel better. It didn't. "They would never go after you for what your dad did. The very idea is ridiculous. And even if they *did*, which they *wouldn't*, the Falcone Mafia doesn't hurt innocents. It's one of their almighty, crap-loaded, self-righteous rules. And they just *love* being self-righteous."

I could practically taste the venom. So Jack knew everything I did, and he had decided to be coy about it. And did that mean he *wasn't* innocent? What exactly had he done to make it onto the Deserves-to-Die list? "Sounds like you know a lot about them. Thanks for the heads-up." *You could have saved me a whole lot of time and swooning.*

"I did give you a heads-up."

"Yeah. A *crap* one."

I sprinted back downstairs, my feet hammering against the steps like thunder.

"Sophie, I really can't get into this now." His voice was weary. "Just sit tight. I've sent someone."

"I'm trying." I slid through the ajar door into the living room and snapped the window shut. I was in the middle of pulling the curtains closed when I heard a voice behind me.

"Hello, Sophie."

I dropped the phone. Gino and Dom Falcone stood up from the couch at the same time, moving toward me with matching gaits.

"How did you get into my house?" I tried to find where my phone had fallen, but the room was almost pitch-black. They both shrugged, their faces disguised by the darkness. Had they rehearsed this?

"You should go." I folded my arms in what I hoped was an act of defiance. I raised my voice, too, hoping Jack was still listening. "I'm expecting visitors."

Gino's laugh was a rasping bark. Dom stopped two feet away from me, and his brother hovered behind him, his ponytail adding two solid inches to his height. They smirked the same menacing smile.

"What do you want, Dom?"

"Ideally, Jack," he said. Behind him, Gino nodded animatedly in agreement. "But we can't waste any more time trying to find him. We're done chasing."

"And following you has gotten us nowhere," added Gino, his unibrow furrowed above fathomless eyes. "It's been so *boring*."

I stumbled backward, hitting the backs of my knees against the window ledge. "You've been *following* me?"

I prayed Jack was still listening from wherever my phone had landed.

"Yes," said Dom matter-of-factly. "When we found out who you were, it was a stroke of luck. We thought you'd eventually lead us to your uncle . . ." The way he said it made it sound like he was disappointed in me for failing at a task I had no idea I was doing. "But you didn't."

Gino started snickering through his nose.

"You've been following me," I said again. My voice sounded far away; it was buckling with incredulity. "For how long?"

"Too long," they said together.

"Nic was against it, if that makes it any easier to stomach. He's been fighting to leave you out of this," Dom said with mock sympathy. "But it is what it is."

"Out of what?"

"Fighting and *losing*," Gino sneered, ignoring my question.

"But," added Dom, "if we hadn't been following you, you probably would have been raped that night after the world's most boring party."

"Oh my God." Horror curled in my stomach. "That's how Luca found me."

"He wasn't supposed to intervene," said Dom, his voice suddenly disapproving. "We weren't allowed to do anything that would disrupt your day *unless* your uncle made an appearance, but Luca broke the rules, like he always does. We didn't even know about it until you came around shouting in our driveway."

I blanched. Gino seemed to disengage from the conversation, and his attention started to wander around the darkened room. At a sound from outside, Dom glanced past me through a crack in the curtains. I seized the brothers' momentary distraction and slid around the wall until I was nearer to the door.

They drifted with me like tracking drones.

"I wouldn't if I were you," lisped Gino. "I don't want to hit a girl. Even if it is you."

"You're going to have to come with us." Dom sounded almost

apologetic, but it did little to soothe my slow-burning hatred for him. Not only had he broken into my house and was trying to take me somewhere against my will, but he had obviously used Millie and then dumped her, and that made him a *total, unredeemable asshole.* I slid into the open doorway, but Gino blocked me in an instant. He shot his arm out, covering the sliver of space.

Dom curled around the other side of me, closing in. He glanced at his brother and gave him a controlled nod. Gino dropped to his hands and knees and slithered across the floor like a reptile, swiping his hand around as he crawled. It was completely, unnecessarily dramatic.

I tried to run, but Dom grabbed my arm and pulled me back. "Don't."

Finally, Gino fished out my phone from underneath the armchair and sprang to his feet, dangling it in the air between us. "Gotcha," he said triumphantly to Dom.

Dom took the phone and held it to his ear. "Jackie boy?" he sneered. The distant sound of shouting filled my ears. "I think it's time we finished this."

Laughing to himself, Gino shuffled to my side. "Time for Sophie to say bye-bye." His smile revealed his two chipped teeth, and his tongue poked out beneath them. I was still straining to hear what Jack was saying when Gino's hands disappeared from my view.

Dom covered the mouthpiece and redirected to his brother. "Hurry up," he said.

The damp rag came out of nowhere.

PART III

♥

"And where the offense is, let the great axe fall."
WILLIAM SHAKESPEARE, *Hamlet*

CHAPTER TWENTY-FIVE

The Valentine Vendetta

I could hear buzzing. It made the world vibrate, pulsing inside my eardrums until it felt like the bees were coming from inside my skull. I twitched awake. The sweetest cacophony of smells hung in the air, coaxing me from the darkness that had engulfed me so completely. I opened my eyes to a white ceiling and felt a horrible tightness in my chest.

I groaned.

"Ah, you're awake, at last. I was wondering how long that would take to wear off."

I didn't have to turn my head in the direction of the voice to know who it belonged to. It was unusually soft for a man's tone, and each syllable was pronounced with overexaggerated precision, betraying his faint Italian accent.

"Felice," I said. I tried to sit up, but I couldn't. My arms and legs were bound together by cable ties; they cut into my wrists and squeezed the bottom of my bare ankles uncomfortably. "Where am I?"

"Generally? You are in Lake Forest. Specifically? You are reclining on my couch."

The leather squeaked as I heaved my clasped hands toward my bound legs and pulled them together, crunching into an upright position. I swiveled my body around, dropping my knees over the couch and placing my hands in my lap as a streak of white sunlight slashed across my vision, making my eyelids flutter.

I was almost level with an open bay window across the room. The sun was beginning to dip in the pink-tinged sky — I must have been out for a long time. I could tell I was at least one story up. Outside, there was an old wooden barn tucked behind a sprawling garden with vibrant flowers that faded into open fields. Tens of small wooden sheds dotted the grass in regimented lines.

"Beehives," I realized aloud. I could just about make out the swarms of bees droning in the distance, and there were at least two more buzzing somewhere inside the room.

"Well noted, Persephone," said Felice. He was sitting bolt upright in an armchair directly across from me, one impossibly long leg crossed over the other.

I rolled my eyes over him and frowned. Everything about him — from his silver slicked-back hair and his Mediterranean complexion to his expensive pin-striped suit — screamed *creepy Mafia dude*. And judging by the house so far, not to mention its location, he was rich.

"It's Sophie," I replied.

"Apparently it is. If only we had been aware of that sooner, it would have saved us quite the confusion. We would have known you from the outset."

From what I could see we were the only ones in the room. Aside from the black leather couch on which I sat, there was nothing else but Felice and his bees. They were flying in wide circles around his head as though they were defending him, and I felt my skin prickle uncomfortably at the sight.

"I must say I'm surprised you haven't screamed yet." He settled an elbow on each armrest and brought his hands together in the middle so that each finger touched off its correspondent.

"Would there be a point in screaming?"

He shook his head. "We are far removed from civilization. It is just you and the bees, Persephone."

I felt a vague semblance of fear somewhere deep inside, but my head was still fuzzy from whatever had put me to sleep. It was hard to arrange my emotions appropriately, and even more difficult not to say the wrong thing. I knew I had been kidnapped, but I couldn't determine the correct response. I zeroed in on the pockmarks along Felice's neck and face. They were shiny and red, and bubbling angrily in places.

"So this is where you live with all your bees? How romantic." I knew I shouldn't have said it, but my brain had disengaged from keeping my actions appropriate. "Pity they sting you so much."

He raised his eyebrows, causing ripples along his forehead. "It is my personal choice not to wear a mesh veil when in the company of my bees. I feel it separates us needlessly; I prefer to be close to them, to feel them on my skin." He flicked his gaze to the bee flying nearest his head and smiled like a proud parent. "It is an honor to be stung by such noble creatures. That they would lay down their lives for a fleeting moment of my attention is extraordinary. There is no creature more majestic than the honeybee."

"If you say so," I said, without registering what I meant. My brain was so cloudy, and the buzzing was making it worse.

"I do say so. The honeybee is already dying out and it is my contention that we must do our very best to protect nature's noble children."

Nature's noble children? I could have knocked myself out again just to keep from dealing with the crazy in front of me. "What do you want with me?"

Felice pursed his lips. It made his chin look unnaturally sharp. He didn't answer. He just stared at me, and I got the sense I had offended him by moving the topic away from his bees.

"Can you at least loosen these ties? They really hurt." My wrists and ankles were red-raw and stinging.

He shook his head; it was almost imperceptible this time. "Not quite yet, Persephone."

"My name is Sophie. I don't call you Fabio."

Felice threw back his head and laughed until his eyes began to water. "Of all the things you could be angry about," he said, wiping them with the back of his hand. "You are a funny one."

I didn't feel humorous, I felt drugged. "I got your honey, by the way. Thanks *so* much."

"I think we both know it was not meant for you, but for the sake of clarity, since I cannot fathom whether you are playing dumb or actually *being* dumb, I shall elucidate. The honey was intended for your uncle."

"I don't think he appreciated it."

"Oh no?" Felice contorted his features into the most elaborate smile I had ever seen. It was as terrifying as it was disingenuous.

"He smashed it," I said, setting my tone to serious. Whatever delirious desire I had to be a smart-ass was fading. I was coming to my senses again.

"It happens." Felice waved his hand in the air dismissively. "I know you're not supposed to tip off your victims, but I just can't help my flair for theatrics. And I'll have you know I prepare the honey myself and it is positively delicious, not that anyone ever bothers to try it."

"I tried it. It tasted off," I lied.

"That's an incredibly rude thing to say." Felice made a point of grimacing at me before continuing. "Still, it does its job. I do think everyone deserves a fair warning so they can get their affairs in order."

"Before you kill them?" I asked. Though I already knew, I wanted him to say it so it would kick my fuzzy brain into gear.

"Of course." Felice smiled, revealing two long rows of sharp teeth. "Head start or no head start, we always catch up in the end. And sometimes, I daresay, the chase is the best part."

A shudder rippled up my spine. Finally, and unpleasantly, the urgency of the situation had settled on me; I had more people than just myself to think about. "Why did you send my uncle the Gift of Death?" My voice cracked, and a wave of fear careened over me. "If it has something to do with revenge for what my father did, he didn't mean it."

Felice raised his finger to hush me. "The death of my beloved brother Angelo at the hands of your father was, of course, regrettable, but I don't believe there was any ill intent on your father's part."

I felt my shoulders dip. "That's good."

"That is not to say, however, that this situation is not about revenge. Because," he said, standing to his full height, "of course, it is."

Felice's tallness suddenly seemed so much more formidable. He began pacing up and down, and I got the sense he did this all the time — intimidation by theatrics. He probably had a special suit for every occasion. His neck scarf cascaded behind him as he glided back and forth.

"I think it is reasonable to ascertain now that you are clearly unaware that your uncle, Jack Gracewell, is a pivotal member of the biggest drug cartel in the Midwest. The Golden Triangle Gang, as they so eloquently call themselves. Would I be correct in assuming so?"

I gaped at him. It couldn't be true. It had to be part of his theatrics.

"Among other things, they have recently begun dealing a hybrid narcotic that, when taken, elicits effects similar to those associated with extreme intoxication, and can lead to an array of unfortunate aftereffects, including paranoia, memory loss, paralysis, and my personal *least* favorite, death." He shook his head at the world outside, like all the birds and flowers had let him down at once.

"No" was all I could muster. Words were failing me. I was dumbfounded and Felice could see it; worse than that, he was thriving on it, like a well-dressed parasite.

He started pacing again. "Of course, we've been monitoring your uncle and his not-so-esteemed business partners for nearly four years — right back to the time when he began using the diner, your homey family establishment, to stash drug shipments between deliveries."

"What?" I spluttered back into life. "Jack used my father's diner for drug trafficking?"

"Well, I would have thought those two dots would have been easy to connect, but maybe I'm too close to the situation, so it's easier for me." Felice hunkered down so he could be closer to me. "Initially there were just three pivotal members of the Golden Triangle Gang operating on this side of the Atlantic, each one positioned at a different key point in the Midwest; points that, when drawn together on a map, form a perfect triangle" — he made a triangle in the air with his fingers — "of ill-earned profit."

I felt a bee buzzing dangerously close to my ear and jerked my head on reflex.

"Careful," Felice warned. He sprang to his feet again. "As the Falcone boss, my brother Angelo was principally in charge of ending this chain of unlawful activities. It was no mean feat, but we have always said, 'The falcon does not hunt flies.' Together we were to change the face of the Midwest narcotics underworld."

Felice's movements turned fluid, one hand tucked behind his back wistfully, as though he were taking an evening stroll down a quiet street.

"My brother was successful in coordinating the demise of founding fathers one and two of the Golden gang in relatively quick succession, not to mention several key members of their respective crews." He widened his colorless eyes and looked toward the ceiling like he was talking to someone beyond it.

"And if I may say, the family made *quite* an artful job of them, but I would hate to offend your sensibilities, Persephone, so I won't go into the details."

I remembered the newspaper article with a jolt. It had mentioned the Golden Triangle Gang. Angelo Falcone had been suspected of their murders — their *brutal* murders — but was never charged. I didn't know whether I could bring myself to believe it, but before I could stop myself I was saying, "And Jack was number three."

"And Jack Gracewell was the elusive third point on said triangle," Felice confirmed, his expression suddenly somber. He cracked his knuckles, one by one, and I noticed they were stung just as badly as his face. "Miss Gracewell, I have yet to meet a more slippery, unconscionable individual than your uncle."

Me too, I realized as nausea rose in my stomach. If everything Felice said was true, I didn't know my uncle at all. Sure, I knew Jack was capable of acting out of line: He drank too much, he had a short fuse, and he had a tendency to disappear sometimes. But these accusations were something else entirely.

"We almost did it, you know — wiped them all out — and that might have been the end of it, but of course it wasn't. Because Angelo ran into the wrong brother that fateful Valentine's night, and then everything changed in the blink of an eye."

I could taste the bile rising in my throat. I thought of my father all alone in the dark outside the diner and how scared he must have been when Angelo Falcone approached him, yelling. He had no idea who was coming for him. He couldn't have. He would never be involved in something like that. Right? I clenched my fists to stop my hands from shaking. Just how many people in my life weren't who they said they were?

"I didn't know Jack had a brother who looked *so* like him until the night I saw him shoot *my* brother. That's terrible research, is it not? I can tell you, a lot of heads rolled after that unfortunate mix-up." Felice allowed himself a fleeting smirk before adding, "Literally."

"You were there?"

He sighed, his bravado diminishing. "It was dark, and Angelo approached the wrong Gracewell. The plan was for my brother to subdue Jack and drag him back into the alley behind the diner so that I would shoot him in private — it was my personal request, you see — but we never got that far, and that is something you do know, at last."

I flinched at the thought of him shooting Jack.

Felice wagged his finger at me, back and forth like a metronome, until I wanted to rip it off and spit it back in his face. "You mustn't conceptualize me as the monster. It was Jack who was *and is* contributing to society's underbelly in the worst way. And it was *Jack* who got your father into such an unfortunate position. If I were ever to traffic drugs, which *of course* I would not, I certainly wouldn't use one of my brother's family establishments for storage."

"Jack isn't into that stuff." Doubt caused my words to falter. They fell out of my mouth, unsteady and forced. "My father would never let him do that. I don't believe you." I would have crossed my arms and stormed off if I could have. Not because I was angry, but because I was afraid of the truth, and what it meant for my understanding of family, of right and wrong.

"Well fortunately for me, it is of no concern whether you choose to believe me. It does not change the truth of the matter."

The more I thought about it, though, the more I teetered toward his version of events. After all, it was strange to think that Angelo Falcone would be skulking, unarmed, around a small suburban diner in the middle of the night. And stranger still was all of Jack's mysterious business in the city. And the money he always seemed to have, the fancy cars and the exquisite suits. There was always something a little off about him: something that caused my mother to keep him at arm's length, something that had kept him from settling down with a family of his own. And then there was his vehement hatred of the Falcones. The more I pieced everything together, the less ridiculous it was beginning to sound. "So if it is true . . ." I began.

"It is," clarified Felice.

"Well, why am I here now, if this isn't about my father? I haven't done anything wrong."

"After the unfortunate death of my beloved brother, Jack's activities experienced a significant decline, so much so that we believed the Golden Triangle to be finished entirely. Of course, we were always going to finish what we started with him — after the appropriate mourning period, that is. I must admit Angelo's death took a heavy toll on all of us, the boys especially. But when we discovered our intel was incorrect and that Jack is now *spearheading* the entire gang from the city, we realized we would have to dispatch of him sooner rather than later. We procured a residence in Cedar Hill, and from there, we have been picking off your uncle's key associates one by one."

Did that explain the drowned deliveryman — was Luis part of this, too? And all the other mysterious disappearances Mrs. Bailey had been so eager to point out — the ones I had been so quick to ignore? All this time, and right under my nose, they were killing people.

"That's horrible," I said, feeling dazed.

"Actually it's competence," Felice corrected me. "And now, with Jack proving to be the final piece of the puzzle — and weakened without his most trusted henchmen — we must end him sooner rather than later, before he can regroup. It must finally come to an end the way my brother intended it to."

I panicked at the thought of what they would do to Jack, wondering just how many of his "associates" had been killed over the past few months, and trying not to think about which ones had met their deaths at the end of Nic's gun. "So you're going to kill him."

"Yes." Felice eased himself into the chair like his bones would snap if he weren't careful. "And that, lovely *Persephone*, is where you come in."

I bristled. "That's *not* my name."

"I don't see why you have chosen to cast it off." He paused as if expecting me to justify something that seemed so unbearably trivial to me now. When I didn't answer, he continued with obvious bewilderment. "Why wouldn't you want to associate yourself with the majestic and beautiful Queen of the Underworld, the wondrous and infernal Goddess of Death? Sophie is so *plain* in comparison."

"Do you really expect me to answer that?"

"The significance of such a name is amusing to me. You have even found your Hades." He smirked, and I got the feeling he was expecting me to be impressed by his knowledge of Greek mythology. I wasn't.

When I didn't reply, he continued. "It was Dominico who found out who you were, when he was with that trivial British waitress, trying to gather information on Jack. By the time Nicoli realized that you were, in fact, *Persephone* Gracewell, he tried to pull away from you, but it was too late. Suddenly you had become the most viable way to lead us to our intended target at a time when we were running out of patience."

I thought of Nic and frowned. All this time he was fighting his desires for my safety, and he was losing. And lying.

"But you didn't see the danger, did you? Because you see only the parts you want to see, and you are blind to all else."

I glowered at him. "I'm not blind to anything." *Except my uncle's secret life as a drug kingpin. And my crush's secret life as a killer.*

"Of course, of course," Felice replied dismissively. "How would an old fool like me know anything about that? I have no doubt you are perfectly in love and that you've counted all the notches on his trigger hand *lovingly*." He leered at me and I hated him for it; but most of all, I hated him because he was right. I hadn't reconciled myself with that part of Nic; I had tried to ignore it. I had even tried to justify it.

"So you see," Felice purred on, "when Jack fled, he foolishly left *you* behind, the very thing that will cause his undoing. We expected you might lead us to him.

"However, since your uncle is smarter than your average deck chair and has inexplicably been able to outrun us thus far, we must move on to a more improvised plan, in which you are *bait*." He clapped his hands together. "If Jack doesn't present himself to us at the abandoned auto parts warehouse in Hegewisch before midnight tonight, then things will take a very unfortunate turn."

"So you're going to kill me?" I asked, feeling completely hollow inside. Was this really how it was going to end? I had fallen down a tunnel of lies, and now there was a gun to my head?

Felice stared at me impassively. "The idea of killing a teenage girl just doesn't appeal to me, but I think you'll really have to ask someone better qualified to answer, Persephone."

"Like who?"

Felice rose to his feet again. "Our boss."

My mouth dropped open. "You're not the boss?"

"Me?" A shadow passed across his face, but before I could focus on it, he lit up, until he looked like a children's cartoon character. "I am not. But thank you for assuming so. I'm flattered."

"What are *you*, then?"

"Me? I'm just a simple beekeeper." As he said it, one of his bees droned into my eyeline, just a foot away from my face, as though he had programmed it to do so.

"And a murderer," I reminded him.

"I do feel we can all be defined by more than one thing."

"Unless you're a killer. Then that's pretty much all you amount to."

"Maybe you should tell that to your father. Or to your handsome Hades, between kisses."

If I could have jumped out of my seat and ripped his face off right then, I would have.

"In any case," he continued in his patronizing way, "I'm just the Falcone *consigliere*. I offer advice, which is usually ignored. I'll find someone more equipped to answer your question. Frankly, I've grown weary of your teenage sarcasm."

CHAPTER TWENTY-SIX

The Boss

I heard him before I saw him — the hardwood floors rumbled as he glided into my eyeline, his hands barely touching the wheels to make them move. He turned with a series of expert flicks and then he was facing me. His frame was narrow, but not hunched as I'd remembered; he was dressed in black pants and a crisp black button-up shirt that pulled across his shoulders. The occasion? My doom.

He shifted his left leg so that it stretched out toward me, grazing the floor. His right leg, which was bony and turned in at the hip, slumped against it so that he looked twisted from the waist down. He released his hands from the wheels and entwined his fingers in his lap. The first time I saw him, he was behind a table, coaxing the emotion from his absentee subjects and showing me a different world with his pencils. Now he was watching me through that delicate azure gaze, his lips set in a hard line.

"You wanted to see me?" That musical voice. I struggled to believe it could be the commanding force of an entire fleet of assassins.

"Valentino," I said, my voice surprisingly steady. I spoke like I had known him for years, but his expression didn't break. It was unreadable. "Please tell me this isn't true."

He shifted in his wheelchair, pulling himself up, and he was taller all of a sudden, his shoulders broader than before. I realized I had been a fool to think him weak. "What isn't true?" he hummed.

"You're the boss of this whole thing?" I said.

He raised his jet-black brows. "By 'thing' do you mean 'family'?"

"Yes."

"Is it so hard to believe?" he countered.

I leaned forward, like I was trying to pierce the invisible wall between us. "Yes. It is hard to believe."

He tapped the right wheel of his chair with his finger. "Because of this?" There was a hint of bitterness in his response.

"No. Because you seemed so . . . empathetic before."

"I am empathetic," he replied. "It's one of my more prevalent traits."

"But you kill people." My voice was wavering.

Again he tapped his chair by way of explanation. "I *order* kills."

"That's not much better."

"It is a necessary evil for a greater good," he answered evenly. "It is what it is."

"Are you really going to kill me?" My voice cracked and a string of tears slid down my cheek onto my neck, dampening it uncomfortably. Still I kept my chin up. If nothing else, I would be brave.

Valentino was slow to respond. He shifted his gaze out the window. "Yes."

"Even if Jack shows up?" I couldn't believe what I was asking; I shouldn't have even entertained the possibility of anyone's life being forfeited for mine, but it turns out my survival instincts were crueler than I was.

Valentino turned back to me. He smiled, just a little. "Even then."

I opened my mouth to speak, but a strangled cry escaped instead. Shaking, I buried my head in my bound hands and wept hard, trying to get it all out at once. I had to pull it together, to try and find a way out of this, but my shoulders were convulsing and my breathing was coming in thick gasps.

"If you would allow me to explain," he said. I wouldn't look at him, but his tone was entirely unaffected by my emotional melt-down. "I don't want to be anything other than fair in this role that was given to me. I try to be as logical as I can when making decisions about life and death."

"But you're *not* fair," I sobbed. "None of this is fair. I'm not a drug dealer! I'm just a girl!"

"A Gracewell girl. And a loose end, I'm afraid."

He let me cry in silence, and he didn't speak again until I finally lifted my head.

"Jack's debt is owed because of his prolific drug activity and the destructive, far-reaching effects it has had. That much is plain to see. But your father's debt to us is owed because of what he did to my father."

"Your father was trying to kill him!" I shouted. I was shaking so bad I felt like I was going to combust. "Of course he defended himself! The whole thing was an accident. Even Felice admits my father didn't do anything on purpose!"

"How do you know?" The impassive nature of Valentino's response caught me off guard. For a laughable moment I found myself feeling foolish for reacting so violently, when he could have had this conversation the same way he would have talked if he were ordering a pizza for dinner.

"What do you mean?" The words quivered in my throat.

"How do you know your father was innocent?" he asked, studying my reaction. "How do you know your uncle didn't confide in him? That he wasn't prepared to do the unthinkable to defend his family?"

"Because . . ." I faltered.

Valentino narrowed his eyes, and I felt colder all of a sudden.

"Because my father would never hurt someone deliberately," I said with renewed confidence. I wasn't sure of much, but I was sure of that. "He's not capable of such a thing."

"Did you think your uncle was capable of masterminding an entire drug cartel before today?"

I hesitated.

"Did you think I was capable of overseeing a dynasty of assassins before the moment in which we now find ourselves?"

I looked away from him, but he didn't relent.

"Did you think, the first time he kissed you, that Nic was capable of drowning a man in his own bathtub?"

"Stop," I pleaded, feeling an overwhelming urge to vomit. "Just stop."

"Masks," said Valentino. "Look what happens when we take them off."

"It's horrible." I buried my face in my hands again so he wouldn't have the satisfaction of watching his words burn right through me.

"Absolute chaos," he reminded me calmly, like he had not just annihilated my family's reputation. "Since it is principally my decision, I think when we have apprehended your uncle at the warehouse, the correct course of action is to settle your father's blood debt, once and for all."

I lifted my head again, feeling dizzy and nauseous. "So you're going to use me to lure him out and then kill me anyway?"

Valentino shrugged. "It is the best plan."

I thought of my mother and Millie and had to choke back another sob. My mother wouldn't survive this, she was barely hanging on as it was. And Millie — she had given up entire friendships to stick by me after my dad went to prison. She didn't have anyone else, not anymore. We only had each other.

When Valentino spoke again his voice was clinical, though the musical edge endured, lilting his words as they stung, one by one. "Nic won't come for you, Sophie. He doesn't know about any of this."

I didn't say anything. I just sat there, feeling the hollowness inside me harden.

"Do you want a handkerchief?" He pulled a silken red square from the pocket of his shirt. His initials were monogrammed in black thread in the corner.

I ignored the gesture. "I thought you liked me. I thought we understood each other."

"I do like you." He tucked the handkerchief back in place, unaffected by my refusal. "If the circumstances were different, I think we'd be friends."

"But you're all set to kill me?"

He spoke matter-of-factly. "The reason I was appointed to this position by my father was because I have always been adept at keeping my personal feelings separate from the Falcone mission. I have the ability to compartmentalize."

"Congratulations," I spat.

"I'm not sure what Nic told you about me." His left leg twitched against his right in a sudden spasm. "But Luca and I were appointed together, did you know that? Two bosses. It was a decision that was unheard of in underworld circles, but for our family it made sense. We have done everything together since before birth, each of us a half of one whole. I would remain cool and collected, making the decisions from afar, and he would ensure they were carried out effectively. That was the idea of it. Together we would be the perfect boss: fair and efficient. Removed and yet completely involved."

"But he's not the boss. He's the underboss," I argued pointlessly.

If Valentino was surprised by my knowledge of their infrastructure, he didn't show it. "That's right." He smiled, revealing a glimpse of his teeth. "He deferred to me entirely shortly after our father's death. He stepped back from his part in this role."

"Why?" I gaped. If any of the five brothers fit the definition of a mob boss, it was Luca. Or so I'd have thought.

Valentino raised his hands, gesturing at the room and everything it encompassed: me, him, a black leather couch, my impending death. "Perhaps because of this. These kinds of maneuvers are particularly difficult to stomach." He paused for a moment, ruminating on something. "Or," he ventured, "perhaps he felt like he owed me." He casually fanned his fingers toward his mangled leg, but his face flashed with something else. "In any case, Luca and I had always worked together in perfect harmony, until this situation came upon us. Of course, I argue with Nic all the time, so it's no surprise we've had to keep him out of this, but this is the first time in my life that I have ever disagreed with my twin brother over anything. And the fact that it's about the fate of a Gracewell girl he doesn't even know is truly beyond me."

I felt an unexpected heave in my chest.

"But I'm the boss," Valentino surmised, the lyrical lilt of his voice veiling the bluntness of his statement. I got the sense he didn't want the flicker of hope inside me growing any stronger.

"So the final decision rests with you," I realized.

"It does," he said solemnly. "And Luca will respect that."

And just like that, the flicker died.

"Have you heard from my uncle?" I wished I could call Jack and tell him not to bother coming for me. If they were going to kill me anyway, the whole thing would be a trap.

"It's difficult to persuade a drug baron, who is selfish by

nature, to trade his life for another's, even if that other is someone very dear to him. But I'm sure when he sees our video of you, he will understand the true gravity of the situation."

"What video?"

Valentino dipped his head, turning from me. "Be brave for Calvino or he will go harder on you."

He left, and I was alone again.

CHAPTER TWENTY-SEVEN

The Video

Sometime later, a door opened and closed behind me, and the sound of heavy footsteps punctuated the silence. A bald, stern-looking man with a thick black mustache stalked across the room. I remembered him from that day at the restaurant — Calvino.

He seated himself in Felice's vacant armchair, contorting his angular features until they looked like prosthetics, and stared right through me.

"I saw you at the Eatery a few weeks ago," I said, hoping that kindling a conversation might offer a way out of whatever he was planning to do to me. "You killed the bee."

His smirk curled into a grimace. "And I'm still paying for it." His voice was rasping and deep, and it occurred to me — however absurdly — that he might make a good radio announcer. If killing people didn't work out, that is.

"What are you going to do to me?"

"Much the same." His expression darkened and he moved his stare back to the door behind me just as it swung open.

A boy of around twelve came to stand behind Calvino, resting his hand across his shoulder like some creepy family portrait setup. The boy was obviously his son. They shared pointy chins that jutted out below thin, pale lips and hooked noses that dominated their faces. Their eyes were dark with heavy lids, and, like all of the Falcones, they shared an olive complexion.

Calvino gestured at the boy, and in response he whipped out a phone — *my phone* — from his pocket.

"Hey!" I yelled, startling myself. They both turned to me, identical looks of surprise making their faces seem impossibly long. "That's my phone, you little shit. Give it back."

"No," the boy hissed.

"C.J.," his father cautioned him. "I said no talking to her."

C.J. frowned. "Tell me when you want me to start recording," he said to his father, clicking into the camera feature on my phone and making the flash on the back of it light up.

Of course. They were going to send the video to Jack from my own phone. Calvino stood and rolled up his black shirtsleeves until the end of a tattoo peeked out on his right bicep. Instinctively I pushed back against the couch and brought my legs higher in front of my huddled frame.

"Should I start now?" C.J. was hopping from foot to foot.

"Yeah." Calvino whipped a knife out of his pocket and flicked the blade open. I recognized it as a Falcone switchblade — it was identical to Nic's.

"Should he be witnessing this?" I gestured at his son as he moved toward me. "He's just a kid."

Calvino raised his thick eyebrows — they matched his caterpillar mustache perfectly. "He is a Falcone."

He retained his shocked expression for five full seconds, as if to indicate that great offense had been taken at my question. I used the time to grapple against the couch; I brought my legs up until they blocked the rest of my torso, and tried to push myself over the top as the knife-wielding madman and his son moved toward me.

"Do you want to introduce it?" his son asked.

Calvino seemed surprised by C.J.'s apparent ingenuity. "Good idea."

A wide grin spread across the boy's acne-fied face.

I pushed against the couch with my bound feet as Calvino zeroed in on me, casually, like he knew no matter how hard I tried, he would get the better of me. He stowed the blade and grabbed onto my arm. I sailed back toward the middle of the couch with one stiff yank. Then he shuffled in beside me so we were both under the phone's lens. He dropped to his haunches and pulled me by the collar of my T-shirt so C.J. could zoom in.

The pungent smell of aftershave rolled over me. I noticed, with horror and an irrepressible sliver of intrigue, that a thick white scar rippled along where Calvino's hairline might have been once upon a time. As he tilted closer toward me, it glowed beneath the lights, making the top of his head look like a lid.

"Jack Gracewell" — like steel claws shredding a bass drum, every syllable scraped at his throat — "I hope this video finds you gravely unwell."

C.J. gave him a thumbs-up from behind the phone. I tried to inch away from his father's shiny head, but he squeezed the back of my neck until he broke the skin with his fingernails, and I let out a yelp of pain.

"As you can see, we have your beloved niece, Miss Persephone Gracewell." He patted my hair in one long sliding motion. I tried to jerk my head away again, but he grabbed my jaw and pulled me back so that it unhinged itself with a small *pop*. I closed my eyes and tried not to scream as I set it back into its socket in one agonizing click.

"As you are aware," he continued to the camera, swatting my flailing hands down in a painful blow, "we were not happy with our conversation earlier and feel your hesitance should result in escalation on our side."

Escalation? The word rang in my head like a car alarm.

Calvino grabbed my hair and twined his fingers in it, pulling roughly. I threw my arms against his chest, pummeling it as hard as I could, but he angled away from me so I was punching at the air.

"Please!" I screamed.

He kept twisting his fingers through my hair, yanking so hard it felt like he was trying to rip my scalp off.

"You have until midnight to come alone and unarmed to the abandoned warehouse on the outskirts of Old Hegewisch, where we will talk about the terms of your business activity and the girl's release."

So they were misleading him twofold: once about his own fate and once about mine. "You lying assholes," I spat.

Calvino flung his hand across my face. The blow stung the tears out of my eyes. Bucking wildly, I hit him in the shoulder; he recoiled and cursed under his breath. Seizing the moment his distraction allowed me, I rolled off the couch and struggled to my feet, hopping toward the door.

Calvino lurched forward and grabbed my shoulders, pulling me back to him and that godforsaken couch. I covered my face with my bound hands as he loomed over me, breathing raggedly through his nose. He bent down until I could feel his breath across my hair, ruffling it away from my forehead as he forced my hands from my face.

He slammed the heel of his hand against my nose, and my upper teeth imprinted on the inside of my lips. The taste of salt and rust oozed away from my gums, mixing with the stream of blood coming from my nose. I wheezed as it trickled out over my lips and down my chin.

"Stop," I begged. I started to claw up over the couch, but Calvino yanked me back again. My head landed against his chest with a thud and he held it there.

"If you don't show up, Jack," he resumed his psycho video voice-over, "we'll kill her. And then we will come for you with every man we have until you are hanging from the ceiling of your restaurant." He pushed me away and I fell back against the couch, aching and trembling.

C.J. scurried up until there was less than a foot between the lens and me, and I could make out every pus-filled zit on his greasy face.

"You see what you make me do, Gracewell?" Calvino paused as if he was expecting Jack to respond. My crying filled the silence. I hadn't even realized I was sobbing until I heard myself. He gestured to C.J. to turn it off.

"Nailed it!" his son chimed. "It's good." Like he had just gotten an A on a test instead of a video documenting the abuse of a defenseless seventeen-year-old girl.

I spat a pool of blood onto Calvino's silk shirt. "You're a monster!"

He raised his hand at me and I flinched away from it. "Watch your tongue," he cautioned. "Or I'll take it from your mouth." Then he stood up and laid a heavy hand on his son's shoulder. "Show the video to Felice and send it through. He'll be leaving soon to set up for Gracewell's arrival. I'll follow later with the girl."

"Can I go, too?" C.J. asked excitedly.

"Next time."

Nice to know this kind of thing was a regular occurrence in the Falcone family.

The boy disappeared, leaving me alone with my torturer. I fell back into a seated position and pulled my limbs into my body.

"Nothing's broken," Calvino informed me in a way that implied I was being overdramatic. He sauntered back to the chair and relaxed into it with a deep sigh.

I wanted to shout profanities at him, but my energy was dying with each breath. I knew I had to escape, if not for me, then for my mother, and my best friend, and my father. And even Jack. Deep down I was still hoping for something that would explain this, something that would make it less horrific than it seemed.

Calvino was watching me, his gaze unblinking. I flicked my attention around the room. I could jump through the window, but I would probably break my leg on landing. And then there were all those bees to think about. Even if I could somehow get the ties off, I'd have to run through the fields at the back or take a chance going through the front of the house. I didn't know how many people were here or how big the place was. The door was behind me. If I was lucky, maybe Calvino would get bored and fall asleep. It was dark out now.

My thoughts were still whirling when he stood again. He rerolled his sleeves.

"What are you doing?" I tried to hop off the couch, but the binds on my legs tripped me.

"I wasn't finished," Calvino replied as I landed against the floor and tried to slither away from him, using my butt and my legs like a caterpillar. "I just needed a rest."

He rounded on me. I scooted furiously until my head banged against one of the walls. He brought his foot back like he was going to kick a ball, but I rolled over at the last second.

I pulled myself across the floor with my hands. He kicked me again, and this time it landed on my right side. I heard a faint crack as the wind left my lungs. Twinkling stars began to cloud my vision as I clawed at the rough wooden floors. There was a labored grunt from somewhere above and I crumpled as another blow hurtled into me.

Waves of nausea rocked back and forth inside me. I pulled my knees into my chest and cradled myself into a fetal position as shrieks of uncontrollable pain ripped through my body. Calvino began circling my frame. This time, instead of kicking me, he flipped me over with his shoe so that I landed under the force of my own body. He started to press against my back with his heel.

"Stop," I wheezed. I tried to claw across the wood, but he stamped down harder, and then I heard the flick of his switchblade from somewhere above me.

"Please," I panted, but to whom, I didn't know. I was on my own, and I had to do something before it was too late.

He rolled me over again, until I lay flat out under the glaring ceiling lights, squinting as his angular face came back into focus.

He brandished the blade, running his thumb along the edge. Slowly, I pushed myself onto my side and pulled my legs back behind me, bending them a little at the knees. This was my last hope. I prayed he wouldn't move before I could swing them forward again, and he didn't; he was too busy staring amorously at the blade as it glinted above me.

It was my only chance: I pushed against the floor with my bound hands and swung the lower half of my body forward with as much force as I could muster, using my elbow and my hips to propel myself. My legs swooped in a semicircle, and by the time Calvino noticed what I was trying to do, they were already knocking his legs out from under him.

In what felt like slow motion, he careened backward, tumbling from his tremendous height. The blade landed with a *ping* beside my shoulder. His head hit the wall behind him with a deafening thump. He crumpled and slid toward the floor a couple of feet away from me, and then, apart from one brief twitch in his leg, he lay perfectly still.

I crunched into an upright position, biting hard on my bottom lip to stop the screams of agony building inside me. I grabbed the knife and got to work on my leg binds, sawing through them as quickly as possible, and glancing at Calvino every few seconds to make sure he wasn't about to lunge at me and choke me out. His eyes were shut, but his chest was still rising and falling, so I knew I was short on time. The ties around my ankles came away.

I curled my hand around the knife and tried to cut backward into the binds on my hands, but I couldn't find the right angle and each attempt was useless. But I had come too far to fail now, with tied wrists or not. I held the knife between my hands and rocked back and forth until I could push up onto my feet.

When I stood up, the pain in my chest tore through me like a flame. I doubled over, clutching the knife inside my fist. Using the wall as my anchor, I slid forward against it, one baby step and then another, forcing my screams into breathless sobs. The door was close enough to touch. Behind me, Calvino's breathing was growing steadier.

Slowly, I started to slump against the wall. I held my ribs tight against my bound hands, but the strength was petering out of my body. I was shuddering with pain, and suddenly escape seemed impossible. He was going to catch me.

I couldn't lift my head, and I couldn't see the door anymore. But I was close enough to feel the surge of air that rippled inside when it swung open in front of me. With every last ounce of strength, I forced my chin away from my chest and fixed my gaze forward.

"Sophie?"

I opened my mouth to yell, but the words came out in breathless puffs. "You. Asshole."

CHAPTER TWENTY-EIGHT

The Escape

Luca and I stared at each other for a long, agonizing moment. I watched his expression darken. I tried to speak again, but I couldn't. I knew I was teetering on the edge of unconsciousness; flashes of pain were pulsing through my rib cage, and every breath was more difficult than the one before. But I knew, too, if I let myself fall into the darkness that was licking at my mind, then I might never wake up again — because Luca was Valentino's underboss, and he had orders to extract a blood debt from me.

I unballed my fist and pushed onward, holding the knife as far from my body as I could and using my shoulder as an anchor to keep me upright.

"Get out of my way." Brandishing the switchblade, I tried to shove against his chest with my other shoulder.

Luca curled his hand around my back and yanked the knife easily from my grip with the other. He flicked it closed and threw it onto the couch, far from my reach. "You can't go through me."

I looked up at him, glaring. I had seen enough of those piercing eyes for a century. "Let go of me."

He didn't. He moved his gaze across the room and let it rest on Calvino's flat-out form. "You do that to him?" he asked evenly.

I nodded.

He studied me, first the dried blood on my chin, and then where I was trying to clutch at my ribs. *"Cazzo,"* he muttered, shaking his head.

My legs buckled, but he caught me. He lowered me to the floor so that I was sitting. I wanted to tell him to get his hands off me, but I didn't because, for a nanosecond, I felt a respite from pain. It was almost manageable in this position, but I knew I couldn't remain in it. I had to escape.

Without taking his eyes off me, Luca pulled out his phone, punched in a number, and lifted it to his ear. "She's still here." A short silence and then, "An hour." He clicked off and returned the phone to his pocket.

"What's in an hour?" My voice was breathless with pain.

Luca didn't respond, and I winced as another ache spread along my chest. He got to his feet and crossed over to where Calvino was beginning to stir on the floor.

"Svegliati," he said, nudging his shoulder with his shoe. Calvino groaned, but he didn't open his eyes. "I'm taking her to the warehouse," Luca continued, as though talking to a semiconscious, moaning man was entirely normal. "I'll try not to let everyone know a seventeen-year-old, tied-up girl with no formal training managed to knock you out. In the meantime, you might want to sleep this off."

Calvino's leg twitched as Luca walked away from him. *"Pezzo di merda,"* he muttered, before returning his attention to me.

"I'm not going anywhere with you," I said.

"It's not up to you."

"Nic will never forgive you." My voice cracked and I cursed the weakness it betrayed, but Luca didn't seem to notice. Or care. He flicked his gaze to Calvino again. "Nic is not my concern right now."

He peered his head around the open door, into the next room. When he turned back I was already on my feet again, swaying. I stumbled forward.

Luca cocked his head. "You're coming with me, Sophie."

"No," I heaved, pushing forward until we were standing together at the door once more. "I told you I don't respect your authority." I staggered on and nearly tripped over the threshold.

Luca caught me again. I tried to hit his shoulder, but I faltered and he grabbed me by the waist, anchoring me to him so that I was half-floating and half-standing. "That doesn't change anything."

I tried to wriggle free, but he wouldn't let go of me. "I hate you," I heaved.

"Then this probably won't help," he replied. Before I could respond, he swung my legs upward and caught them beneath one arm, pulling my body into his with the other. I kicked out as hard as I could, but he only held me tighter, crushing me against his chest.

He carried me through a second, larger room. It was a dimly lit sitting area strewn with empty pizza boxes and cans of Coke. There was a muted poker tournament playing on a huge flat-screen TV, which was surrounded by wide leather armchairs.

I continued to struggle as agony coursed through my body, pushing through my vocal chords in banshee moans.

"Shut up," he cautioned as he opened another door and we plunged into the darkness along the second-story landing. I didn't shut up. I screamed until my voice cracked and my throat stung.

We reached the top of a winding staircase that parted into two identical paths. Luca descended quickly, his footfalls tapping against the marble until we were at the very bottom, standing in a large circular foyer with a white stone floor. In the center, a glass chandelier illuminated a mosaic of the Falcone family crest carved into the stone at our feet. My kicks were getting weaker and weaker.

"Please," I said, looking up at him. My head lolled against his shoulder as exhaustion crashed over me. "Please don't do this."

Luca's mouth was a hard line, stretching the faint scar above his lip. He didn't look at me.

We reached the front door and stepped out into the night. Luca hurried into a jog. The house rose into the dark sky behind us; it was a gargantuan three-story mansion made of white stone. In the middle, the roof rounded and protruded from the rest of the house, supported by a semicircular row of columns.

The driveway was torturously long and dark. When we finally stopped, Luca hitched me away from his body and opened the door of his SUV, propping me into the passenger seat and shutting me in before I could try and tumble out. He jumped into the driver's seat and started the engine. It roared to life beneath us. The clock on the dashboard read 10:04.

"Where are we going?" I already knew. I just wanted him to speak to me, to acknowledge what he was doing. Even yelling was better than the stony silence that stretched out between us. The quiet meant he was too focused on what he had to do, and that my pleas weren't causing him to waver.

We drove in silence for a long time, speeding along deserted roads I didn't recognize, until finally strands of civilization edged back into view. I tried to stay alert, but I could feel myself slipping in and out of consciousness as the pain ebbed and flowed through my body.

I tried everything to get through to Luca: I cried, I pleaded, I yelled, but he never replied. He never even looked at me. He just stared, face-forward, at the road, grinding his jaw and gripping the steering wheel so hard his fingers turned white.

And then when the clock read 10:57, almost an hour after leaving Lake Forest, we stopped. Luca turned off the highway and pulled around the back of a small service station. He parked the car, and for the first time since we had started driving, he turned to me. I stared back into his fathomless blue eyes, and waited as he shifted in his seat. He pulled something out of his back pocket, and my stomach curled with terror as he leaned toward me. He dropped it into my lap and for a moment I felt no pain, just surprise. It was a fifty-dollar bill.

Then he spoke quickly and quietly: "I took you from Felice's house against your will. When we made it into town, I stopped at a red light and you escaped. You ran into a service station. I couldn't come after you because there were too many people inside. I couldn't risk getting caught. You called a cab to pick you up. You went home to your mother and you both fled Cedar Hill immediately."

I started to shake, first my hands and then the rest of me. He was setting me free. He wasn't going to kill me. "What about my uncle . . ." I said as tears pricked the back of my eyes.

Luca's expression was unyielding, his voice dark. "You will not return home until after your uncle's funeral. Valentino won't keep us in Cedar Hill just for you. He won't like it that you escaped, but he will be able to move past it once Jack Gracewell's debt is settled."

"But if — "

"Sophie," Luca cut me off. "You will never see your uncle again."

"Please," I whispered. "Please, you have to help him."

"There are certain mistakes I can afford to make," he replied evenly. "And certain mistakes I can't."

"Do you mean they'd kill you if you tried to help him? But they're your family."

"I mean I wouldn't try," he said plainly.

I swallowed my words. Not only could Luca not help Jack, I knew he wouldn't. In his heart, he believed he should die, and there was nothing I could do to change that. How could a boy who was raised to believe that bad people are wholly bad possibly understand the idea that within bad there can be good and, more important, the potential for good? Luca and his family were looking at the world in black-and-white.

With a quick glance over my shoulder, Luca pulled his switchblade out of his pocket and cut the ties around my wrists. I watched as they fell apart limply. He pressed the handle of the blade into my hand and closed my fingers around it. "You stole my knife and took it with you in case you needed protection."

I looked down at the inscription: *Gianluca, March 20th 1995*. He was really giving me his blade, his personalized blade. And what's more, he was trusting that I wouldn't use it against him. It felt cold and unnatural in my hands, but I kept it, stuffing it in a pocket of my shorts alongside the fifty dollars.

"Thank you," I said, because I couldn't manage anything else. I didn't know whether to be grateful or horrified. I was exhausted, I was numb, and I was shaking. But he was setting me free, and whatever else was happening around us, that meant something. He was going against his family. He was giving me my life back.

"You'll never see us again, Sophie." There was a devastating finality in his words, but there was still nothing in his expression. It was, as ever, carefully controlled.

Before I could respond, the handle of the passenger door clicked and I turned to find Nic standing there, in the small parking lot at the back of the service station, holding it open for me. I stepped out of the car. We looked at each other, and I could see every shred of heartache bound up in his dark eyes.

He studied me — the bruising on my face and the lopsided way I was holding myself, my hands clutched beneath my ribs. He shut his eyes, there was a sharp intake of breath, and I swore both our hearts cracked just a little in that moment.

"I'm sorry," he said, opening his eyes again.

I couldn't tell him it was OK. It was a million miles away from being OK. But I offered him something small: a soft, watery smile for the boy who had kissed me like I had never been kissed before. He had goodness in him, even if it was buried far beneath the codes he lived his life by.

I stood back from Nic and he brushed by me, taking his place beside Luca in the car. He reached out for my hand and I gave it to him. He held it carefully, like it was made of porcelain, and traced the red marks on my wrist with his thumb. Then he lifted it to his lips and kissed it. *"Riguardati,"* he murmured against my skin.

And then the Falcone brothers were gone from me, and I was doubled over on the ground, crying so hard I could barely breathe.

CHAPTER TWENTY-NINE

The Warehouse

The more I cried, the more I thought about everything that had happened, and slowly, my resolve grew steadier than all the pain swimming inside me. If all the Falcones did was put people in the ground, then how could they know the benefits of second chances and what they can do for someone? How much good were they doing by ripping the potential out of a man before he could find the good in himself?

Luca and Nic might not have had a choice about killing Jack, but *I* did. I didn't know his number to call him — never mind that my phone was presently in the possession of thug-in-training C.J. — but I knew where they were going, I had a weapon, and I had money to get there. If I abandoned my uncle now, I would never forgive myself, and I would never think of Nic with anything other than contempt. I had made a promise to my father to look after Jack, and if his brother died like this I knew he would never recover. He was barely hanging on already.

But there was still time, I could still do something. I could stand between Nic and my uncle, I could stop him from killing him. I might not have been able to convince Luca, but I knew Nic would listen to me. He wouldn't devastate my family so completely, not after everything we had shared with each other.

I picked myself up and did my best to clean my face, wiping the blood from my chin and pulling my hair around my eyes to hide the bruising. I forced my body to straighten, walked into the service station, and broke the fifty-dollar bill so that I'd have one measly quarter to call a cab. I waited in the service station bathroom until it arrived, studying my reflection. I pulled my matted hair back from my face and stifled a horrified gasp. Deep bruises pooled out from under my swollen eyes. The bridge of my nose was crooked, and my cheeks and chin were red-raw from where I had scrubbed the blood away. I gripped the sides of the sink as the pain in my ribs surged. A few weeks ago, my biggest problem was the stifling July humidity. How had it come to this?

Somewhere along the way, there had been a gross misunderstanding. Everything had spiraled out of control. I couldn't just think about the drugs or the money or the dark parts of my uncle's soul without thinking about the good parts of him, too — the parts I knew existed. My uncle was not the one-dimensional villain the Falcones thought he was — how could they make allowances for themselves and not him? It wasn't right. Even if I couldn't convince them of that before it was too late, I still had to try.

Twenty minutes later, and to the bewilderment of the cab driver, I got out at a vacant lot on the outskirts of Old Hegewisch. Along the periphery, plastic bags floated like ghosts over sideways shopping carts. The old auto warehouse was halfway across the lot; it was a huge, faceless structure, its cracked concrete walls stained with rust and pigeon crap. On either side, shipping containers were precariously stacked like giant LEGOs, orange, beige, and blue. Along the top, a worn sign reading GREENE'S AUTO SUPPLIES swung precariously from its final screw. I walked briskly toward it, feeling less scared than I should have been. I was running entirely on adrenaline now, and I could feel my pulse in my fingertips.

I walked along a row of corrugated steel containers until I found an alley barely wider than a car. It was pitch-black and completely hidden from the entrance to the parking lot. At the end of the alley, I turned right and found two of the Falcones' SUVs, parked and empty. So Luca and Nic were here already, but who had come in the other car? It was obvious why they had chosen the spot. It gave them a secret entrance and an immediate upper hand for when Jack arrived.

At the back of the warehouse, a small door was hidden behind several stacks of wooden crates. It was partially ajar. The lock had been broken, but I doubted its necessity — the door itself was already crumbling at the edges, and probably could have been kicked in by a child.

I tiptoed between the crates and slid through the door. The space inside was mostly empty; it was cold and dirty, and damp. The smell of mold hung in the air and around the edges, more stacks of termite-eaten crates were piled haphazardly, regurgitating strips of plastic packaging. A single wire cage lamp illuminated a circular space at the front, and another smaller lightbulb had been strung near the center, where the Falcones were standing, partially shielded by a tower of crates that came up to their chests.

Luca was arguing with Felice, while Gino and Dom hovered behind them, fidgeting with their guns. Nic was several yards away, waiting just inside the front entrance. If only I could get his attention, maybe he would listen to me without being influenced by his brothers.

I started moving around the side of the warehouse, clutching at my sides as I bent low behind the boxes. Rats scurried in and out of crates, and I had to bite hard on my tongue to keep from yelping every time one skittered by my sneakers.

I stopped creeping and listened as the faraway rumblings of a car grew louder.

The activity in the warehouse fell deathly quiet.

The engine cut somewhere beyond the front entrance. I heard a car door shut. *Jack.* My heart was pounding hard and fast in my chest. Suddenly all I could think about was my uncle's face when he walked into the guns that were about to be leveled at his head.

Then something unexpected happened: I heard another door shut, and another, and finally a fourth. Jack wasn't alone.

Nic peered around the warehouse entrance and then pulled his head back in a blur. "He's got company," he announced to the others, backing away from his post and coming to stand beside Luca. Both of them looked uneasy, but no one seemed particularly surprised. I don't know why I was so shocked: Walking into a dark warehouse alone was suicide. Jack was smarter than that, and, to my dismay, he was obviously used to this world and how things worked in it.

"They'll have guns," said Dom casually.

"Classic Gracewell," said Felice with a mirthless laugh. "There is never any honor in his agreements. We always knew he would come heavy. How many are there?"

"It's too dark, I couldn't tell." Nic's voice was tight with frustration. He pulled out his gun and double-checked to make sure it was loaded. How could I get to him now when he was so close to his brothers? Maybe if I made it to Jack before he came inside, it would stop him from trying to come in at all. All this time I had been so worried about my uncle that I hadn't stopped to think about the possibility he might come prepared, too. And that meant Nic and Luca weren't any safer than he was.

Stupid vendetta.

I became more deliberate about my steps as the crates grew fewer and far between. They were getting trickier to hide behind and, with each shallow breath like a stab in my cracked rib cage, I was finding it harder to exert myself. If I could just make it through that front door before anyone came in, I might be able to stop a massacre.

"I knew this would get messy," Felice was ranting. "And if he sees we don't have the girl anymore, then he won't hesitate to shoot first. We need to be on our guard — we've lost the upper hand."

The shadows of Dom and Gino murmured their agreement. Luca's voice was too low to hear, but by the way his hands were gesturing, I guessed he was protesting his innocence. From my vantage point, it looked convincing. I hoped it was.

"And you're not even fully protected." Felice motioned toward Luca's and Nic's chests. "Go out back before you get injured.

Valentino's angry enough already. We can't afford to have anything else go wrong."

Neither of them moved. "We'll see this through," said Luca.

Nic rolled his neck around until it cracked. He squared his shoulders and clenched his jaw. If this was him in soldier mode, it was damn effective. And that made me want to pull my hair out of my scalp, because he was preparing to kill my uncle.

The Falcones fell out of their conversation; no one wanted to argue anymore. They grew silent, each of them boring holes in the door with their eyes, waiting for Jack to make his move. They knew he was out there; he knew they were inside. Both sides had backup and both sides, presumably, had guns. And I was stuck, crouching in rat piss behind a stack of moldy crates in a warehouse in the middle of nowhere, wondering which of the people I cared about would die first, and whether I would survive long enough to try and forgive the ones that didn't. If this wasn't rock bottom, I shuddered to think what was.

I was trying to sneak across a gap between two toppled crates when the door to the warehouse creaked open, first one notch, and then another. I froze. The Falcones raised their guns at the entranceway. I was too late. I had failed.

"Hello," said a quiet, nervous voice.

My whole body turned to ice.

No one answered her.

"Hello?" she said again, the word just a wavering tinkle in this huge, barren space.

In one echoing click, they set their guns ready to fire, and aimed them at my mother as she edged into the warehouse.

CHAPTER THIRTY

The Choice

Her hair was falling in messy strands across her ashen face, and she'd pulled her old cardigan over her pajamas. She was still wearing her slippers.

Suddenly it felt like all my nightmares were colliding with each other and exploding into one dreadful spectacle. And this? *This* was my rock bottom.

If I thought I'd known anger before, this was something else entirely. Heat surged through me, and I could barely keep from screaming. What was Jack *thinking*? How could he do this to my own *mother*? To his brother's *wife*? I felt sick, and suddenly I didn't know what side I was on anymore. Luca was right; I should have gone home. I should have left Cedar Hill with my mother. I should have kept her safe. She was the only person in my family I could rely on, and I had been a fool to think anything different.

When she saw the guns that were pointed at her, my mother let out a strangled gasp. Her hands flew to her mouth and she stumbled backward.

The Falcones hesitated, glancing at one another, but they didn't lower their guns. I couldn't understand why they would see anything remotely threatening about her. She was five feet tall, a hundred pounds, and shaking like a leaf.

I bit the back of my hand and tried to center myself, but I was screaming on the inside. I crept closer — as close as I could get to her before I couldn't hide behind the dwindling crates anymore. It still wasn't close enough. I desperately wanted to spring from the shadows and pull her out of there, but I knew I'd probably be shot before I got to her.

My mother shuffled forward again, cradling herself. "I'm here for my daughter." The fear made her voice unrecognizable. "I'm here for Sophie."

Luca lowered his gun. "What the hell does Gracewell think he's doing?"

The others didn't move.

"Keep your defenses up," cautioned Felice. "This is clearly a trap."

"It's her mother," said Nic, turning to spit on the ground. "He's using her goddamn mother."

"There are more of them outside," said Felice. He narrowed his eyes and started scanning my mother as if making sure she wasn't an illusion. "I don't know what this is, but if Jack Gracewell thinks we won't shoot you, then he's sorely mistaken."

"Wh-Where is my daughter?" My mother wasn't focusing. Her attention had fallen away from the guns and she was whipping her head around, searching the warehouse frantically. For me. "Where is she?" she asked, dread drowning out the fear in her breathless voice. "He said she was here. What have you done with her?"

"Where is Jack Gracewell at this moment?" Felice started toward her, leveling his gun at her forehead. "Tell me what he's planning or I'll kill you right now."

"Stop!" shouted Nic. He flung his arm out across his uncle's chest and Felice skidded to an unexpected halt.

"Nicoli," he hissed. "You need to learn to pick your battles."

"She's not part of this," he snapped.

"Of course she's part of this, she's standing right here!"

"We said no more innocents. You're as bad as Valentino!"

"Nonsense," said Felice, indignantly. "Of course we should kill her."

Luca stepped between Nic and Felice. "Do you really wish to derail this family further, Felice?" he asked, his voice carefully controlled. "This is not what my father would have wanted, and we all know it."

"Then perhaps you shouldn't have shunned his last request. You would certainly be in a better position to complain now."

Luca's expression grew faintly hostile, but his voice remained unchanged. "I'm sure I don't need to remind you, Felice, that regardless of my decision, I still outrank you."

Felice grimaced and lowered his gun slowly. The feeling returned to my jelly legs.

"S-Sophie?" My mother inched forward, craning her neck to see behind the crates ahead of her. But she wouldn't find me there, and the more she tried, the harder it was to watch her fail. Silent tears were streaming down her cheeks, catching in the half light. "Sophie?"

"Where is Jack Gracewell?" Felice repeated. He was so caught up in studying her that he didn't hear the dim thud coming from the back of the warehouse. None of them did.

I felt myself jump and the pain in my rib cage soared, as if an invisible hand had decided to braid my insides. I fell back onto my haunches and followed the noise. Four figures were sneaking through the hidden back door. They started navigating their way through the crates, crouching low to the ground. A shock of crimson hair alerted me to Eric Cain's position. Of course Jack's best friend was involved in this, just like everybody else seemed to be. Beside him, I recognized the gait of my uncle as he pulled himself across the ground, stalking toward the Falcones.

I started to panic, caught between shouting out to draw attention to Jack so Nic and Luca could be forewarned and keeping quiet so Jack could save my mother from Felice's increasingly steady aim. Maybe he did deserve this, but she didn't. I patted my hand against Luca's knife in my pocket and the angriest part of me imagined using it on Jack. What good was showing up to rescue me if he was prepared to use my own mother, knowing she could get hurt, too?

"Enough of this!" It was Gino; Gino the Unstable. He lunged forward, barreling past Felice and Nic, his gun held high.

My mother yelped, stumbling backward and almost tripping over herself.

"Gino!" Nic's scream drowned out my own, and no one seemed to notice the threads of our voices intertwining. Luca lunged at the same time and in a heartbeat he was standing in front of my mother, his palms raised toward his brother.

"Gino, no," he echoed, but calmer.

"She's a distraction," Gino lisped, madly waving his gun in the air. "And she's Michael Gracewell's wife! At least this way we can get the blood debt that you and Calvino screwed up."

"Watch what you say, Gino," Luca said without budging.

The shadows at the back were lurking ever closer. I caught a glint of Jack's buzz cut several crates across from me. I decided to go for him. If he knew I was OK, maybe he could sneak away and then Luca could convince them to let my mother go, too.

I dragged myself across the cement, glancing over my shoulder as I crept as quickly as possible. My mother had buried her face in her hands and her sobs were echoing around the warehouse. I watched Luca turn and whisper something to her. She straightened up and began to wipe her face with shaking hands. She said something in return. He nodded and she released a watery smile, her face twitching with relief. She knew I was alive.

When I turned back, my uncle was no longer in my sights, and the lurking shadows were no longer shadows. They were men. And they were standing up, arms outstretched and guns in hand. I screamed at the top of my lungs, but it was too late.

In the movies it's always so dramatic when someone gets shot. Time slows, the music ebbs and flows around the moment. When the bullet hits, the body buckles — each limb reacting in perfect unison — as it sails backward through the air, and even though it's supposed to be horrifying, there's always something quietly artistic about it, too.

It wasn't like that with Luca. He just crumpled. One minute

he was on his feet, standing in front of my mother, and the next he was lying on the ground in a pool of his own blood.

The pop was still echoing in my eardrums when she started screaming, and then the shouting followed, and all hell broke loose.

Eric Cain, the man who had shot Luca, dropped to the ground and rolled behind a line of broken crates. Dom started shooting at him, putting holes in the crates as he sprang up and leapt between them like a gazelle, weaving toward the back of the warehouse. Another man — who was little more than a curtain of white-blond hair — was trying to dart in wide circles around Gino, while Felice cornered the fourth, all of them firing at one another between crates.

Nic went straight for Jack, his gun readied, but Jack shot first. The bullet lodged in the crate beside Nic's head. He shot back, but Jack dodged it, leaping behind a tower of crates and disappearing from my view. And then I couldn't see them anymore, but their shouts rose up with the others'.

I slithered across the cold cement, following Luca's blood like it was a trail and ignoring the pulsing pain in my rib cage. My mother was already crouched down, trying to drag him away from the chaos with one hand and protecting her head from stray bullets with the other. Someone screamed my name, and I braced myself for the impact of a bullet that never came.

Behind us, a door slammed and most of the shouting moved outside. I reached Luca and threw my hands onto his waist to stop the bleeding that was coming thick and fast from an entry wound in his side. It bubbled angrily beneath my hands as blood oozed over my fingers, coating them in sticky warmth.

"Sophie!" my mother cried, grabbing onto my shoulders. "Sophie, you have to leave!"

"No." I pressed down harder, feeling my own ribs shriek in protest. Luca's eyelids were fluttering and his complexion was drained. It was strange to see him so pale. "Call an ambulance."

My mother released me and started patting her sweater frantically. "I don't have a phone. I didn't think," she dithered. "Everything happened so fast, and Jack said we had to leave urgently if we were to have any chance of . . . Oh, and I was so worried I could barely think . . ." She trailed off into senseless mutterings. We were close to the front of the warehouse now. She started pulling nearby crates around us — building a makeshift barrier.

There was no sign of Nic or Jack. Before, I could hear them barking at each other, but now there was nothing. Inside, the rest of the shooting had ceased. Someone had had the sense to lure the chaos away from us, and I couldn't be sure which side had thought to do it, and whether it was for my benefit or for Luca's, but in that moment I was profoundly grateful.

Outside, three more shots rang out and an engine roared to life. Someone was leaving in a car at the front of the warehouse, and I didn't know whether to be relieved or terrified.

"We have to get help." I started to drag Luca toward the entrance with my free hand. He gurgled and a stream of blood bubbled from his discolored lips, staining his chalk-white skin.

"It's too dangerous, Sophie," my mother whispered. "We don't know what's going on out there."

The sound of another engine startled me. It was farther away, coming from the back of the warehouse. Tires squealed, and I knew it meant at least one Falcone was taking off.

"Those bastards," I spat. "They're leaving him here to die."

"They probably think he's already dead." The way my mother said it betrayed her own grim expectations. "He very nearly is."

The tears stung my eyes, but I blinked quickly so they would fall away from them and clear my vision. "If you hold the wound, I could try to find — "

The front entrance was kicked in. Jack stomped into the warehouse, his shirt pooling with sweat and his face blotchy and red. He had his gun raised in front of him, his eyes darting around the warehouse for possible threats.

"You're safe," he said without looking at my mother and me. He was still scanning the warehouse. "We have to go."

"Where are the others?" I asked.

"Carter's dead. They got him twice in the head. Grant's still out there with one of them. Cain's been shot in the arm, but he rallied and — "

"The Falcones," I interrupted. "Where are the Falcones?"

Jack didn't register the urgency in my question; he probably thought it was fear. "Cain's leading them on a wild-goose chase across the city; those dumb goombahs think they're chasing me. They thought it would be so easy, but once again they've underestimated me. They have no idea what they've started. I'm going to pick those little shits off one by one. No one lays a hand on my niece and gets away with it." The pride in his voice was horrifyingly misplaced; I guessed it often was in this strange underworld, where morals were warped beyond reason. "We've got to get you two to safety before that other Falcone comes back in here. I've called Hamish and he's on his way; we're meeting him at the edge of the lot. We'll just have to write Grant off as an expense. He was new any — "

Jack stopped mid-rant. For the first time, his attention focused on our little heap behind the crates. He zeroed in on Luca, his eyes growing. "Shit," he said, grimacing. "Move aside."

He pointed his gun at Luca's head.

"Stop!" I screeched, shifting so I was in his firing line instead.

He came closer, stomping through Luca's blood like it was a puddle of water. He softened his voice in an effort to comfort me. "You don't have to look."

"Jack!" my mother cried hysterically. "Don't shoot the boy!"

Jack didn't understand. Luca was just another fallen chess piece, and he was distracting me from our getaway. "Celine, if she doesn't come now, we won't get her to safety."

Luca was unconscious, but I could still hear labored wheezes seeping from his chest. I pulled my body over his, bringing our foreheads together so that my hair fell around his head, shielding him. I stretched my free hand across his body, covering his heart, while keeping the other one tight against his wound. "No."

"He has to go, Sophie. He's the underboss." The gentleness in my uncle's voice was turning to frustration, his patience to urgency. "Don't make me pry you off him."

"Jack," my mother tried again. "We need to help him."

I could hear his knees crack as he hunkered down beside me. "Don't be ridiculous, Celine."

I held on tighter.

"Come on, Soph." He grabbed me by the shoulder and pulled me away from Luca's body in one stiff yank. "Turn away."

I clawed forward, but he pushed me back, sliding me across the ground until my bare legs were stained with Luca's blood and I was too far away to stop him. I screamed as he cocked the gun at his head.

There was an almighty *pop*. It was louder this time, and it seemed to change the particles in the air around me, pushing them against each other in small vibrations. My mother and I screamed, but Luca, who was barely Luca now, remained intact.

Instead, the gun flew out of Jack's hand, and skidded along the floor past me.

"Son of a bitch!" he cursed. His head was lolling, his expression dazed. The bullet had gone right through his hand, and now the tear was pumping blood down his arm. Jack shrank to the floor, gasping and clutching his crimson fingers. I kicked his gun away. It slid across the floor, coming to a stop between two bullet-riddled crates, far away from his reach.

At the back of the warehouse, Nic was sprinting toward us, his face spattered with dirt, his clothes soaked with what must have been someone else's blood. The gun was still in his hand, half-raised at my uncle, like he was planning to shoot at him again. I guess he wasn't kidding about that perfect aim.

"Both your friends are dead!" he shouted.

Jack started scrabbling backward toward the entrance, pulling himself across the floor with his uninjured hand. "Sophie!" he shouted, but he wasn't focusing; he couldn't see me. But I could see him; his pale face was awash with terror and his blood was mixing with Luca's as he dragged himself through it.

Nic stopped running and raised his gun again. "Stop!" he commanded.

"Nic, don't!" I yelled. "He's not armed. Just let him go!"

Nic's head twitched like there was something buzzing around it. He hesitated. Jack was at the door now; he stuck his good hand through and tried to pull himself up. He was almost there.

And then Nic shot him.

My mother and I screamed. Jack slumped against the doorway, and a blood-red star started to swell across the left side of his shirt.

Nic skidded to a stop beside Luca. He didn't even look at Jack. He stowed his gun and crouched down beside his brother, checking the pulse in his neck. "We need to get him to the hospital," he said to my mother. She was visibly shaking, but she was still plugging the wound.

I was too numb to move. I was still staring at my uncle and the new, terrified expression in his eyes. He was still alive, and he was looking at me, his body slumped half in and half out of the warehouse. I scanned the entry wound — it was just below his left shoulder. Not quite his heart, although it could easily have been. By all appearances, from where my mother and Nic were huddled, my uncle seemed very much dead, but I could see the alertness in his expression, and the fear in his eyes. Had Nic shot to kill or to wound Jack? And if he knew what I knew then —

that the bullet had missed my uncle's heart — would he finish the job?

"Sophie," my mother said, her voice heaving. She and Nic had started to hoist Luca between them. "Can you help us? We need you to plug the wound while we move him."

Did Jack deserve my forgiveness? No. Did he deserve to die? That wasn't my decision to make; it wasn't anyone's. I didn't have any time to think. I stood up without saying anything, sticking my hand out to help, and blocking their view of my uncle's body as I came toward them. Then we moved quickly, all three of us in tandem, toward the back of the warehouse, away from all the blood. I didn't turn around to see if Jack was still there.

My mother and Nic carried Luca into the remaining SUV, while I stumbled along beside them, clutching my ribs with one hand and plugging his wound with the other. And then we took off, Luca and I lying side by side in the backseat, my hand pressed tight against his torso as our labored breathing mingled in the air between us.

As Nic sped through the darkness, lost in hurried conversation with my mother, I drifted away from the pain inside me, and into the darkness that had been creeping up on me all evening.

CHAPTER THIRTY-ONE

The Hospital

For the second time this summer, I awoke in a hospital room. Everything around me was strange and discolored. Cartoonish images danced back and forth in my brain as I lay still, feeling a million miles above the earth. I pulled my hand up around my chest and felt a subtle pinch as my eyes rolled back in my head.

"Sophie?" A tinkling bell infiltrated my bubble.

I rolled my head around and landed on my right cheek, which throbbed dully beneath me, like the pain was just outside of my body, looking in. I tried to groan, but it caught in my throat and wheezed out in pathetic puffs of nothingness.

"Sweetheart?" My vision sharpened until my mother's face loomed just inches from my own. Her eyes were glassy and her face was drawn. "How are you feeling?"

I tried to speak, but I couldn't find the words, and I knew even if I could, I wouldn't be able to push them out. I scrunched up my face and blinked over and over until my mother's movements became disjointed.

"The doctor has given you morphine. You have two broken ribs and a broken nose. Don't worry if you feel a little strange." She reached over to my unobscured hand and squeezed it tightly. The sensation was little more than a slight tickle.

For every moment I lay there, feeling high and low all at once, memories flashed across my addled brain. I remembered the pain of every Calvino-inflicted blow; the argument with Luca at Felice's mansion; a long, meandering drive to nowhere. I pulled my hands under the blankets and, dimly, I became aware of the hospital gown I was wearing. Beside me, on the bedside locker, my tank top and cutoffs were folded in a pile. The top of a switch-blade peaked out from my front pocket. There were more flickers of confusion and then something real, another disjointed memory. It was Luca's knife. But why did I have it again? I scrunched my eyes shut and tried to reach inside the darkest parts of my mind.

When I opened them, Nic had appeared inside the room, looking like he hadn't slept in a very long time; his hair was tousled across his forehead and dark circles had spread out under his eyes. He handed a paper cup of coffee to my mother and sat next to her so that their faces appeared side by side. For a second I could have sworn they were nothing more than floating heads, but then the morphine crest subsided enough for me to register some level of reality.

"You're awake." He released a small smile.

I moaned breathlessly in response.

Nic leaned in until his dark eyes dominated my limited field of vision. "You are stubborn, Sophie Gracewell," he chided softly.

"I don't know what I would have done if something happened to you."

I tried to remember more. The faint memory of shouting filled my brain, but it floated away again. I stared at Nic so hard I felt tears stream from my eyes and slide back into my hair.

He gently traced his forefinger under my swollen eye; I desperately wanted to feel his touch, but I couldn't. "I'll make this right," he said. "I promise."

I closed my eyes, remembering the old, dank smell of the warehouse with a start. I saw a line of scattered crates stretch out before me into the darkness. Nic and his brothers were standing in a solitary patch of light, arguing.

When I opened my eyes again, Nic was lifting his hand away from my face, but his attention was still trained on me. "Forgive me," he whispered.

In my botched peripheral vision, I could make out my mother; pools of tears were spilling into the corners of her eyes. "Sweetheart, I'm so sorry. I didn't know about any of this. I thought you were with Millie until Jack came banging on the door. I had no idea what he was doing. I had no idea about any of this."

I could see her then, in another time and place, weeping as she was now, wearing the same pajamas, and slippers I had gotten her for Christmas.

I reached out and patted her arm in what I hoped was reassurance, but I could barely feel the gesture because of the morphine. When I felt satisfied with the feeble attempt, I tried to sit up.

"Stop," Nic murmured, putting his hand on mine. "Don't try to move just yet, OK?"

Stop. Nic had yelled that in the warehouse. That was right before he shot Jack. *Jack.* "Jack," I wheezed. It barely made a sound, but my mother understood.

"It appears your uncle made it out alive." There was no emotion in her voice. I wasn't sure if she was relieved or disappointed. Cautiously I flicked my gaze to Nic. His expression was unreadable. I couldn't tell if he was surprised or not by the news, but he wasn't looking at me anymore. I looked away from him, too, but our fingers remained entwined.

When my head hit the pillow again it seemed to lift the rest of the fog in my brain. My memory flashed; the bullets were raining down around me as I huddled with my mother on the floor. I saw Jack, first holding a gun, and then clutching his hand as spurts of blood ran down his arm. Below us, Luca's eyelids fluttered, his chest heaving unsteadily. He was lying in a pool of his own blood, and my fingers were *inside* his body, holding him together.

Suddenly the image of Luca crumpling to the ground crashed into my mind, and every single harrowing memory of our escape littered my thoughts. I gasped so hard it stung my chest. I threw my hands out, flailing them helplessly, until Nic returned his attention to me. He grabbed them and settled them back by my side, brushing his fingers across mine. "It's OK," he soothed.

"Luca?" I wheezed. "Where is Luca?" My breathing quickened to match my heart rate and suddenly the room began to spin. Nic was reaching for something in his pocket. The pain in my ribs resurfaced and rattled against my skin. A strangled scream sprang from my chest.

My mother was on her feet, settling me. "He survived," she said. "He's alive as well, sweetheart. He's alive."

Nic unfolded the piece of paper he was holding. "He's down the hall. He lost a lot of blood, but he's recovering. We got him here just in time."

"You saved him," I said, feeling myself smile. It felt heavenly not to have to worry anymore. "You shot Jack's gun out of his hand."

"It really was remarkable," my mother echoed. I could tell by her tone that she couldn't decide whether to be impressed or disapproving.

"*You* saved him," said Nic. His expression was sheepish, his eyes dark. "You stopped the bleeding."

"You were so brave, sweetheart." My mother started to stroke my forehead. "I'm so proud of you."

"Here," Nic said, handing me the note he'd already opened. "He's not able to walk around yet, but he wanted me to give this to you when you woke up."

I grabbed it more fiercely than I intended to, almost ripping it. It was simple and short, written in neat black lettering. It took me a while to read it:

I told you to go home.

I felt myself grin. Nic was watching me intently; two dimples punctured the skin above his brows and his mouth was pursed. I caught his eye and the sternness disappeared. He smiled at me encouragingly.

"Pen?" I asked him.

My mother rustled around in her purse and handed me one. I turned the note over and wrote on the back. It took me far longer than it should have, and when I finished, the morphine-guided script was wobbly and disjointed, veering up and down the paper like a six-year-old had written it:

Aren't you glad I have no respect for your authority? ☺

I folded it over and handed it to Nic. "Will you give this to him, please?"

His frown returned, and this time he didn't hide it. "Sure," he said, glancing at the piece of paper as he stepped out of the room. "I'll be right back."

My mother leaned over me and dropped her voice. "The police were here earlier asking questions. I expect they'll be back."

"No statements," I replied, falling back into my pillow. I wanted to say more, but I was losing my energy again.

My mother didn't appear surprised by my answer. She shook her head. "No, I don't think so, either."

"Welcome to *omertà*," I murmured. My tongue was thick and heavy in my mouth.

"*Omertà*," she repeated quietly, and I could tell by her tone she already knew what it meant.

ACKNOWLEDGMENTS

Thank you to Samantha Eves — You have been an instrumental part of this journey. I can't tell you how much I appreciate your tireless enthusiasm, your honest feedback, and your readiness to read the book over and over ... and *over*, at every stage. Thank you for the midnight Skype sessions and Niagara dinners where many of the characters and their journeys took shape.

Thank you to Jessica Hanley, Katie Harte, and Susan Ryan for flat-out refusing to acknowledge my fear that you wouldn't embrace my book, and for insisting on being my first readers. From the start, you have been the greatest friends and supporters I could have asked for.

Thank you to my dad for thinking so convincingly like a Mafia boss and for rivaling my excitement at every step of this process. I am only sorry I couldn't have a winking cartoon bee on the cover, like you so desperately wanted.

Thank you to my mom, for making me take part in many library read-a-thons as a child, and for ensuring I actually *read* the books instead of just ticking them off the list ... like my brothers did. I am especially grateful for the way you sneakily convinced me to accompany you to those creative writing courses two years ago. I see now, with perfect clarity, you were not going for yourself — you never even did the homework! You were really introducing me to a world I always wanted to be a part of but was too scared to enter alone. You are an amazing mother, and a truly talented meddler.

Thank you to my brothers. Conor, I know you wanted to write your own acknowledgment to yourself but this will have to do instead. You have been such a great CEO. Thanks for personally appointing yourself the Boss of My Life. You were the first person I told about my publishing deal, and even though you insisted on making a sandwich before celebrating with me, I can't think of anyone I would have rather told first. Really, you are a great brother ... but don't let it go to your head. Colm, thank you for your unwavering belief in me, and your insistence in spurring me on when I felt like giving up. Thank you for your cheerful company on all my London visits, for giving me your bed, your time and your optimism . . . and for not letting those birds eat me at the zoo!

To Claire Wilson, thank you for making my dream come true, and for being an incredible agent. To Lexie and everyone else at Rogers, Coleridge & White, thank you for championing *Vendetta* so well. Thank you to my fellow STAGS, Alice Oseman, Lauren James, and Melinda Salisbury, for sharing your journeys with me and for being part of mine. I see a lot more magical moments and beach Pimms ahead!

Thank you to everyone at Chicken House — to Barry Cunningham and Rachel Hickman for welcoming me so wonderfully and offering my book an incredible home. Thank you to Rachel Leyshon, for adding your magical editorial touch to *Vendetta* and making it better than I ever thought it could be. Thank you to Jasmine Bartlett, Laura Myers, and Laura Smythe for introducing *Vendetta* to the world, and for being so amazing along the way.

Thank you to Siobhan McGowan for your humorous and insightful copyedits, and to Emellia Zamani and the Scholastic team for championing *Vendetta* on the other side of the Atlantic.

Thank you to Aoife, my soul sister-cousin and fellow writer, for all the late night conversations about bees and dragons, and everything in between. Thanks to Sinéad for introducing me to Young Adult fiction all those years ago in school and for not hounding me too much about all the books I still have to give back. Aidan, thanks for *that* line and for the ones I'm sure I'll be "borrowing" from you in future. Remember our deal — you're not allowed to sue me.

Finally, I am so grateful to everyone at Salmon Poetry, and to all my amazing friends and extended family, for being part of this journey and for sharing in the excitement with me at every stage. I feel very fortunate to have you all in my life! ♥